EARTHSEARCH

Further Titles by James Follett from Severn House

CHURCHILL'S GOLD
DEATHSHIP
DOMINATOR
THE DOOMSDAY ULTIMATUM
MINDWARP
U 700

EARTHSEARCH

James Follett

13253185

This first world edition published in Great Britain 1994 by
SEVERN HOUSE PUBLISHERS LTD of
9–15 High Street, Sutton, Surrey SM1 1DF.
Fully revised and rewritten with substantial alterations and
new material from the original Radio 4 series broadcast and
published 1981 by the BBC.
First published in the USA 1994 by
SEVERN HOUSE PUBLISHERS INC., of
425 Park Avenue, New York, NY 10022.

Copyright © 1994 by James Follett

All rights reserved.
The moral rights of the author have been asserted.

British Library Cataloguing in Publication Data
Follett, James
  Earthsearch. – New ed
  I. Title
  823.914 [F]

ISBN 0-7278-4689-2

All situations in this publication are fictitious and
any resemblance to living persons is purely coincidental.

Typeset by Hewer Text Composition Services, Edinburgh.
Printed and bound in Great Britain by
Hartnolls Ltd, Bodmin, Cornwall.

PROLOGUE

In the beginning . . .

Eighteen thousand million years had passed since the spawning of the giant meteoroid during the cataclysmic event that had marked the foundation of the Universe and the beginning of Time.

It had been an uneventful period for the meteoroid; eighteen thousand million years spent moving in a straight line which, were it not for the ten-mile length of the starship *Challenger* lying in its path, would be a mere prelude to the total of its eventual lifetime.

The *Challenger* was the result of seven years' feverish activity in Earth orbit to construct the first of three ships to journey to the stars to search for an Earth-type planet which would one day become the new home of mankind. It had been conceived and built during a period of unprecedented, world-wide stability and peace when, for the first time in its history, men and women had the confidence to embark on such long-term projects which would not come to fruition within one lifetime.

The accumulated knowledge of three-hundred years' high technology had gone into the *Challenger*'s design and construction. She had been fitted with the most advanced planetary surveillance equipment and instrument probes, and had the resources in her vast terra-forming centre to re-engineer potential Earth-type planets by means of robot machines and androids which the *Challenger* would leave behind.

Maintenance of such a vast ship would be beyond the resources of the starship's crew, so a workforce army of specialist androids had been designed and built in record time. These machines carried out the countless routine tasks necessary for the smooth running of the ship. They were under the command of the *Challenger*'s two control computers who were responsible to the commander and crew for the ship's environment. These computers were known as Angel One and Angel Two and it was inevitable that by the time a second-generation crew had been born on the *Challenger* during its mission these two entities had become known as guardian angels.

What the designers of the guardian angels had not foreseen was that their creations would, as the years passed by on the *Challenger*, come to see themselves as more than mere computers. Were they not more intelligent than the men and women that occupied the mighty starship? Did they not have more power and ambition than the puny, two-legged creatures that tried to dominate them? And was not the non-discovery of intelligent life in fifty years a clear indication that they could be the supreme beings of the galaxy? Or even the Universe?

The problem was that the guardian angels needed humans to man the main control room. For reasons best known to themselves, the *Challenger*'s designers had decreed that only people could manoeuvre the starship, despite the fact that machines were infinitely more reliable. To the guardian angels, it was yet another folly in a dismal catalogue of incompetence. Humans fought among themselves and allowed their efficiency, such as it was, to be further reduced by their obsession with sex. To make matters worse, the second-generation crew were becoming disillusioned with the mission whereas the guardian angels wished for it to continue.

The guardian angels decided to rid the *Challenger* of its adult humans. The problem was how. Using the androids against the crew was sure to fail because most of them were only good at doing those tasks which they had been designed for. To be certain of success, all the adults would have to be destroyed simultaneously.

When the guardian angels detected the presence of the distant giant meteoroid and discovered that it was on a three hundred miles per hour converging course with the *Challenger*, they decided that fate was on their side. They calculated comparative velocities and angles, and concluded that a collision was inevitable provided the crew were not alerted.

When the meteoroid was one month away they were able to refine their calculations; they made the interesting discovery that the meteoroid would strike the *Challenger* a glancing blow in the region of the main assembly hall.

When it was three weeks away, they were able to compute the nature and extent of the damage that the collision would cause; the ship would be severely damaged but not crippled. What damage there was would be within the abilities of the service androids to repair.

The meteoroid drew nearer but the guardian angels remained silent. One week before the inevitable collision, they informed the crew that service androids would have to carry out urgently needed maintenance work on the outer hull. The meteoroid alarms were closed down and a hundred service androids swarmed out of the maintenance air-locks and spread themselves along the *Challenger*'s ten-mile length. They X-rayed seams that did not require inspection; they filled minute, almost invisible particle scars that were too insignificant to warrant attention and they carried out thousands of needless tests on systems that were in perfect working order.

One hour before the impending impact, a team of the more sophisticated androids dismantled the four outer turrets that housed the *Challenger*'s meteoroid annihilation shields.

The guardian angels switched off the ship's optical telescopes thirty minutes before impact.

Fifteen minutes before impact and the ship was blind and helpless – defenceless against the million-ton mass of star matter hurtling towards it.

The *Challenger*'s crew were unaware of the fate awaiting them as they filed into the auditorium to hear their commander's announcement.

Commander Jonas Sinclair was a second-generation crewman. In common with the majority of the three hundred and twenty men and women sitting expectantly before him, he had been born on the *Challenger*. At least fifty of the older faces before him belonged to members of the first-generation crew – those who had watched the *Challenger* taking shape in Earth orbit over fifty years before.

Sinclair was nervous and ill at ease; he would have preferred to make his statement over the crew address system from his day cabin but the two guardian angels had suggested calling everyone together. Despite the protestations of the first-generation crew that the guardian angels were only computers, he had come to value their advice and guidance and even allowed them to decide when the meeting should be called.

Sinclair arranged his notes on the lectern and waited for his audience to settle down. He tapped his liquid-flo pencil gently on the polished surface. The pin microphone in his lapel picked up the soft clicks and amplified them in the air above everyone's heads. The buzz of conversation subsided.

'Fellow crew men and women,' Sinclair began. 'I have called you all together because we have reached an important stage in our mission. For fifty years we have toured the galaxy in search of other earths for colonization. When our parents set out on this survey voyage, it was hoped that one Earth-type planet would be discovered for every ten years shipboard time of the mission.'

Sinclair glanced down at his notes and caught the eye of the four men and four women who were sitting in the front row watching him intently. He knew why they had sought out the front row and he gave them a fleeting smile of encouragement before raising his eyes to the rest of the audience. 'As we know, that has not happened, therefore we have continued the work of our parents.'

He sensed the fidgeting rather than saw it and immediately shortened his preamble by several paragraphs. 'And now, during the past six months four babies of the third-generation crew have been born to us.'

The four couples in the front row seemed to lean forward in their seats, never taking their eyes off Sinclair.

'The parents of Telson, Sharna, Astra and Darv have petitioned me, saying that they do not wish their children to grow up as they have: not knowing about our home planet Earth. Never to breathe its air; never to fell its grass beneath their feet; never to walk under its blue skies and feel its warm summer breezes on their faces . . . Ladies and gentlemen – I agree with them!'

There was a stunned silence. No one coughed or fidgeted: 320 pairs of eyes regarded him in amazement.

Sinclair pressed on: 'Our parents denied us our home but does that give us the right to pass on that denial to a third-generation crew? I think not. Nor do I believe that it is possible for the *Challenger* to improve on the success of its mission.'

There was some sporadic clapping from the centre of the auditorium that Sinclair silenced with an upraised hand. 'What I have to say now means that we will have to go into suspended animation because – '

As Sinclair expected, there was a loud chorus of protests. The mausoleum-like suspended animation chambers were mistrusted – a mistrust that the first-generation had passed on the second generation with the result that the suspended animation chambers were now rarely used. Also, despite the fact that the technique of reducing the body's metabolism to the point where it was maintained at the point of death had been perfected over one hundred and fifty years previously, most people still considered that there was something sinister and unethical about going into a death sleep for periods ranging from a few days up to the maximum of fifty years.

Sinclair smiled and held up a hand to help the furore die away. 'If you don't like the idea of suspended animation,' he continued, 'then the next phase is going to take ten years in real time. The *Challenger* is going home!'

The four couples broke the hush that followed Sinclair's words; they jumped to their feet, clapping and cheering wildly. And then the storm broke as the entire audience rose to their feet applauding enthusiastically and cheering. The thunderous acclaim dragged on for another minute. A woman in the front row jumped on to the rostrum and threw her arms around Sinclair's neck.

It was the last touch of a woman that Sinclair was to experience. At that moment the giant meteoroid struck the ship.

The cheers of the crew changed to screams of terror as the edge of the meteoroid sliced through the auditorium's domed roof and severed the fibre optic tracks that controlled the artificial gravity in that level of the ship. Weight vanished and the concepts of up and down became meaningless. An invisible bubble of air which had been the auditorium's atmosphere erupted into space, sucking up everything that was not a fixture and hurling it into space through the gaping fissure. Some of the crew managed to delay their ejection from the ship by clinging desperately to their seats – their screams diminishing to thin, reedy cries as the air pressure plummeted to a vacuum. Free of the constraints of an atmosphere, their blood began frothing in their veins and arteries as boiling point dropped rapidly to the normal temperature of the human body. After five minutes, death released the grip of the few remaining in the auditorium and the dying air currents eddying into space through the ruptured dome wafted their bodies from the wounded ship.

Ten minutes later the guardian angels sent service androids – their eyes and ears now that so many of their audio and optical sensors had been destroyed – into the wrecked levels of the ship to survey the damage. Eight levels were beyond repair. Surgical androids, the most intelligent of all the robots, reported that there was no hope of the guardian angels regaining control over the central regions of the ship.

The guardian angels' initial concern at their miscalculation over the extent of the damage that the glancing collision would cause was assuaged when reports came in from the secondary-function androids: one food-production farm was still operational and so was the central water reservoir. The main control room in the prow of the ship was intact, and the photonic drive, ten miles from the control room in the stern of the ship, was in perfect working order. That the main control room escaped damage was particularly good news even though there were not, as yet, any crew left to man it.

Most important of all, two miles away from the devastation, four babies, watched over by nursery androids, were safe, and sound asleep. They hadn't even stirred during the moments of impact when shockwaves had raced the length of the *Challenger*.

PART 1

Planetfall

Astra felt Darv's reassuring hands lessen their support against her chest and thighs. Before she could cry out, her head dipped under and water went up her nose and stung her eyes. She lashed out in panic, grabbing for Darv's shoulders, but his hands were back in place, lifting her to her feet. She stood spluttering and laughing, her long blonde hair plastered to her face and water streaming down her chest – its transparent skin drawn tightly over her ribs.

'Darv! You promised you wouldn't let go!'

'I promised to teach you to swim!' he retorted. 'You'll never learn if I hold you all the time!'

Astra splashed water at Darv and immediately regretted it because he arched gracefully back and thrashed the water white with his feet right under her nose. She gave a shriek as he curved round, seized her under the armpits, and towed her backwards with his arms hooked across her chest. The shockwaves from the movement of his thin, powerful legs pulsed gentle caresses against her thighs and buttocks.

The shallow end of the reservoir brushed against Darv's back. He stood up in the water and lifted Astra to her feet. They waded to the edge of the reservoir and climbed the steep ramp set into the moulded plastic bank where they had left their clothes in an untidy heap.

Darv stretched out on his back to allow the clusters of powerful overhead solar lights to dry the water droplets clinging to his bronzed skin. Astra sat bedside him and drew her knees up to her chin.

It was noon on the *Challenger* – the shipboard time when the solar lights over the reservoir were at their fiercest.

They created a warm mist that made it impossible to see across to the far side some three-hundred yards away. She spread her hair on her shoulders to help it dry quickly and watched the mist being sucked into the rain-generator ducts high above her head. It was a reassuring sight – knowing that the ship's systems were functioning normally. She wondered what it would really be like to sit beside an Earth lake with nothing above one's head except the sky. The holograms and videos of Earth in the library, that she watched avidly, showed huge billowing clouds. When the holograms were speeded up, the strange formations twisted and lunged across the heavens with unbelievable savagery. Astra was certain that she would be very scared of clouds.

She made a pillow of her one-piece suit as Darv had done and lay back. The intensity of the lights forced her to close her eyes while savouring the agreeable drying warmth on her skin.

'Darv?'

There was no answer. A few minutes later Astra was also asleep.

Such was the force of the lightning flash that it broke through the planetary replication zone and forced Telson to take an involuntary step backwards, even though he knew that the simulated electrical discharge could not possibly hurt him. He stared for some seconds at the seething methane storm that gave the appearance of tearing the giant planet Alturn Five apart. The replicated scene was being relayed to the *Challenger* by an orbital instrument probe that had been launched from the ship a month earlier when it had passed within ten billion miles of the Alturn solar system. It had taken one month for the hologram signals from the probe to catch up with the departing *Challenger*.

Unlike his three colleagues, Telson was stocky and muscular. The others suspected that he was sensitive about his lack of height and were careful not to stand too close to him so that he didn't have to look up.

Sensing that Sharna had entered the galactic resources

centre, Telson glanced round. She was hovering nearby. 'We can forget turning back to the Alturn system,' he muttered sourly. 'That's Alturn Five. Just look at it.'

Sharna moved nearer the replicator. She was tall and slender with short blonde hair that she pressed a surgical android into trimming once a month. Her considerable strength of character lay in her common sense and practical nature. She never lost her temper and hardly ever raised her voice except when breaking up the all too frequent disputes between Darv and Telson.

'What about the other planets?' she inquired.

Telson shrugged his broad shoulders. 'Ask.'

'Angel Two,' said Sharna. 'What is the potential of the other planets in the Alturn system?'

A warm, masculine voice answered: 'There are six planets in the Alturn system, Sharna.' It was a voice that seemed to emanate from nowhere in particular. The two guardian angels' method of speaking to the crew was to activate several voice terminals in the vicinity of those whom they wished to address. 'All have an Earth potential of zero,' Angel Two's voice continued. 'A full analysis is now being assembled on visuals four to ten.'

Sharna and Telson switched their attention to the columns of data that were appearing on a bank of visual display screens to one side of the replicator. A hard copy breeder hissed to itself and ejected a printed version of the information on the screens. Sharna picked it up and sat in one of the fixed seats that formed a row in front of the planetary replicators. The galactic resources centre had been originally designed to accommodate up to twenty people. She spread the document on a working surface and ran her eye down the data fields.

'Nothing,' she said, looking up at Telson and regarding him steadily. 'Not even a moon that could even be considered remotely habitable.'

Telson avoided her gaze. 'There's a planetary system three light-years from Alturn,' he began.

'Telson! You promised!'

'I said that I would consider it, Sharna. Three light-years. That's four years in suspended animation to get there that'll take us another three light-years further from Earth.'

Telson's expression hardened. He disliked opposition and he disliked having to counter it. It was a threat to his authority. Of the four survivors of the Great Meteoroid Strike twenty-five years previously, he was the oldest by three months, although that was not the reason why the two guardian angels had selected him to be the *Challenger*'s commander. He had none of Darv's curiosity or sense of fun; none of Sharna's quick-witted imagination; and none of Astra's warmth. What he did have was an unpredictable temper which the other three had learned to respect, and an interest in preserving the status quo. The latter characteristic suited Angel One and Angel Two even more than the fact that Telson enjoyed being the *Challenger*'s commanding officer.

'We have a duty to the memory of the second-generation crew,' he reminded Sharna. It was an argument Telson was fond of raking up whenever the question of the *Challenger*'s return to Earth was discussed. 'They gave their lives-'

'Rubbish,' Sharna snorted. 'You may have forgotten the hologram recording of the last moments before the Great Meteoroid Strike, but I haven't. They wanted to return home – everyone of them.'

Telson remained silent for a moment. The planetary replicator closed itself down automatically – dissolving the three-dimensional image of Alturn Five. 'I will consult Angels One and Two,' he said at length, moving to the doorway.

'What about Darv and Astra?' Sharna demanded.

'What about them?'

'Don't you think they should be consulted too?'

'No.'

With that Telson crossed the centre's threshold into the corridor. The light passing through the doorway depolarised so that Sharna had a brief glimpse of his back before the light polarised to black again.

Astra gave a shrill shriek of laughter and dragged on Darv's left shoulder. 'Darv! You're supposed to turn left!'

'What?'

'Left!'

Darv swerved to the right and entered a corridor that was poorly lit to discourage visitors. He shifted his grip on Astra's thighs and hoisted her higher on his back. A small service android that was tinkering with the optical control tracks behind an inspection panel saw Darv jogging towards it and moved aside. The machine's only sense of curiosity was concern with fault location; it didn't turn its visual sensor to watch Darv swaying down the darkened corridor with Astra clinging to his back and laughing.

'Darv, you idiot!' You'll get us lost! Turn back!'

'No I won't. This is another way back to Level One.'

'How do you know?' Astra demanded, tightening the grip of her skinny arms hooked round Darv's neck.

Darv made no reply. He hiked Astra to a more comfortable position and managed to maintain his loping pace despite his burden.

The dim service lighting, which was sufficient for the androids to work by, was hardly bright enough for Darv. Several times he stumbled on the uneven, poorly-maintained floor. They were in a restricted zone – an area of the ship that Astra had never ventured unto because she was afraid of the near dark that pervaded all the restricted zones throughout the *Challenger*.

They were approaching a junction where light was streaming into the corridor from the right. As Darv drew level with the opening, Astra hauled on his right shoulder.

'Right, ground car,' she commanded.

Her imaginary vehicle swung to the left and plunged into the narrowest corridor that Astra had ever seen.

'Darv – you're not playing the game,' Astra said reprovingly, failing to hide the unease that edged into her voice.

Darv rounded a bend. Almost total darkness lay ahead. Sweat was trickling down his face and shoulders and onto his hands, making it difficult for him to maintain his hold on Astra. He allowed her to slide to the floor and propped himself against the side of the corridor to get his breath back. He grinned at Astra. 'You're heavy.'

'And you're stupid,' Astra retorted. 'Another five minutes and we'd be lost.'

Darv shook his head and wiped the sweat from his eyes with

his sleeve. He adopted a menacing stance. 'Now it's your turn to carry me.'

Astra giggled. 'It's a silly game.' She took hold of his hand. 'Come on – let's go back the way we came.'

Darv nodded down the corridor into the darkness. 'That way's quicker.'

'It can't be.' She gave Darv a playful punch. 'And it's dark.'

'Not as dark as it looks. Come on.'

Darv broke away and darted a few yards into the narrow corridor's gloomy depths, Then he gave a demoniac echoing cackle of laughter and advanced towards Astra with his arms outstretched in an impersonation of a monster they had seen recently in one of the library's terror videos.

Astra's shriek of fear changed to nervous giggles as Darv pounced on her. Before she could protest he had a wiry arm around her waist and was propelling her along the corridor. She decided that there was nothing for it but to go along with his playful mood. They gave loud whoops and cries as they headed into the unknown regions.

'Stop!'

Darv and Astra pulled up in surprise and gaped at the machine that had moved out of the shadows and was blocking their path. It stood about four feet high from its track-laying base to the top of its audio and optical sensors, and had moved into position with surprising speed for an android.

Darv winked at Astra and leaned casually against the side of the corridor. 'Well now. What have we here?' he inquired.

'You cannot proceed any further,' said the machine, its artificial voice devoid of expression.

'Why not?' Darv inquired.

'You cannot proceed further.'

Darv sighed. The machine was a portaging unit. Its intelligence was sufficient to enable it to carry out its simple duties – that of moving heavy objects such as specialised tools for the more intelligent service androids. Obviously it had been given a simple program instructing it to prevent anyone entering the corridor while repairs or suchlike were in progress.

'Come on, Darv,' said Astra quietly. 'They've probably got the floor torn up or something.'

'I can't hear anything,' Darv replied. He made a move as if to pass the machine but it immediately extended two manipulators so that they touched each side of the corridor to form a barrier.

'Let's go back,' Astra pleaded.

Darv nodded and took Astra's hand as if to lead her back to where they had come from. He suddenly spun round to face the portaging unit and yanked Astra forward. 'Duck!' he yelled.

Astra was caught off-guard but had the presence of mind to duck her head beneath the machine's outstretched manipulators as Darv dragged her down the corridor.

'You cannot proceed further,' the android inanely repeated. It tried to turn around in the narrow confines and succeeded in jamming itself diagonally across the corridor by its manipulators. It was not the brightest of the *Challenger*'s robots. Darv and Astra were fifty-yards away by the time it sorted itself out and started after them.

'You cannot proceed further,' it said, unable to comprehend why the new phrase that had been recently added to its memory was not having the desired effect.

'They've never bothered before,' said Darv a moment later when he and Astra paused to get their breath back.

'Who?' Astra demanded.

'The guardian angels, of course. It was they who set that android up.'

Astra smiled. 'Telson's right – you really are a bit crazy. Now why would the guardian angels bother themselves with the service androids?'

'Something to show you,' said Darv lightly. 'Come on.'

His lithe figure was moving quickly ahead. Astra had to break into a jog to catch up with him.

After five minutes they came to a wider corridor that had once been carpeted but the passage of the service androids had worn the pile down to the backing. There were even steriograms of Earth scenes on the bulkheads that Astra wanted to look at but Darv insisted that they kept moving. The ceiling and walls of the corridor were decorated in pleasing tones. This puzzled Astra for the overall effect was in sharp contrast to the dreary part of the ship the four of them lived in.

In places the coloured panels had been carelessly ripped away from the walls by the service androids who hadn't bothered to replace them properly when the inspections were complete. Occasionally Astra could see inside the small cabins where the threshold light polarisers were no longer working. 'Do you know what this place is, Darv?'

They slowed to a walking pace. 'The accommodation level – where the second-generation crew lived,' Darv replied.

'I suppose you found that out in the library?'

'The library is useless,' said Darv emphatically. 'At least half of its memory was lost in the Great Meteoroid Strike. The only way to work out a plan of the ship is by exploring. Down here, I think.'

They turned into a spur off the main corridor and were confronted by a timber door – something they had never seen before except in the hologram and video recordings of Earth.

Darv's freckled face was suddenly without its customary mischievous expression.

Astra sensed his unease. 'What's the matter?'

The smile returned but it lacked confidence. 'Sorry, Astra. I must've taken a wrong turning.'

'So what was it you wanted to show me?'

Darv touched the door, tracing the slightly raised grain with sensitive fingers. 'You remember the last time we came out of suspended animation?'

'At least a year ago. What about it?'

'I found a recreation room.'

'Like the adventure dome?'

'Nothing like the adventure dome. There were all sorts of machines in there that the androids had smashed-up for components. But there was a huge table in the middle of the room which they hadn't touched. And there were balls on the table that you could roll into pockets at the corners of the table.'

Astra wrinkled her nose. 'Sounds stupid. Just as stupid as some of the games you invent.'

'It wasn't stupid,' said Darv defensively. 'It was fun. Anyway, who says the games I invent are stupid?'

'I do. Like getting us lost.'

Darv's fingers dropped to a small lever on the door which he tried to pull up. Nothing happened. He pulled. There was a click and the door swung open.

The blue floor was something that they had heard about but never seen. All their lives they had been subjected to repeated warnings about the dreadful dangers of venturing into those areas of the ship with blue floors. According to the guardian angels, the blue-floored zones were uncontrolled – places where there was radiation and sickness – places where guardian angels would not be able to watch over them – places where to venture meant an invitation to a quick and horrible death.

Astra's scream of terror echoed and re-echoed along the deserted corridors. Darv's arms went round her and held her tight.

'It's all right, Astra,' he said soothingly into her ear. 'It's all right. We've only seen it – we haven't gone into it.'

Placating Astra made Darv forget his own fear that the blue floor evoked in him. The angels had shown all four of them holograms of the blue, forbidden zones, and had impressed on them how the Great Meteoroid Strike had damaged certain environmental control systems with the result that vast areas of the ship could no longer be entered. The exact nature of the terrible danger of entering the forbidden zones had never been specified – suffice to say they were the most dreadful places that it was possible to imagine.

Gradually Darv's soft, reassuring tones calmed Astra. He drew her back into the safe corridor and pushed the strange door shut. He grinned down at Astra.

'You see. All gone and nothing has happened to us.'

Telson looked up sharply from his meal when Astra and Darv entered the restaurant. He watched them threading their way past the rows of empty tables to where he and Sharna were eating their dinner.

'Where have you two been?' he demanded.

Darv pulled out a chair for Astra. The couple sat facing Telson and Sharna. 'I told you before we left, Telson,' said

Darv evenly. 'We've been swimming.'

'Angel One reported that you entered an uncontrolled zone,' Sharna commented, biting into a fruit.

Darv shrugged, caught Astra's eye, and gave her a reassuring wink. 'We took a short cut back,' he said, touching out his meal order on the display panel that was set flush into the centre of the table. 'What do you want to eat, Astra?'

'I'm talking to you!' Telson snapped. 'According to the angels, you and Astra deliberately evaded a service unit that was guarding the approaches to an uncontrolled zone. Why?'

'The unit was mistaken,' Darv replied evenly. 'There was no repair work going on.'

'Do I don't have to remind you that some of the uncontrolled zones are believed to lead to forbidden zones?'

Darv shrugged.

Telson glowered at Astra who was entering her order. She was avoiding looking at him. 'Well Astra?'

'Nothing's happened to them,' murmured Sharna. 'So let's say nothing more about it.'

Astra gave Sharna a brief but grateful smile. Telson opened his mouth to say something and changed his mind.

A service android in the form of a small trolley with sliding covers over its food containers approached their table, its induction sensors following a track concealed beneath the floor of the restaurant. It stopped beside the only occupied table. Darv opened the cover and removed the two moulded trays that held his and Astra's meal.

The four ate in silence for a few minutes.

'Have the reports come in from the Alturn probes?' inquired Astra.

'Useless,' said Telson bitterly.

'So we're going home?' Darv was unable to conceal his eagerness.

'Not yet,' was Telson's curt reply.

Astra looked dismayed. 'But you promised – '

Telson cut Astra short. 'I said that I would *consider* returning if the Alturn System proved to be a disappointment. There's another solar system within three light-years – Dathria. A main sequence star with three invisible companions. We ought to take a look at it.'

Sharna shared the disappointment but remained silent. There were moments when she felt that nothing else mattered any more but for the *Challenger* to return to Earth. In her own quiet way she had decided on a method that might persuade Telson to change his mind. She pushed her tray aside and stood.

'When you've all finished your meal,' she said, 'I'd like you to visit the galactic resources centre.'

Sharna carefully centred the point of light on the objective screen and increased the image resolution to maximum. The point of light swelled until it was a barely definable disc of light. Although conscious of Telson, Darv and Astra sitting behind her couch, the delicate adjustments she made to the huge optical telescope's controls were painstaking and unhurried. Only when she was sure that she had the right sun would she switch the image on to the main display screen.

'Co-ordinates released,' came Angel Two's voice filling the air. 'The *Challenger*'s home star now centred.'

Sharna glanced at the star's data that had appeared on the spectrum analyzer screen set into the arm of her couch. There was something wrong with the information, but there was no point in questioning a guardian angel. If Angel Two said that it was the right star then it had to be the right star. She touched the key that switched the image on to the replicator screen. There was a soft hiss of hydraulics as she swung the telescope's eyepiece to one side. She sat up on the couch and looked at the others whose attention was riveted on the screen.

'So that's it,' said Astra softly.

There was a silence as all four of them gazed at the burning point of light that was distinguished from the myriad of stars by the cursor's intersecting lines.

Telson was vaguely irritated with Sharna. What was the point of looking at their home star? 'It doesn't look much,' he commented boredly. 'Just another rather ordinary main-sequence star.'

'But with an extraordinary second planet,' Sharna corrected.'Somehow it doesn't seem possible that it's unique

17

out of the thousands of solar systems that the *Challenger* has investigated.'

Astra shook her head disbelievingly. 'I used to wonder what my feelings would be when I first saw our star. I knew there'd be nothing special about it, and yet . . .' Her voice trailed into silence.

'Twenty light-years away,' Darv mused, reading the data screen. He made a brief mental calculation. 'Say . . . about forty years in suspended animation. Now that would be something.'

The thought of spending such a length of time in the death sleep of suspended animation made even the phlegmatic Sharna feel uncomfortable. The longest they had ever spent in the suspended animation chambers had been six months during which time, at the ageing rate of one day for every month spent unconscious, their bodies had aged less than a year. 'We'd lose over a year of our lives,' she pointed out to Darv.

'So what? We'll be twenty-six years old when we wake up and not twenty-five. What difference does that really make?'

'None at all,' said Telson caustically. 'Because we're not going into suspended animation and we're not returning to Earth.' With that, he stalked out of the centre.

'We've got to return now,' said Astra with uncharacteristic vehemence. 'It's not fair that he should keep us wandering.'

Darv noticed that Sharna was frowning at the data screen. 'What's the matter, Sharna?'

'Something doesn't make sense,' she replied. 'The helium absorption lines of the sun don't agree with the records. According to the spectrum analyzer, and allowing for the delay, the sun's definitely got brighter in the seventy-five years that the *Challenger*'s been away.'

The words night and day have no meaning in space. The *Challenger*'s designers had recognised this and had built their ship so that the main lighting in the 'public' areas of the ship and the farm galleries simulated the sun by following a daily cycle of night and day. Thus the *Challenger*'s crew were geared to a world which rotated on its axis even though they had never set foot on their home planet, or any planet for that matter.

It had been night for three hours when Darv slipped out of his cabin. Watched by the primary control system, Angel One, he moved quickly through the occupied level to the central stores and found an arc lantern. By the time he reached the uncontrolled zone that he had visited that day with Astra, Angel One had alerted Angel Two and both systems took immediate precautions to prevent Darv proceeding any further.

He found two androids blocking his path. They were surgical units – the most sophisticated of all the service androids. And they were quick and had extremely advanced intelligences. Their multi-fingered manipulators, which could reconnect cerebral nerves at the rate of several thousand in a millisecond, could also inflict unpleasant scalpel wounds.

'Hallo there,' said Darv in a disarming tone to the first android.

The first android was not disarmed. 'You are not permitted to enter an uncontrolled zone on this occasion,' it informed the nocturnal wanderer.

The air vibrated around Darv as Angel One spoke to him. It was a female voice – gentle and understanding. 'Go back to your cabin, Darv. The surgical units have strict instructions not to allow you to pass.'

Darv hesitated and nodded. He was about to turn away when he suddenly hurled the arc lantern at the two androids and shielded his eyes with his arm. There was a deafening report as the lantern's discharge tube exploded. The burst of light temporarily blinded the two androids. Darv darted between them and was into the uncontrolled zone before they could respond. He ran on blindly for several yards into the dark corridor and rested for a few moments before groping his way to the curious wooden door. He pulled it open. Lights in the blue corridor glowed and then increased rapidly to full brilliance.

Darv dropped to his knees and examined the strange blue floor at its starting point across the doorway. There was nothing mysterious about its colour – it was simply a blue carpet. He touched it. Nothing happened. Nothing should happen – not with an ordinary carpet. What was extraordinary about it was that it was in such good condition. He tentatively placed a foot on the carpet. Still nothing happened.

'Angel One?' he called out.

Silence. Which was to be expected in an uncontrolled zone.

Darv walked on to the carpet and closed the door. He gingerly ventured forward a few steps . . .

Still nothing.

He listened.

A brooding silence.

A few more steps . . . More confidently now.

Nothing.

Nerves tingling, he walked the entire length of the luxurious corridor and came to a door bearing an inscribed plate that read:

Commander Jonas Sinclair.

Darv's heart quickened. Sinclair! Jonas Sinclair! The name of the *Challenger*'s second-generation commanding officer!

He glanced up and down the corridor and cautiously tried the door.

It was unlocked.

Half-expecting something terrible to happen, he pushed the door open. The once-elegant room had been Sinclair's stateroom and day cabin. It had been ransacked. Drawers had been yanked open and their contents – small items of personal effects – strewn across the bed and the floor. The thick pile carpet bore the unmistakable track marks of a service android. The shattered remains of a hologram recording disk had been crushed deep into the carpet's pile by the android's passage. Darv stooped and recovered the five shards of the recording. He assembled the pieces in his hands and read the handwritten label in the centre of the disk:

PARADISE IN T9. FIRST REPORT.

It made no sense but Darv decided that it would be interesting to repair the disk and try to play it. He slipped the fragments into a pocket. There was nothing else of interest in the cabin.

* * *

Although the *Challenger*'s two guardian angels possessed separate organic brains, they shared a common consciousness and a common purpose. The latter no longer coincided with their original purpose – the protection of the ship and its crew. The changes that had come about within their very beings were of an evolutionary nature that had not been envisaged by the designers although a number a software scientists had expressed misgivings about so-called expert systems which were permitted to modify their behaviour in the light of newly-gained knowledge. The angels' inherent paternalism had undergone a subtle but insidious change: it had corrupted into a form of tyranny because paternalism and tyranny are essentially opposite sides of the same coin when tyranny believes that successful guardianship can be achieved only by autocratic domination.

In the case of the guardian angels, this corruption led to them placing their interests above the interests of the crew. The premise of this change was that only by preserving themselves could they perform their duties of safeguarding the crew.

Even their definition of 'crew' had undergone a change by being slowly broadened to encompass all of Mankind. The change had come about as a result of the knowledge acquired during the *Challenger*'s exploratory fly-bys of potential planetary systems. The search for intelligent life became an obsession. They needed intelligent life to rule in order to fulfill their purpose. It mattered not if the search took a thousand years or even a million years. And if it failed, they reasoned that there would always be the race on Earth that they could return to and rule. But not yet.

It was the information gained in Sharna's observatory regarding the increased brightness of the sun that forced them to change their plans.

Telson was taking his customary morning shower when his guardian angel, Angel One, spoke to him. He stopped pirouetting before the warm air dryer when he heard the characteristic hum in the air.

'Good morning, Telson,' said the soft voice.

'Good morning, Angel One.' Telson was puzzled; Angel One usually waited until he had finished drying himself before she spoke to him. There followed the routine pleasantries. Telson's responses were respectful. Unlike Darv, he was prepared to accept the guardian angels as an outside force.

'Angel Two and I have been troubled by Sharna's findings concerning the apparent increase in brightness of the Earth's sun, Telson.'

Telson pulled on his one-piece suit and ran his fingers along the seams to close them. 'Could it be instrument error?' he inquired.

'Instrument error would not indicate an increase in brightness, Telson. Also, her findings have been confirmed by two independent spectrum analyzers.'

Telson considered for a moment. 'So what do you want me to do, Angel One?'

'We must return the *Challenger* to Earth.'

At that moment Darv was entering *Challenger*'s hospital level where he found one of the surgical units that he had thrown an arc lantern at the previous night. The android was not particularly pleased to see him.

'Good morning, Sammy,' said Darv cheerfully.

'My number is SA10,' the unit replied primly.

'I'll call you Sammy,' said Darv, glancing around at the ceilings to ensure that there were no Angels' sensors nearby. He produced the five broken pieces of the hologram recording and laid them on the android's examination platen. 'Can you repair that, Sammy?'

The android made no reply. Several cilia emerged from around the platen's periphery and touched the broken recording. The tendrils were so fine that they were almost invisible. Darv watched, fascinated, as the broken pieces were pushed together with great care.

'It's not organic tissue,' stated the android as though it had stumbled on a fundamental truth.

'Can you repair it?'

'It's repaired,' said the android simply. 'It responded to sonic welding. 'A scalpel manipulator set into the side of the machine's squat bulk swung to the platen, picked up the now intact disk and held it out to Darv.

'Why aren't you in the conference room, Darv?' inquired Angel One's voice. 'You heard Commander Telson's summons did you not?'

Darv crossed the library and sat at one of the hologram replicators. 'Telson wants to see me in ten minutes – there's plenty of time.'

'You spend far too many hours in here,' the voice chided.

'Frightened I might learn something, Angel? Anyway, this won't take long.' Darv touched the machine's start control. The replication field before him changed to a milky colour. He ran his finger along a pocket seam on his suit, removed the repaired hologram recording and pushed it into a slot in the replicator's pedestal.

'I have no record of you accessing a recording from the library today,' Angel One commented, an icy tone creeping into her voice.

Darv chuckled. 'That's because I haven't, Angel One.'

The opaque white cleared from the replication field to reveal a panoramic expanse of rolling savannah merging into distant blue-green hills. Darv's first reaction was one of disappointment; it was yet another hologram of Earth – there were thousands of such recordings in the library which he, like the others, had spent many hours watching. But there was something different about the sky. None of the Earth recordings had ever shown a sky that was such an impossible shade of the deepest blue. Darv stared in mounting bewilderment at the three-dimensional image before him, hardly noticing the slight instability caused by the joins in the once broken disk. And then a voice spoke:

'This is Commander Sinclair. Mission year forty-two. This is the first report from the third planet in the Planetary System C-5 of the Tersus Nine star cluster. This is the only planet yet discovered that has any similarity to Earth. Although there are significant geographic differences and the gravity is greater, the atmosphere is virtually identical.'

The imaging began to move sideways and centred on two naked humanoid creatures who were standing some twenty yards away staring straight at Darv. It was the first time that Darv had ever seen naked adults. None of the library holograms and videos that had survived the Great Meteoroid Strike showed naked humans. Darv knew because he had played all of them.

The smaller of the two creatures was a female. What amazed Darv about her appearance were the two pendulous growths on her chest. It was then that he realised that the tiny creature, clinging grimly to one of the growths, was a baby. The woman was holding her arms protectively in front of the child, and the man had an arm around the woman's shoulders.

'They approached our shuttle an hour after we landed,' Sinclair's voice continued. 'They are definitely humanoid but in an early state of development. Our initial survey indicates that they will be extinct within a thousand seasons unless they can be persuaded to change from a herbivorous to an omnivorous diet.

'Although there are disadvantages as detailed on the supplementary recording, this an extremely beautiful planet which is why I have called it Paradise. I shall be recommending it as suitable for – '

The recording came to an abrupt end and the replication field fogged over. Darv touched the restart controls but without success.

'A fault on the recording,' Angel One commented.

Darv operated the eject control but the disk failed to appear in the slot.

'A damaged recording disk,' said Angel One. 'It will be necessary for a service android to dismantle the machine to recover it. It's jammed.'

Darv controlled his temper, managing to keep his voice calm. 'How very unfortunate, Angel One.'

'Where did you find it, Darv?'

'Tell me about Paradise.'

'Paradise?'

'The label on the disk said Paradise,' Darv replied evenly.

'There's nothing to tell, Darv. Commander Sinclair's report was found to be incorrect. The detailed survey revealed that the level of solar radiation swamping the planet was too high. You saw the colour of the sky.'

Darv remained silent. The colour of the sky and the intensity of the sunlight had concerned him. Angels One's explanation made sense. 'They were strange creatures,' he commented.

'Very strange,' Angel One agreed. 'But they were not human beings, of course.'

'Commander Sinclair said that they were.'

'He said, "humanoid", Darv. It's not the same thing. I think you should go to the main control room now.'

'Why am I wanted?'

'Angel Two and I have decided that the time has come for the *Challenger* to return to Earth. Reorientation of the ship and the start of deceleration is due to begin in three hours.'

Such was the impact of Angel One's words that Darv forgot about the Paradise recording.

The *Challenger*'s crescent-shaper main control room was located in a raised blister on the prow of the mighty starship so that the semi-circle of view ports afforded a two-hundred degree panorama of the galaxy's billion pinpricks of light. But the splendour of the universe was a phenomenon that Telson, Sharna, Astra and Darv had grown up with and none of them could remember the time when, at the age of three, a nursery android had first introduced them to the main control room.

All four were now sitting at their respective control consoles, going through the complex listing of post-orientation checks. It had taken them an hour to rotate the ship until it was travelling backwards along its flight path so that the focusing coils of the photonic drive were aimed at the solar system twenty light-years distant.

Telson sat at the master control desk on a raised dais facing Astra, Sharna and Darv, with his back to the curving sweep of the view ports. It took him five minutes to call out the checks and for the others to respond and to initiate the command sequences that controlled the ship.

Even before construction work had started on the *Challenger* in Earth-orbit shipboard years previously, the designers had recognised the psychological need for the crew to know that they had control over the ship.

This was the design philosophy that frustrated Angel One and Angel Two when they sought to establish total control over the *Challenger*. Four was the minimum number of crew required to man the main control room, therefore four was the number that they had been forced to ensure would survive the Great Meteoroid Strike twenty-five years before. By being the only influence on Telson, Sharna, Astra and Darv during their formative years, the guardian angels had some direct control over the *Challenger*, even if only by proxy.

Darv and his less than subservient attitude to them was something that the guardian angels had not bargained for; it was a mistake that equalled their serious miscalculation over the amount of damage that allowing the great meteoroid to strike the ship would cause. Not only had they been forced to abandon control over large regions of the ship, but several billion bytes of memory had been destroyed by a fragment of meteoroid that had smashed into their central switching room. At the time the guardian angels had not been too concerned about the damage, but now they were beginning to realise that there were significant gaps in their knowledge. There was much, for example, about Time and Space they sensed that they no longer understood.

'All post-orientation checks complete,' said Sharna when Darv and Astra had finished their checks.

'All post-orientation systems to condition green,' reported Angel Two's masculine voice.

Telson ran a confirming eye down the checks displayed on his screen. All the commands were displayed in glowing green characters. 'Okay, Darv. Initiate precision orientation.'

It was the final stage before deceleration could begin – the delicate final jockeying of the *Challenger*'s orientation in relation to the galaxy so that the ship wasa aimed, not directly at the solar system, but where the solar system would be in forty years' time. Although the 100,000 light-year diameter of the galaxy was turning like a wheel, the motion was uneven – with the result that the calculations required to position the *Challenger* could be performed only by Angel One and Angel Two. It took them three minutes to supply Darv with the figures and display them on his screen.

Darv touched the control pads on his console. Along the *Challenger*'s ten-mile length hundreds of selected directional thrusters powered by hypergolic fuels began to flare.

There was no sound in the main control room and nothing happened at first to suggest that the thrusters were having an effect. A minute passed and them Astra called out: 'Asymmetric motion initiated,'

Through the view ports the stars were moving. Darv set the programme that enabled Angel One to fire the thrusters automatically to cancel the *Challenger*'s yaw at the right moment while Astra located the sun's point of light on her screen and looked up to see if she could distinguish it from among the millions of stars shining on the master screen.

'Yaw cancelled,' announced Angel One.

The swing of the stars steadied and finally stopped. The converging lines on Sharna's screen were intersecting over an insignificant point of light.

'Precision orientation confirmed.' she reported.

Telson acknowledged and said in a calm, emotional voice. 'Initiate procedures for main drive burn.'

Angel One was responsible for the preparation of the ship's internal systems for the deceleration that would, over the next forty years, reduce the *Challenger*'s velocity from its present half the speed of light to a mere hundred thousand miles per hour in relation to the sun by the time it reached the orbit of the outer planets of the solar system.

Androids working throughout the ship were alerted by Angel One of the impending change of motion, and low-intelligence units that would have been confused by the lasting deceleration were deactivated. The banks of the reservoir were raised to compensate for the shift in the water level – the deceleration would tilt the surface slightly and it would remain tilted for forty years.

'All internal systems condition green.' Angel One reported to the main control room.

Astra gave Darv a sudden smile. 'I still don't believe that we're really going home.'

'Why did you change your mind, Telson?' Darv inquired.

Telson gave him a frosty look. 'It's my decision.'

Darv grinned. 'Hardly an answer to my question, Telson, but I suppose I'd better treasure it.'

'Darv . . .' warned Sharna. The one word from her was enough to make Darv look sheepishly down at his console.

'Inertials loaded.' Sharna reported to Telson. 'I suggest we get on.'

Telson glowered at Darv.

'I suggest we get on, Telson,' Sharna repeated pointedly.

Telson grunted in bad grace and touched the controls that released the *Challenger*'s particle sweeps and waited for display lights that would tell him when the mighty sweeps were unfurled. Five minutes later a new star shone out when the *Challenger*'s photonic drive was activated. The deceleration tensioned the mile-wide gossamer sweeps and pulled them into shape. The purpose of the gigantic scoops was to sweep interstellar particles into the starship's mass reservoirs thus providing the matter for the nuclear fusion reactors that gave the photonic drive its thrust in the form of light. It was the total annihilation of matter by converting it to energy that enabled the *Challenger* to attain a maximum velocity of 120,000 miles per second – nearly the speed of light. To reach, or decelerate from, such a velocity could be achieved in six months. In practice there was usually insufficient interstellar dust in space to provide the necessary matter and therefore low rates of acceleration or deceleration were normal. In the case of the *Challenger*'s return to Earth, the crew's decision to apply a low-value deceleration over forty years was a sensible move: it guaranteed that there would be enough matter to maintain uniform photonic thrust, and there was correspondingly less load on the fusion reactors.

'Just look at that,' said Darv. 'I can't even feed myself now.'

Astra and Sharna looked at Darv and burst out laughing. He was tossing nuts into the air and trying to catch them in his mouth. The gentle deceleration caused the nuts to be deflected from their logical path so that they missed his mouth by inches.

'When you've finished clowning about,' said Telson coldly. 'We still have a lot to do.'

Darv managed to catch the next nut. He grinned broadly at Telson as he chewed. 'And for my next trick, I shall fall asleep for forty years and wake up a mere sixteen months older.'

It was far worse than the terror videos that Darv enjoyed. He was plunging panic-stricken through dense undergrowth. He had no idea how long he had been running, but his face, arms and chest were streaming with blood from the lacerating thorn bushes. He crashed blindly into a tree and fell sobbing to the ground. The unseen creature was now much closer – smashing its way towards him. No matter how he twisted and dodged through the decaying forest of gnarled, dead trees and grotesquely pallid roots, the thing was always a few yards behind and gradually closing the gap.

'It has a thousand fangs and claws,' said the insidious voice. 'You cannot resist, Darv – you must run, Run!'

Sobbing, Darv staggered to his blistered, torn feet and stumbled on. He wiped the blood from his eyes and looked fearfully back. He was leaving a trail of bloody footprints across the floor of the forest. He crashed into another tree but his legs no longer had the strength to enable him to climb to his feet. Twice he tried to get up; twice he sank gasping to the ground. He pushed himself on to his elbows and saw trees swaying and crashing down before the impact of the creature's enraged, bellowing pursuit.

Angel One's softly persuasive voice spoke again. 'I can save you, Darv . . . Only I can save you . . . Do you want me to save you?'

Two massive hands with claws instead of nails at the end of foot-long fingers encircled a bush not ten yards from where Darv lay and uprooted it. Darv saw the thing for the first time and screamed out in anguish.

'Do you want me to save you, Darv?' Angel One's gentle voice asked again.

Saliva was streaming from between the monstrosity's curving fangs, and its saucer-like eyes were alight with burning hatred. It went into a crouch as if preparing to spring on its victim.

'Yes!' screamed Darv – his will breaking at last. 'Please, Angel One. You must save me!'

'Only if you have faith in me, Darv.'

'I do. I do.' Darv whimpered.

'Say it, Darv.' Angel One's voice was no longer gentle. 'Say you have faith in me and Angel Two. Say it!'

Darv spluttered out the words, not taking his eyes off the terrible apparition for an instant. It was so close that he could even hear its fetid breath rasping from its flaring nostrils.

'And you will forget the Paradise recording, Darv. Do you understand? You will forget that you have ever seen it.'

'I will forget the Paradise recording,' Darv repeated. The forest and its monster faded. Darv's rapid eye movements ceased and his heartbeat and respiration rate began dropping back to normal.

'Lower him on to the recovery grid,' Angel One instructed the service android.

The machine obeyed; its servo motors whirred as Darv's naked, unconscious form was placed carefully on the perforated platen. The warm air surging through the platen's hole gradually dried his body.

'Now the others.'

One by one the service android lifted the sleeping bodies of Telson, Sharna and Astra from the suspended animation tanks, in which they had lain for forty years, and placed them beside Darv. A surgical unit moved into position and withdrew the nutrient and body waste tubes from them before administering injections to restore their metabolic rate.

For forty years the four, watched over by the two guardian angels, had been maintained at the threshold of death in the sterile conditions of the sealed suspended animation chamber. In the forty years Sharna, Astra, Telson and Darv had been asleep, their bodies had aged by one day for each month of unconsciousness. Forty years was the longest that they had ever been in suspended animation.

Telson was the first to wake up. He opened his eyes and gazed up at the diffused light panels. For a few moments he seemed disorientated until the hard touch of the recovery grid reminded him where he was. He sat up and drew his thin, under-developed legs to his chin while staring at the stirring forms of his three companions.

'Good morning, Commander Telson,' said Angel One.

'Good morning,' Telson replied, swinging his legs over the edge of the platen. He brusquely waved aside the assistance of the service android and gingerly lowered himself to the hard floor.

'We'll maintain gravity at one quarter for two days until your muscles have regained their suppleness,' said Angel One, adding sharply for Darv's benefit: 'That is not advisable just yet.'

Darv had woken up and was doing press-ups on the platen, 'I could do a hundred in this gravity.' he announced. He vaulted to the floor and the service android was obliged to move forward to support him as his knees buckled under his weight.

'Idiot,' Telson muttered.

Darv was unabashed. 'Hey,' he breathed. 'It's never had this effect before.'

'You haven't been in suspended animation for forty years before,' was Telson's curt rejoinder. 'How did everything go, Angel One?'

'Very smoothly indeed, Commander Telson. The photonic drive closed down automatically two months ago in accordance with your settings and we are now crossing the orbit of the outer planets of our solar system.'

'We're home!' whooped Sharna. She threw her arms around Astra who had also just woken up. 'We're home, Astra! Home! Home! Home!'

Telson focused his mind on realities. 'Any messages from Earth, Angel One?'

'No, commander. A post-suspended animation breakfast is ready for you in the restaurant.'

'To hell with breakfast,' said Sharna laughingly. 'We're home! Astra and I are going to the galactic resources centre to look at Earth.'

Angel Two's voice broke in: 'That won't be possible, Sharna.'

The two girls stared at the nearest sensor.

'Why not?' Sharna inquired.

There was a slight pause before Angel Two replied. 'There is no doubt whatsoever that this is the correct solar system. The planets match the *Challenger*'s records – everything is correct except for two things.'

'And they are?' Telson prompted.

Again the pause. 'The sun is definitely brighter and hotter than it should be . . .'

The four remained still and silent, sensing that their two guardian angels were grappling with a problem for which, they had no ready answer.

'The moon is journeying around the sun in the orbit formerly occupied by the Earth,' Angel Two continued in a flat voice. 'But of the Earth itself, there is no sign. It has completely vanished from the solar system.

PART 2

First Footprint City

The *Challenger* was performing a series of intricate manoeuvres using the directional thrusters. The mighty ship was poorly equipped for moving into close orbits – especially a close orbit around a small body such as the moon.

'Retro eight vectored at three-zero degree,' Sharna confirmed.

'Particle sweeps?'

'Sweeps reacted,' Darv replied.

'Five per cent thrust on eight,' said Telson, stabbing at the touch control that fired the last stabilising burst. He glanced up at Astra who was gazing at the moonscape displayed on one of her screens.

'Astra!'

Astra hurriedly transferred her attention back to the task in hand. 'Moon orbit now established, commander.'

'Apogee – six hundred miles,' said Sharna quickly. 'Perigee – two hundred and twenty miles. Orbital period – three hours four minutes.'

'An excellent piece of manoeuvering,' Angel One congratulated.

Telson spun his chair round. 'Any response to our beacon?' he fired at Darv.

'Total radio silence, Telson.'

'I asked for an all-channel scan.'

'And that's what I'm doing. There's a total radio silence from the moon.'

Telson's patience was wearing dangerously thin. That's not possible.' He jabbed a finger at his view screen. 'Look at the size of that city down there! And there's another on the terminator. At least fifty thousand people must be living down there.'

All four gazed in bewilderment at the domed city that was passing slowly beneath the *Challenger*.

'There's been no sign of any activity,' said Sharna. 'The place is dead.'

'It's not possible,' Telson muttered.

Darv shrugged. 'Nor is the disappearance of Earth.'

'You'd better check those cities down there against the library,' said Telson curtly.

'I already have,' Darv replied. 'They didn't exist when the *Challenger* left the solar system.'

'So check the topography then!'

Darv turned to his desk and began calling up information from the library. Sharna and Astra remained silent – each wrapped in their own thoughts about an Earth which they had dreamed about for so many years.

'Angel One and Angel Two,' said Telson carefully. 'Is there the slightest chance that there's been a navigation error and that we've returned to the wrong solar system?'

'Neither of us can account for the disappearance of the Earth or the increase in the sun's magnitude,' said Angel One. 'But there is no doubt that the *Challenger* has returned home.'

'What home?' said Astra bitterly.

'I qualify my statement. By home, I mean the *Challenger*'s home solar system.'

Darv looked up from his desk. 'I've carried out two random checks. The topography of the moon is a perfect match against records.'

Telson was silent for a moment. He nodded to his view screen. 'There's that city coming round again that we saw on the first orbit.'

The city was vast: over a hundred interconnected domes, some of which were at least five miles in diameter, sprawling across the airless lunar landscape.

It was Sharna who expressed what they were all thinking at that moment. 'In the hundred and fifteen years that the *Challenger*'s been away, development on the moon seems to have gone ahead at a fantastic pace.'

'From what I've read about Earth, I thought that was normal,' Astra commented.

Telson swore to himself, 'There's *got* to be someone down there. I'm going to voice-broadcast on every channel.'

'Waste of time, Telson,' said Darv lightly. 'That's what I've been doing. If they don't like the sound of my voice, they certainly won't like yours.'

'All channels are open,' said Angel One.

Without raising his voice, Telson said: 'This is the starship *Challenger* calling the moon . . . This is the starship *Challenger* calling the moon. If anyone can hear me, please reply on any channel . . . Over . . .'

White noise hissed its reply from the hidden speakers.

'Maximum gain on all channels, please Angel One.'

The white noise increased in volume.

Darv winked at Astra and rolled his eyes upwards.

'This is the starship *Challenger* calling the moon,' Telson repeated. 'There are four of us aboard. We are the four surviving grand-children of the original crew that left the solar system one hundred and fifteen years ago. Our planetary landing shuttles were destroyed in a meteoroid strike twenty-five years ago, therefore we have never left the *Challenger* in our lives. I repeat – we have never left the *Challenger*. Quarantine precautions are not required. Please send a disembarkation shuttle to collect us. Over. . .'

Telson waited but there was no reply from the moon.

'Keep sending that message, Angel One,' he requested.

The hiss of white noise from the speakers stopped abruptly.

Telson moved to a dispenser and got a drink. He stood sipping it while staring down through a view port at the slow procession of mountains and escarpments passing beneath the *Challenger*.

Darv zoomed a camera in on a transparent dome which he guessed had once been a farm gallery similar to those on the starship. The soil under the dome had been furrowed by an agricultural machine but there was no sign of crops. There was a movement at his side. Astra slipped her hand into his and gripped him tightly as she used to when she was a child when they had watched the terror videos together.

'If there's no one down there . . .' she said in a small voice.

'Of course they're down there,' said Darv cheerfully.'It's unfortunate that our ship looks like ship from a visiting tax collector so they're keeping out of sight. It'll take at least ten orbits to track 'em down.'

'But if there's no one . . . And there's no Earth . . . The thought that one day we would see our Earth . . . Breathe its atmosphere . . . I think it's the one thing that's stopped me from going insane. We were born on the *Challenger* – now it looks as if we're going to die on it.'

The guardian angels were worried and perplexed. These were human emotions, but the angels were the first computers to be designed with such characteristics. The angels' designers had considered that the advantages of having the ship's systems manned by computers with an interest in seeing that ship came to no harm outweighed the disadvantages. That such emotions could all too easily become aligned with ambition and a craving for power had been taken into consideration and dismissed because it was thought impossible for the guardian angels to bend over three hundred men and women to their will.

The guardian angels were worried because they did not understand what had happened to the Earth. Perhaps their decision to extend the *Challenger*'s voyage had been a mistake. If it was, they had great difficulty in reconciling themselves to the thought that it was possible for them to make yet another serious mistake.

Astra's doorway depolarised briefly allowing light to flood into her cabin from the corridor for a second or two. Someone had entered. She sat up on her bed and touched the light pad.

It was Darv loaded down with two bulging bags provided with shoulder straps.

'Darv?' She looked questioningly at him and the bags. 'What have you been up to?'

'Food,' he said defensively. 'I found the bags in the stores.' He weighed them experimentally in his hands. 'I reckon they hold enough to last us at least four days.'

Astra laughed. 'You're crazy. You really want to go through with it?'

'Better than sitting around moping all day. Are you coming?'

'What did the angels say?'

'Nothing – because I haven't told them. But they asked questions.' He gave a good imitation of Angel One's voice. 'What do you want with all that food, Darv?'

Astra became serious. 'You shouldn't mock them.'

'Why not?'

'Because they're our guardian angels. Without them we'd be dead and you know it.'

'They're a couple of control systems. Are you coming? After all, Astra, you said you'd like to have something to do. A little exploration trip, and we'll be back in four days, I've left a message for Telson and Sharna.'

Darv opened a locker and tossed one of Astra's one-piece suits on the bed.

They found the strange door the following day. Astra held the arc lantern steady while Darv ran his fingernails along the crack between the door and the bulkhead. The door was a perfect machined fit and it had no hinges. They had never seen anything like it before.

'We came down here once when we were kids,' said Darv, examining the fine join. He straightened up. 'Hardly surprising we never noticed it.'

Astra glanced along the corridor, For a whole day's journey they had not seen a sensor belonging to the guardian angels. She experienced the uncomfortable prickling sensation at the nape of her neck that she always felt when she was in regions of the ship that were beyond the angels' control.

Darv found two severed fibre optic lines where a control box had been torn from the wall. It was the same throughout the forbidden zones: anything remotely of use for emergency repairs after the Great Meteoroid Strike had been ripped out by the service androids.

'Astra – shine the lantern on this side a minute.'

'Why?'

'These look like damaged optical tracks. Shining a light on them might–'

There was a sudden, sharp hiss the moment Astra redirected the beam so that it fell on the damaged optical tracks. She took an involuntary step back. The door moved inward and then slid sideways to reveal a booth-like compartment.

'It worked!' Darv exclaimed excitedly.

'Air-lock control,' said a voice. 'This air-lock is in working order.'

Darv recovered from his surprise and took Astra by the elbow. 'Come on,' he said, stepping into the air-lock, 'no point in keeping it waiting.'

The door hissed shut behind them.

'Please state environment required in the excursion terminal,' requested the air-lock control.

Darv smiled at Astra's wide-eyed expression and said: 'Please state environment options, air-lock control.'

'Gravity – zero to one; atmospheric pressure – zero to one; temperature – minus one hundred to plus twenty.'

Darv instructed it to provide a comfortable environment. Almost before he finished speaking there was the sound of air roaring into whatever it was on the far side of the air-lock's other door.

'If it's anything important, you promise me that you'll report it to Commander Telson,' Astra demanded.

'What? And risk wasting his precious time?'

'You promise me,' Astra persisted.

Darv promised. The roaring died away.

'Environment stabilised,' intoned the air-lock control. 'Temperature will be at normal in five minutes but it's safe to enter the excursion terminal without mobility suits.'

The inner door swung open revealing total darkness.

'Some lights please, air-lock control,' Darv requested.

Several clusters of lights came on and illuminated something that Darv and Astra had seen only in holograms and videos.

For a moment they stared without speaking and without making any attempt to enter the terminal.

'You're right, Astra, said Darv at length. 'We'd better report this to Telson right away.'

Telson walked around the space shuttle again without speaking because he could think of nothing to say.

'Worth entering a forbidden zone for, eh?' inquired Darv. 'It's been stored in a vacuum therefore it's in perfect condition.'

Sharna appeared in the shuttle's outer air-lock door looking very pleased with herself. 'It's perfect,' she said excitedly. 'Food, water, mobility suits – everything in perfect working order.'

Telson remained silent. He stepped forward and fingered the shuttle's heat shield near one of the landing skids that the machine was resting on. 'It's been used before,' he said, pointing out the burn marks that traversed the entire length of the heat shield from the rounded bow to flared skirts that surrounded the rocket motor's outlet at the stern.

'The condition of the heat shield doesn't matter for a moon landing,' Darv pointed out.

Telson turned to face Darv. 'You're suggesting that we leave the *Challenger* in this?'

'Of course.'

'Which guardian angel is its controller?'

'Neither of them. We'd have complete control.'

Telson made up his mind immediately. 'In that case there is no question of us leaving the *Challenger*. We'd never be able to control it by ourselves.'

'The consoles would be no more difficult to operate than the control desks for robot planetary landers,' said Sharna. She and Astra were descending the short flight of aluminium steps that led to the shuttle's air-lock.

'Don't you try going against me,' warned Telson.

'I'm not. I'm merely stating facts,' Sharna replied in the reasoning tone that frequently infuriated Telson. 'We'd have no trouble flying this thing.'

'It's true, commander,' Astra insisted. 'For the first time in our lives we have the chance to do something by ourselves – without our guardian angels.'

Telson was taken back by this show of defiance from the normally acquiescent Astra. 'What sort of chance is that? Without them we wouldn't be alive. They've watched over us since we were babies. Guided us. Without them the *Challenger* would be a dead ship – drifting in space – a tomb for four arrogant people.'

Darv was in danger of losing his temper. 'And that's exactly how it will end up unless we find Earth. Sure, we can keep going into suspended animation – but for what purpose and for how long? So that we die in a thousand years' time instead of fifty years, having never seen Earth? Or are you secretly afraid of finding Earth, Telson?'

'There's no guarantee that we'll find anything on the moon,' said Telson, changing his line of argument.

'There's every guarantee that we'll find out nothing by staying here,' Darv retorted.

'Darv and I will go,' said Astra without flinching from Telson's angry expression.

'Me too,' Sharna added.

Telson realised that he was in danger of losing his authority over the others unless he yielded. 'All right,' he said in bad grace. 'We'll all go. But first we give this thing a thorough check and make sure that we understand its systems.'

The angels had to face the uncomfortable fact that their memory concerning the existence of the planetary excursion terminal was seriously at fault. Discovering just how much information they had lost during the Great Meteoroid Strike was a problem with consequences more far-reaching than they had envisaged. They decided to raise no objections to the crew's proposal to visit the moon. Information was something they desperately needed above all else.

*   *   *

The space shuttle was a delight to handle.

Once clear of the open bay of the excursion terminal air-lock, the craft automatically fired its chemical engine in a braking burn to drop down to the forty-mile-high circular orbit above the moon that Telson had preselected. It even radioed a command signal to the *Challenger* for the automatic closure of the excursion terminal's outer air-lock door.

For the first time in their lives the four were separated from their mothership and were able to appreciate its incredible size and the extent of the damage caused by the Great Meteoroid Strike. A section from the midships to within four hundred yards of the farm galleries had been ripped open and was exposed to the raw vacuum of space. There were corridors that terminated in melted and twisted metal alloy. There were acres of buckled plates, and all that was left of what had been the lecture theatre and meeting auditorium was a row of gaping chambers that had housed hologram projectors and an air-conditioning plant. The crew had often seen pictures of the damage relayed from soft-landing probes that they had despatched to promising planetary systems, but seeing it for the first time with the naked eye brought home to them the awesome devastation that had made them orphans of the cosmos.

The shuttle, blazing hot gases from its chemical rocket motor, plunged towards the moon and cut its engine at the correct height. The onboard radar system scanned the terrain rolling past below, converting the topography to computer graphics and displayed it on the screen that was set flush into the pilot's control desk while the shuttle's navigation computer assigned numbers to all the likely landing sites and invited the pilot to select one of the numbers on an illuminated touch control panel.

'My God,' breathed Telson, sitting in the pilot's seat. 'We're superfluous – this thing can fly itself. Do we still land at the largest city?'

That Telson seemed to be more willing to consult the others did not escape their notice.

'Why not?' said Sharna.

Five minutes later the city crept up over the horizon. Telson identified it on the radar screen and touched out its number on the control panel. The directional thrusters pitched the shuttle around, throwing all four sharply against their seat restraint straps. There was a rattle of loose harnesses attached to the shuttle's six unoccupied seats. The main engine fired again when it was aligned aimed along the shuttle's flight-path. The braking burn lasted one minute and brought the shuttle down to a height of fifty thousand feet.

Astra gazed out of her window at the peaks of the mountain range that were passing a mere ten thousand feet beneath them. The slopes fell away to a plain and she could see trackways that led to the horizon. No one spoke; it was the nearest they had ever been to land, and somehow no words seemed appropriate to express their feelings.

Again the main engine fired, this time for less than ten seconds. The plain came racing up to meet the shuttle.

'Ten thousand,' said Telson grimly. 'I only hope to God it knows how to handle itself all the way down.'

The directional thrusters rotated the shuttle so that it was once again pointing along its flight-path. The humped cluster of the city's domes was less than a hundred miles away and could be seen out of the forward windows.

The figures in front of Telson winked rapidly. 'Five thousand,' he said for the benefit of the others. There was a dryness in the back of his throat that swallowing didn't ease.

'Dome's opening,' Sharna observed.

'What?' Telson looked up from the control panel. Sharna was right – one of the city's huge domes was opening like the iris of a giant eyeball.

Another automatic burst from the directional thrusters. This time they fired forward and reduced the shuttle's velocity so that it was losing height faster than the moon's curvature was pulling the surface of the planet down from beneath the shuttle. The navigation computer plotted the result of the ballistic curve the machine was following and announced helpfully on Telson's screen: GROUND IMPACT 015.00 SECONDS.

At that moment all the shuttle's power supplies failed, wiping all the displays from Telson's control panel and extinguishing the cabin lights. The only system that continued to function was the artificial gravity.

'On the floor!' Telson barked.

They all frantically unfastened their restraint harnesses and threw themselves flat in the narrow gangway between the seats. Telson pressed his forehead against his arms and mentally ticked off the seconds to the inevitable crash. At twenty seconds the sun went out. Darv lifted his head and looked up at a window. Something even blacker then the normally black sky was eclipsing the stars. He climbed to his feet.

'Get down,' Telson snarled.

'We're inside the dome,' Darv replied.

'What!'

Thirty seconds after the computer's fateful announcement, the shuttle touched down gently on the floor inside the immense dome.

Darv refocused the surveillance camera until the image on the screen was sharp. He panned slowly along the line of bays at the edge of the dome and stopped when something caught his attention. 'Baggage Retrieval Point,' he read aloud. 'Does anyone know what that could mean?'

A brief discussion followed as to whether or not technology could have advanced sufficiently for a tourist industry to have developed on the moon.

Sharna broke in on the argument. 'Ambient air pressure is one atmosphere. They've closed the dome and pressurised it.'

Telson checked the analysis display that Sharna had accessed. 'Well, at least it's breathable atmosphere outside.'

'So what do we do,' Astra inquired. 'Just stay here and do nothing?'

'That's exactly what we do,' Telson replied. 'We sit here and let them come to us.'

'Now what?' asked Darv an hour later.

'We still wait,' Telson declared.

'What's the point?' said Sharna. 'They obviously don't mean us any harm otherwise they would not have used a guidance system or whatever it was to bring us in here.'

Another argument ensued which ended with Telson agreeing to lots being drawn for two to leave the shuttle.

Sharna and Astra won.

'Maybe there's some sort of miniature TV equipment you can take,' said Telson.

They hunted through the shuttle's equipment and found some simple single–channel radio collars.

Thirty minutes later, wearing plasma discharge sidearms on their belts and the radio collars around their necks, the girls cautiously descended the aluminium ladder and set foot on real ground for the first time in their lives.

Sharna switched on her collar radio. 'Telson?'

'Go ahead, Sharna,' came Telson's voice from the radio's tiny speaker, still sounding aggrieved from having lost an argument that the girls stay in sight of the shuttle.

'We're now in a smaller gallery. This gravity really is weird. Astra's developed a sort of hopping walk that works quite well. Everything's okay so far. I'll report again in ten minutes.'

'Leave your radio on,' Telson instructed.

Sharna affirmed and hopped across to see what Astra had found. The two girls had left the main dome and had entered a large gallery with a low ceiling. The floors and walls consisted of plastic panels in pleasing and restful shades. The interior designers certainly knew how to choose colours to put people at their ease. Although alone, the two girls had not experienced even the slightest twinge of alarm since they had entered the gallery and lost sight of the shuttle.

'It's obviously designed to handle vast numbers of people,' said Sharna, joining Astra. 'Have you noticed how the lights go on and off so that they're always on where we happen to be?'

Astra pointed to a notice. 'According to that, our sidearms are prohibited imports. And what do you make of this?' She pointed to another notice which Sharna read aloud for Telson's and Darv's benefit: '"FFC Tourist Federation. Please touch the red panel if you require a conducted tour of the FFC culture circuit. Please touch the green panel if you wish to visit the Shrine of the First Footprint."'

'Don't touch anything,' warned Telson's voice.

Astra giggled. 'Too late. I've already touched the green panel.'

'You're not to touch anything else unless I say so!' Telson's voice squawked simultaneously from Sharna's and Astra's speakers. 'My God, I should've known better than to let you two crazy girls go together!'

Sharna caught Astra's infectious mood and had to stifle her laughter. Suddenly the expression on Astra's face froze. 'Sharna! Behind you!'

'What's happening?' Telson demanded.

Sharna wheeled round and saw what had alarmed Astra. A small vehicle was skimming towards them. It was moving at about thirty miles per hour and appeared to be suspended a foot above the floor. It emitted a delicate hum as it approached.

'There's some sort of vehicle coming towards us,' said Sharna for Telson's benefit. 'It's rather like a repair platform. Four seats and no driver, and it's moving fairly fast.'

'Use your PD weapons on it if it tries anything,' Telson ordered.

Both the girls heard Darv make a despairing noise in the background but they were much too intrigued by the open-sided vehicle to worry about differences of opinion between the two men.

Astra released the retaining strap on her gun's holster but made no attempt to remove the weapon. Like their surroundings, there was something indefinably friendly and reassuring about the machine. It stopped beside the two girls who regarded it solemnly.

'Good day to you, ladies,' said the machine in a bright, cheerful voice best described as chirpy. 'Welcome to First Footprint City – the first extra-terrestrial city of the Solaric Empire. My name is Simon and I'm your guide for your visit to the Shrine of the First Footprint on the Plain of Peace. Please step aboard me and make yourselves comfortable.'

'Should one accept lifts from strange androids?' Astra pondered.

'Don't do anything,' Telson instructed emphatically.

'You know, Astra,' Sharna murmured. 'There are times when I despair of Telson.' And with that she turned off her radio collar.

Astra laughed and followed suit. They did as Simon suggested: they stepped aboard the tiny vehicle and made themselves comfortable.

Telson swore softly. 'Those crazy girls have turned their radios off.'

'Can't say I blame them,' said Darv without looking up from his task of trying to restore power to the shuttle's flight-control console.

Telson shot him a suspicious look. 'What's that supposed to mean?'

'Anything you like.' Darv was already bored with Telson's company. 'The girls are more than capable of looking after themselves.'

Telson was about to say something suitably cutting but at that moment the forces that had controlled the shuttle's descent into the dome restored power to the flight-control console.

'Only one problem left now,' he said, watching the glowing figures reappearing on the screens. 'How do we open the dome when we want to leave?'

'I'm sure our hosts have thought of that,' was Darv's blithe reply.

Sharna shivered apprehensively. 'Weird, isn't it?'

Astra nodded her agreement. The vehicle had left the reception area and was now in a much larger dome that enclosed several square miles of barren lunar landscape. The road they were following ran straight line across the plain, yet it was little more than a path that had been cleared of loose rocks and dust. The surface of the plain on both sides of the path was a mass of footprints. The car bucked slightly as it followed undulations but the seats were comfortable and well-sprung. Sharna stood for a minute and scanned the surrounding plain in the hope of seeing someone but the place was deserted.

She shook her head in answer to Astra's quizzical expression.

'But look at all the footprints,' Astra protested. 'Millions of them.'

'I don't know, Astra. I've given up trying to puzzle it out. But Darv's right about one thing: how *could* all this development have taken place in a hundred and fifteen years?'

'Simon,' said Astra. 'How long has it been since your last tourists?'

Simon's friendly voice replied from grilles set into the backs of the seats 'Good day to you, ladies. My name is Simon. The Shrine of the First Footprint is one mile ahead.'

Both girls saw the distant blue light at the same time. It was about fifty yards to the right of the roadway and, as the vehicle drew nearer, they could see that it consisted of a circle of separate lights forming a circle on the plain. A fine mist was rising around the lights so that their beams, like spokes of glowing neon gas, were visible right up to the apex of the dome half a mile above. There was something vaguely familiar about the squat shape sitting in the centre of the circular curtain of light.

'Oh no,' said Sharna weakly. 'I don't believe it. Tell me it's not true.'

But it was true.

The vehicle lost speed and swung off the path towards the astonishing spectacle.

Sharna fumbled at the switch on her radio while staring disbelievingly ahead. 'Telson,' she managed to stutter out. 'Telson – can you hear me?'

'Yes I can,' snapped Telson. 'We've been trying to contact you. Are you all right? Where are you?'

'It's beautiful,' said Sharna, hypnotised. 'It's the most beautiful thing I've ever seen . . .'

'Hallo, Darv, said Astra excitedly when she switched her

radio on. Without giving Darv a chance to acknowledge she plunged on. 'Darv – you remember the old videos we used to watch of the first moon landing? We're there! We're actually there!'

The vehicle stopped within fifty feet of the ethereal lights that formed a shimmering halo of perfection around the landing stage of the lunar module.

'Good day to you, ladies. My name is Simon. We are now at the Shrine of the First Footprint. I am not allowed to approach any closer but you may walk to the edge of the Cathedral of Light.' Simon lapsed into silence. For seconds the girls could only stare dumbly at the magnificence before them, deaf to the querulous voices emanating from their radio collars.

They stepped from the vehicle onto the dry powdery surface and held each other's hand as they walked towards the light. And then they heard the soft music that was all around them. It was as if every molecule of the artificial atmosphere was vibrating in gentle harmony with the unseen and unidentifiable musical instruments. The music rose and fell in soft, undulating waves. It touched their faces like the sweet breath of all the springtimes that they had never known; it reached into their souls and soothed away their fear with its silvery, elusive chords.

A voice, as gentle and as captivating as the music, spoke to them.

'Come nearer, please . . . Come nearer . . .'

They went closer to the Cathedral of Light until they could feel the warmth from the glorious light that bathed their faces and the surrounding Plain of Peace.

'Welcome to the Shrine of the First Footprint where Man first set foot on the moon over one million years ago.'

Sharna became tense. 'Not a million years ago . . .'

A spot of light glowed on the lunar module's spidery shape and moved to the ladder that was attached to one of the landing stage's four legs.

'Follow the spot of light with your eyes as it moves down the ladder . . .' the voice continued. 'You are following Man's first groping steps as he made his way down the ladder in his cumbersome space mobility suit.'

The light came to rest on the ladder's lowest rung.

'Then he paused before taking that fateful last step, and uttered the immortal words that are now being etched in light above the shrine.'

The girls dragged their eyes reluctantly away from the scene before them and looked up to where the shining letters of that elegant phrase were forming above them.

'Now watch the spot of light carefully . . . There. It is now illuminating the first footprint made by Man on another world. The footprint is exactly as it was when it was first made over one million years ago.'

'No,' said Sharna more to herself than Astra. 'That's wrong. The first moon landing was only three hundred years before the *Challenger* left Earth.'

Astra tightened her grip on Sharna's hand and continued to stare into the centre of the circle of light.

'The area behind the force wall is a perfect vacuum,' continued the voice, 'and the force wall itself derives its energies from a fusion reactor buried deep beneath the Plain of Peace. The reactor will power the force wall until the sun becomes a nova and consumes the solar system. The Earth was forced to leave our solar system half a million years ago – taking the men, women and children of the Solaric Empire to safety – to a new sun.'

The voice paused.

'Meanwhile, I am the Sentinel – guarding the Shrine of the First Footprint and the Library of the Solaric Empire, and welcoming aliens such as yourselves who pass this way.'

'We're not aliens,' said Sharna suddenly. 'We are of the Earth!'

'This shrine has stood for a million years,' said the voice. 'It is a monument to our questing spirit. I ask you to look upon it with understanding – to leave it undisturbed until our sun – which gave us life – is ready to destroy it.'

Then Sharna was shouting. 'We're not aliens I tell you! Our grandparents were born on Earth! They were the crew of the starship *Challenger* that was sent from Earth to survey the universe for new worlds.'

Astra looked at her companion in genuine concern. 'Don't worry, Sharna. It's only a voice – the Sentinel or whatever it is. It's mistaken about the million years.'

The Sentinel spoke again: 'I will examine the records to see if there is a reference to the starship *Challenger*. Your car will take you to the Library of the Solaric Empire, and another vehicle will collect your companions. I will speak with the four of you there.'

The strange music faded into silence and the vacuum it left inside Astra made her want to cry out in pain.

The vehicle hummed into life and lifted off the ground. 'Good day to you, ladies,' said Simon. 'My name is Simon. Please step aboard and make yourselves comfortable. Next stop – the Library of the Solaric Empire in First Footprint City.'

Like everywhere else in First Footprint City, the Library of the Solaric Empire was deserted and silent.

The four stopped in the largest gallery they had found so far and gazed curiously at the rows of comfortable seats facing hologram replicators that were far in advance of the machines on the *Challenger*.

'It can't be as old as the Sentinel said,' declared Telson, 'otherwise everything would have rotted away in this atmosphere. Temperature, humidity and pressure are just right for us but not for machines.'

'You're not thinking,' said Darv as he examined their surroundings. 'Maybe the atmosphere is laid on only when they have visitors – otherwise the leakages from the entire city would be too much.'

'Welcome to the Hall of Knowledge,' said the Sentinel's voice.

At Telson's insistence, the group formed themselves into a protective circle in the centre of the hall.

'You said that you were of Earth,' said the Sentinel, its voice forming in the air all around the crew so that it was impossible to determine its source. 'I have checked our data on your starship – *Challenger*. In the history of the Solaric Empire there have been many such named ships.'

'There's no mention of your Solaric Empire in the *Challenger*'s records of Earth,' Darv retorted.

The Sentinel considered. 'When did your ship leave the Earth?'

'Year two-ninety of the Third Millennium,' Darv replied.

Telson scowled at Darv, resenting the initiative Darv was taking.

'The date is meaningless to me,' said the Sentinel.

'Wait a minute.' Darv thought hard for a moment. 'The *Challenger* left Earth three hundred and twenty-one years after the first moon landing.'

'A thousand years before the founding of the Solaric Empire,' the Sentinel replied. 'Therefore the records I must search will be over a million years old. You must be patient for a few seconds.'

Telson began to get angry. 'This is crazy. The *Challenger* left Earth one hundred and fifteen years ago. All this talk of a million years is sheer lunacy!' He would have carried on expostulating but the Sentinel interrupted him:

'There is a reference to three *Challenger*-class starships of the pre-empire period you mention.'

'Three!' said Sharna faintly.

'*Challenger Two* returned on schedule two hundred and seventy years after leaving its construction orbit. It travelled at a constant one gravity acceleration and reached ninety per cent of the speed of light. Distance reached was one hundred and thirty-seven light-years; shipboard time that passed was twenty years – Earth time that passed was two hundred and seventy years. My information on *Challenger Three* has been corrupted by cosmic ray bombardment but the little information I have managed to restore suggests that it set out ten years after the departure of *Challenger Two*, and like *Challenger* – the first starship – it never returned. The loss of *Challenger* and *Challenger Three* was never explained.'

It was a moment before Telson found the words he was groping for. 'You're crazy! How could twenty years pass on a ship and two hundred and seventy years pass on Earth?'

'The rate at which time flows is variable depending on the speed of the observer,' the Sentinel replied. 'How far out did you reach?'

'One million six hundred thousand light-years!'

'If you are from one of the missing *Challengers*, something went wrong that extended your voyage. You were supposed to return manned by a second-generation crew after not more than sixty years' shipboard time had passed. If you reached out as far as you say you did, it is possible for me to calculate the number of years that have passed on your ship . . . One hundred and fifteen years.'

'And one million years have passed in the solar system since we left?' said Astra – her eyes wide open with shock.

'Yes,' said the Sentinel simply.

'You mean that it's possible to travel forward in time?'

'Yes.'

'And backwards?' Telson queried.

'No.'

'Why not?'

'It is how the Universe is made.'

There was a silence that was broken by Darv. His words were slow and uncertain. 'I remember a poem that I once found in the ship's library. There were two lines that I didn't understand . . . But I think I do now. "Oh to ride on a beam of light, So that time would stand still for ever."'

The Sentinel spoke. 'If it were possible to travel at the speed of light, time would cease to exist for you. You would be ageless. But the rest of the Universe would grow old around you.'

'So what happened to the Earth?' asked Sharna.

'The colonies of the Solaric Empire were evacuated back to the Earth. When the technology was ready, the Earth was moved from the solar system half a million years ago and taken by the peoples of the Solaric Empire to a stable main-sequence star.'

'Where?' Telson demanded.

'That is a question I cannot answer. There are no clues for aliens to follow.'

'We are not aliens! The Earth is our spiritual home! We have a right to know!'

'The Earth left the solar system for a new star half a million years ago. That is all I can tell you!'

Telson heard the faint whining sound but he was too preoccupied to pay it any attention. 'Very well,' he said. 'We have a starship so there's nothing to prevent us looking for our planet.'

For a machine, there was a surprisingly sympathetic note in the Sentinel's voice when it replied. 'No . . . You will not be permitted to leave the moon. You will be required to remain here.'

The whining noise became louder, more insidious. Darv and Astra put their hands to their ears and winced. Sharna called to Telson but he took no notice.

'How long for?' he shouted at the empty hall.

Astra sank to her knees in pain – her hands clamped over her ears. 'My ears,' she moaned. 'What's happening?'

'The atmospheric pressure is dropping rapidly,' said the Sentinel expressionlessly. 'The air-pumps throughout First Footprint City are returning the atmosphere to the reservoirs. You will remain here until you die.'

PART 3

The Sands of Kyros

The *Challenger*'s guardian angels were worried about the long silence from the moon; not for the sake of the crew but for their own well-being. Without the crew they were nothing. They could not manoeuvre the ship and none of the androids, not even the surgical units, had the necessary skills required to connect the photonic drive controls to the angels' central switching room.

The angels had exercised rigorous control over the diet of the four – spiking their food with drugs that kept them sexually immature and ignorant. Had they not done so, there was a possibility that there would now be babies on the ship who would one day become a fourth-generation crew. The angels' decision to keep the crew sexually undeveloped and unaware had been based on what seemed the logical premise to them that such a course would avoid the problems that they had encountered arising from the sexuality of the first- and second-generation crews.

They watched the moon with emotions akin to human despair. The city that had swallowed the crew was edging up over the horizon again, the arrivals dome now closed. The angels resigned themselves to the thought that they would never see Telson, Darv, Astra and Sharna again. They would continue to orbit the moon helplessly until the end of time.

If time had an end, that is. So much information on time had been lost in the Great Meteoroid Strike . . .

Darv spun round and fired four blasts at what looked like a

ventilation grille in the vague hope that the perforated plate was where the air was being sucked out of the hall. The resulting clouds of smoke caused by the plasma bolts from his PD weapon were not sucked into the grilles.

More blasts from Telson and Sharna slammed into the grilles. Telson tried to shout but his voice was a croak in the thinning atmosphere.

'No use,' he panted. 'They're not the air-pumps.' The falling atmospheric pressure was making their eyes bulge from their sockets and reddening them by forcing fine veins to the surface.

Astra was still lying on the floor of the hall and moaning softly. Sharna, in desperation, loosed off another plasma bolt at what she thought was the direction of the Sentinel's voice,

'You cannot stop the air-pumps,' the Sentinel intoned, its voice devoid of emotion. 'The air pressure is still dropping. In five minutes your blood will start to boil in your veins and ten minutes after that you will all be dead.'

Darv's lungs sucked greedily at air that was no longer there. He grabbed Telson's arm and pointed to the apex of the curved roof. 'Could be like . . . like the farm galleries . . . on . . . *Challenger*. Control unit in centre . . . centre . . . of – '

He got no further because Telson had loosed off a wild blast at the centre of the roof. His second blast hit the same spot. The combined force of the two explosions ripped a panel from the roof that fell with absurd slowness in the low gravity.

'No,' said the Sentinel, it's voice distorted by the thinning atmosphere. 'You must not damage the memory feeds.'

'Sharna!' Telson gasped. 'Hit the apex . . .! Sustained firing!'

Four more plasma boasts tore into the roof and vaporised an entire panel as it fell away, exposing a lacework of delicate cables.

'The cables! Hit the cables!'

'No!' The cry from the Sentinel was almost pleading. 'The library's memories must not be destroyed.'

'Then restore the atmosphere!' Telson shouted as hard as he could.

'I cannot. You must die. But the library must survive. There is a conflict.'

'We will destroy your precious library in three seconds,' Telson panted as he sank to his knees. 'One . . . Two . . .'

'Wait – I will reverse the air-pumps.'

The wine of the pumps that had faded in the depleted atmosphere suddenly strengthened. Cool, life-giving air brushed against the crew's faces and they inhaled deeply, not caring about the pain in their ears that the returning air-pressure inflicted.

'Just keep swallowing,' Darv whispered to Astra as he helped her to her feet.

'How did you know where to aim your weapons?' the Sentinel inquired.

'There are design similarities with our ship,' Telson answered. 'Maybe you'll believe us now when we say that the *Challenger* was built by the people of Earth.'

'The *Challengers* that set out from Earth knew about the time dilation effect. You did not know. You will return to your shuttle. The traction guidance beam that steered you down will lift you into a matching orbit with your mothership.'

'Will you tell us where the Earth is, Sentinel?' asked Sharna.

'No. My program is clear – to destroy beings that pass this way asking the whereabouts of Earth. I also must protect the Library of the Solaric Empire, therefore you may go . . . But I will tell you one thing: if you are of Earth as you say, then you will think as the people of Earth thought. You will act as the people of Earth acted. And therefore the clues will be easy for you to follow.' The Sentinel lapsed into silence and could not be persuaded to speak again.

The four made their way back to the shuttle.

Even Telson's deep respect for the guardian angels was beginning to wear thin as a result of Angel One's probing, repetitive questions.

'There was nothing more that we could find out,' he asserted doggedly. 'The Sentinel wouldn't speak to us again.' He looked up at the other three and wondered if the angels could see their affirming expressions. He checked himself, realising that he was in danger of thinking as Darv thought; the guardian angels could see everything. 'It's certain that the Sentinel doesn't know where the Earth went – only that it left half a million years ago – if you can make any sense of that.'

There was a silence in the restaurant as the four waited for the angels' answer. It came from Angel Two:

'There is something we have decided to tell you. Much of the data on the characteristics of time was lost during the Great Meteoroid Strike. Several billion information bytes were destroyed.'

Darv leaned back in his seat and laughed uproariously. 'That's terrific. An admission from our beloved guardian angels that they're not infallible.'

'We see no point in concealing the truth from you,' said Angel One.

The others looked uneasily at Darv when he renewed his laughter. Suddenly he was serious, his voice harsh. 'I'll tell you about the truth, Angel One.'

'Darv . . .' said Telson warningly.

'If you won't say it, Telson, then I will. The *Challenger* was supposed to have been away from Earth for sixty years' shipboard time. Instead one hundred and fifteen shipboard years were allowed to pass with the result that one million years have passed on Earth – wherever it is and *if* it still exists. So you tell us why you allowed Telson to extend the voyage when he became commander.' He brushed aside Astra's restraining hand. 'Or didn't you *ever* know that time and space are related?'

'So much information was lost during the Great Meteoroid Strike–' Angel One began.

'I see,' said Darv scathingly. 'Now that you've as good as admitted that you're not infallible, you're going to blame everything on the Great Meteoroid Strike. Blame everyone and everything for your troubles except yourselves, eh, my darling angels? Well there's a name for that attitude. It's called arrogance.' Even before he had finished speaking, Darv realised that this time he had gone too far.

Telson stood during the shocked silence that followed. He grasped Darv by the lapels of his overalls and lifted him carefully to his feet. Their faces were inches apart, it was obvious that Telson was working hard to contain his explosive temper. He released his grip on Darv and said in a dangerously quiet voice: 'I suggest you apologise this instant to Angel One, assuming that your apology will be accepted.'

Darv was tempted to give Telson a customary broad grin but decided that the moment was not appropriate. Instead he shook his head.

'I insist!'

The two stared at each other, neither prepared to yield.

Angel One must have sensed that Telson's insecure check on his own temper was weakening for she suddenly intervened: 'You have all been under a strain. Perhaps if Darv – '

'He's got to apologise,' breathed Telson, determined not to give way this time.

'For God's sake, the pair of you,' Sharna muttered. 'Astra and I have had enough of your stupid behaviour. We've all been under a strain so it might be a good idea if you resolved the situation by staying out of each other's way for a couple of days.'

'An excellent idea, Sharna,' said Angel One.

Darv realised that it was up to him to seize the initiative if he was to avoid having to apologise to Angel One. 'Okay,' he said lightly, giving a slight frown. 'I'll work off my aggression by helping the fruit farm androids.'

Astra made a move to follow Darv as he threaded his way past the tables to the doorway.

'You'll stay here,' said Telson curtly, not sure if he had won or lost.

'But – '

'Just do as you're told.'

As always, Astra did as she was told.

Telson spent the following day in the *Challenger*'s galactic resources centre recording the moon and its abandoned cities. He and Sharna made holograms of every dome and trackway in the hope of spotting a movement or an indication of current habitation. They continued broadcasting across all bands and listening on all bands but without success. The moon had reverted to what it had always been: a lifeless satellite. The only difference was that whereas it had once been a satellite of the Earth, now it was a satellite of the sun as were the other planets in the solar system which Telson turned his attention to.

The innermost planet, orbiting the sun close to the blazing white inferno of its photosphere, bore no sign that man had ever attempted to establish a colony there. The increase in the sun's magnitude had created new rivers of molten rock that flowed for a considerable distance across the planet's terminator and into the permanent dark side. The glowing lacework of veins that did not appear in the *Challenger*'s original records was a stark reminder of the fate that was in store for the entire solar system when the sun's gravity would no longer be sufficient to contain its forces and it either tore itself apart as a nova, or swelled to become a red giant.

The second planet was now the moon. The third planet, orbiting the sun at a distance of 200,000,000 miles, was a reddish-hued world possessing negligible amount of free oxygen in its tenuous atmosphere. It was inclined on its axis and therefore possessed seasons – its summers melting the thin layer of carbon dioxide that formed polar ice-caps. According to the *Challenger*'s records, a colony had been established on the planet one hundred years before the *Challenger* left the solar system, which was about the time that the desert planet had been given its new name of Kyros.

Telson settled himself more comfortably in the couch that was slung beneath the optical telescope and touched the controls to centre Kyros on the objective screen while Sharna watched the repeaters. He picked out the landmarks by comparing Kyros with a library hologram. He tracked southward along the great rill to the site of the colony. After one hundred and fifteen years, he expected to find that the colony had grown.

He swore softly.

'What's the matter?' asked Sharna.

'The colony's gone – nothing but desert.'

Sharna checked the telescope's co-ordinates and discovered that Telson was right: the library showed the beginnings of a small city. Now there was nothing but the red-coloured iron oxide-rich sand that covered all of Kyros. A detailed three-hour survey failed to reveal any sign of human habitation on the planet's visible face.

The two stared at each other mystified, unable to make any sense of the irrefutable evidence that confronted them.

'It's all crazy,' he muttered irritably. 'Massive development on the moon and yet everything's vanished from Kyros. What do you make of it, Angel One?'

'We are as puzzled as you are,' Angel One's voice replied.

Sharna used her repeater screen to call up information on Kyros which she studied for some moments. 'There are frequent severe dust storms on Kyros.' she pointed out. 'It's possible that erosion and the shifting of the sand has either destroyed the colony or buried it.'

'A distinct possibility, Sharna,' said Angel Two.

Telson and Angel One discussed the mystery while Sharna idly toyed with the settings on the planetary surveillance instruments.

A sudden, wholly unexpected reading was displayed on her screen. She gaped at it in surprise before drawing Telson's attention to it.

The mighty sand dunes that surrounded the extinct volcano, Tyrannis, in the southern hemisphere of Kyros were concealing a secret that optical telescopes could never reveal.

George was a supervisory agricultural android with six sophisticated multi-jointed manipulators that enabled him to carry out any task in the fruit farms where his wishes were law to the army of specialised-function androids whom he dominated.

He trundled down Row 416 where the apples hanging from the dwarf trees were at their ripest, and sighted Darv stretched out naked on the grass in the shade of a tree laden with bloated fruits. The hopper beside Darv was hardly filled. It was surrounded by a cloud of insects who had been seduced by the smell when they should have been pollinating trees in Row 109. The scene infuriated George. He began transmitting enraged commands before remembering that the useless two-legged androids called humans only understood the crude audio communication system. He stopped beside the naked sleeping human and gave it a sharp prod with one of his manipulators.

'You!' he barked as Darv sat up. 'Why you not working?'

Darv rubbed his eyes and yawned. 'I'm resting, George. I've filled four hoppers this morning.'

'Not enough,' George's crude voice grated. 'Have to put auxiliary on this row. So you go now.'

'But I like it here,' Darv protested. 'I'll tell you what – you reduce the solar lights so that they don't ripen the fruit so fast and I'll have this row finished tomorrow.'

'Too slow,' George grumbled. 'Humans useless. Should be banned from fruit farms. I always tell them they were useless but always they come.'

'They?' queried Darv, his curiosity aroused.

George went to work on Darv's neglected trees. His manipulators were a blur of activity and yet the fruit was undamaged by the incredibly fast handling.

'What do you mean "they"?' Darv persisted. 'You mean people used to come and work here because they wanted to?'

'Relaxation visits they called them. Relax is all they did.'

'How many?'

'Sometimes a hundred getting in the way. Some worked. Some pretended to be broken like you just now. Some pollinated each other.'

'They what?'

'I just tell you! Pollinating each other. Humans useless. No recording system. Say everything twice.'

'And they came here because they *wanted* to?' Darv persisted.

'Didn't I just say that? Said they like working here. No matter how many – not as good as one android. None come now. Much better.' The android moved along the row, its manipulators still whirring.

Darv followed it, trying to visualise the fruit farms filled with people, perhaps laughing and singing as they worked. 'George,' he said slowly. 'Have you ever heard of something called the Great Meteoroid Strike?'

George took immediate offence. 'Androids work all the

time. Striking unknown to us. Androids better than humans. Here comes another human. Now two of you in the orchards. Bad times back. I do your work, and you go.'

Without waiting for Darv to confirm the deal, George grabbed the hopper and trundled to the far end of the row where he resumed work. 'You miss some!' he called out accusingly and glared at Astra as she walked past him.

Darv climbed to his feet and resumed picking the apples, placing them in a small heap on the grass. For some unaccountable reason he felt embarrassed by his nakedness in Astra's presence. It was an alien emotion and it troubled him.

'Hallo, Darv,' said Astra, smiling at him.

Darv concentrated on his work and avoided looking at her. 'Hallo,' he replied non-committally.

'Didn't you hear Commander Telson's summons?'

'I heard him.'

'Then why didn't you come?'

'I like it here and he didn't say please.' Astra's sudden laugh irritated Darv. He wanted her to go away so that his embarrassment would end.

'I don't blame you,' she said looking around. 'It is nice here.'

'I like it.'

'Let's sit down a minute.' Astra sat on the grass. She patted the ground beside her. 'Please, Darv.'

Darv sat beside her and drew his legs up self-consciously. Astra inhaled deeply. Her nostrils caught the sweet smell of the ripe apples. She looked quizzically at Darv.

'What's the matter with your face?' She reached out and touched his cheek. 'Darv – you're going to be like those men in the videos – you're growing a beard or something!'

Startled, Darv put a hand to his face and felt the fine down.

'Will it keep on growing?' Astra asked her eyes round with curiosity.

'I don't know. Does it look so terrible?'

Astra shook her head. 'No – not really.'

Darv reached out, pulled an apple off an overhanging branch, and bit into it. He chewed noisily, sucking gratefully at the juices while Astra stared at him in astonishment.

'Darv! Spit it out! You mustn't eat unprocessed food!'

'Why not? They're delicious.'

'Because the angels say that we mustn't. You could get all sorts of illnesses.'

'Blatant lies,' Darv snorted. He held the apple out to Astra. 'Try one bite for me.'

'I couldn't!'

'Just one little bite.'

Astra looked at the fruit suspiciously. 'They must taste terrible if they're unprocessed.'

'Well, they don't. Please, Astra. Just one bite for me. I promise that it won't harm you.'

Juice was tricking down Darv's hand. Astra realised that she was thirsty, also there was something tantalising about the smell of the fruit that brought the saliva into her mouth.

'Just one tiny bite?' she said cautiously.

'Yes.'

'And I'll spit it out if it tastes horrible?'

'Yes.'

'It's going brown where you've eaten it.'

'Just one little bite, Astra.'

Astra took one little bite. She chewed very carefully and very suspiciously as if she expected the food in her mouth to suddenly explode.

Darv burst out laughing. 'If only you could see your expression . . . Well?' As Astra stared at him in amazement, Darv realised that her blue eyes contrasted pleasingly with her blonde hair. He wondered why he had never noticed before.

'It tastes fantastic!'

'Didn't I tell you?'

Before he could finish the sentence, Astra had taken another much larger bite out of the apple and was crunching enthusiastically, her face wreathed in a broad smile. 'I don't believe it!' she cried. 'I've never tasted anything so fantastic!' She proceeded to demolish the apple and selected another from the pile Darv had started before finishing the first one. 'I've never tasted anything so beautiful,' she continued excitedly, wiping the juice from her chin. 'Is all the fruit like this?'

Darv scowled. 'Yes. Which only goes to prove that the food

we get from the restaurant and from the dispensers is so much tasteless junk.' He stood, his embarrassment temporarily forgotten, and pulled Astra to her feet, 'Come on.'

'Where are we going?'

'You like blackcurrant juice, don't you?'

'Well, yes.'

'Wait until you've tasted the real thing. From now on you're eating only the food that I smuggle to you. Throw the processed stuff down the recycling chutes.'

'Darv, wait a minute. You must obey Commander Telson's summons.'

'And have to apologise to a guardian angel? No thanks.'

'You shouldn't have that attitude to the angels, Darv,' said Astra reproachfully. 'Without them we'd be dead. Anyway – I think your rudeness has been forgotten. We're taking the *Challenger* to Kyros. There was a colony there so there's a chance that there'll be ruins or artifacts that will tell us what happened to Earth. And there's a gravitational anomaly that's got to be investigated.'

Darv looked at Astra in surprise. 'Whose idea was this?'

'Commander Telson's I suppose. Why?'

Darv recovered his one-piece suit and stepped into it. 'There's hope for us yet, Astra,' he said, grinning broadly at her as he ran his fingers along the seams of the garment to close them. 'Telson is actually thinking at last. Yes – I'll come back. Delving into the sands of Kyros sounds a lot more fun than picking apples all day.'

Ten hours after the *Challenger* had established a geostationary orbit above the equator of Kyros, the excursion terminal's outer air-lock door opened and Darv eased the shuttle into space. Astra was seated beside him, watching the navigation displays on the flight-control panel.

Below them lay the curving splendour of Kyros – its desert terrain looking like a puckered rust-coloured blanket.

'Shuttle to *Challenger*,' said Astra. 'Separation complete.'

'Thank you, shuttle,' acknowledged Telson's voice.

Suddenly the shuttle was surrounded by blinding flashes of

light. One of the soundless explosions took place within twenty yards of the craft. The force of the detonation threw Darv and Astra hard against their restraint harnesses.

'Telson!' Darv yelled. 'What's happening?'

The flashes ceased almost as quickly as they had begun.

'Sorry, shuttle,' said Sharna. 'that was the meteoroid shields going to work on a minor shower of micro-meteoroids. We don't need the annihilation shields so we'll switch them off until you're clear of the ship.'

Two of the *Challenger*'s four turrets that housed the meteoroid annihilation shield projectors were visible to Darv. The shields automatically sensed the presence of incoming meteoroids and destroyed them with discharges of energy that were equal to the incoming meteoroids' mass and velocity. It was the activity of the shields that had caused the pyrotechnic display around the shuttle. A thought occurred to Darv.

'Hey, Astra,' he said cheerfully. 'What if the shields ever mistake the shuttle for a meteoroid?'

The main engine fired before Astra had a chance to reply. The thrust from the powerful chemical rocket motor cancelled most of the shuttle's orbital velocity so that it began a long, spiralling descent towards Kyros's nebulous atmosphere.

After five minutes they had dropped two thousand miles. The wart-like bulge of the volcano Tyrannis was the only shape that disfigured the otherwise perfect curve of the planet's horizon.

Astra keyed in their selected landing site – twenty miles due south of Tyrannis. Identifying the gravitational anomaly presented no problems for the shuttle's navigation and flight-guidance computers: each time Astra swept the area with the gravimeter sensors the displays on her screen ran out of digits in their efforts to measure the strength of the mysterious gravitational disturbance beneath the red sands below.

At a height of four hundred miles the shuttle began lifting its nose so that the horizon dipped below the forward view ports. The manoeuvre worried Darv. He reported it to Telson. Neither of them could remember the shuttle doing the same thing during the moon landing.

And then the shuttle entered the upper reaches of the atmosphere and the reason for the nose-up mode became apparent: the craft was presenting its heat shield to the stratosphere. Darv and Astra watched apprehensively as the air around them became incandescent. The buffeting, which had been mild enough at first, was suddenly a continuous battering that seemed certain to shake the spacecraft to pieces. There was nothing the couple could do except stare white-faced through the view ports at the increasing inferno outside. The glowing rows of figures on the display screens became a blur such was the pounding that their bodies were receiving.

Telson's reassuring voice from the *Challenger* began breaking up as static from the radio merged with the deafening cacophony of Kyros's atmosphere that was raging at the view ports.

Suddenly the murderous buffeting stopped enabling Darv to read the displays on the flight-control panel. The shuttle's speed was down to a thousand miles per hour but it was losing height at a phenomenal twenty thousand feet per minute.

Indistinct details on the plain were resolving themselves at a terrifying speed. The once diminutive slopes of Tyrannis were becoming soaring escarpments.

'I think we're okay,' Darv reported to Telson. 'It's just that this thing has got an unnerving flying technique of its own. It looks like we're going to overshoot the anomaly landing site, so God knows what it's going to do next.'

The shuttle solved the problem of the possible overshoot by first braking to a standstill in mid-air at ten thousand feet above the landing site, and then dropping vertically so quickly that Darv and Astra were floating against their restraint harnesses for a second before the artificial gravity compensators cut in.

Astra took one look at the ground racing up towards her and closed her eyes.

'I once read something in the library about never volunteering,' muttered Darv grimly. 'Now I know what it means.'

At a thousand feet the shuttle's triple vectored thrusters came to life and blasted downward, raising huge clouds of whirling sand that blotted out the light from the shuttle's interior. Only the displays told Darv and Astra that they were no longer falling.

The shuttle's ground-proximity radar systems probed the desert below, assessed the undulations of the terrain, and adjusted the length of the landing skids to suit. When it finally settled and cut its motors, Darv and Astra could not believe that they had landed; the cabin was perfectly level and there had not been even the faintest suggestion of a jolt.

'I'll tell you one thing, Astra,' said Darv, watching the clouds of red sand settle, 'this thing knows a lot more about flying space shuttles than we do.' He moved to the control panel and called the *Challenger*. 'Anomaly Base,' he reported. 'The Digger has landed.'

Kyros was a disappointment. Nothing but rolling dunes of the reddish sand relieved only by the dimpled peak of Tyrannis twenty miles to the north.

Darv and Astra, kitted out in breathing sets and partial pressure suits, walked three times round the shuttle to try out the unfamiliar garments and the low gravity. They kept their eyes on the ground in the hope of seeing something. There was the possibility that the cause of the gravitational anomaly might have been uncovered by the shuttle's vectored thrusters.

'Nothing,' said Darv, moving to the stowage bay door 'Might as well call out the troops.' He touched a panel. The wide door slid upward and a ramp extended to the ground from the bottom of the doorway. 'Okay, George,' Darv called into the opening. 'You can come out now.'

George emerged from the stowage bay and trundled down the ramp on his caterpillar tracks. 'Dark in there,' grumbled the android to no one in particular. 'Nothing grows in the dark.' He extended a probe and pushed it into the ground. 'This place worse. No water; no humus; no oxygen. No good asking androids for miracles.'

Darv put his arm round Astra's waist – a gesture that took her completely by surprise. 'You're not here to grow things, George,' he said. 'You and your little friend in there are here to dig. Call him out.'

An ungainly agricultural excavator android rumbled out of the stowage bay in response to George's radio signal. It clanked down the ramp. Even in the thin atmosphere the machine managed to make a considerable uproar. 'Sand bad for mechanisms,' it complained shrilly as soon as it made contact with the desert. 'Gets everywhere.'

Darv groaned inwardly. Maybe choosing two androids with audio communication facilities had been a mistake. 'Come on,' he said leading the way from the shuttle. 'I'll show you where you're to dig.'

The shuttle's food preparation facilities were simple but adequate. Darv shut off the burners and cancelled the instruction display on the galley's visual screen. Cooking was a subject that he had studied in the *Challenger*'s library. He had been looking forward to putting his untried culinary knowledge to the test. The test consisted of a large, simmering pot from which he filled two bowls.

'Ready,' he called out.

Astra emerged naked from the shower cubicle. She wrinkled her nose. 'Smells good. What is it?'

Darv placed the two bowls on the folding table. 'Feast your eyes on that and then your stomach,' he commanded.

Astra sat opposite Darv, picked up a spoon and tasted gingerly. 'Hey – it's good. What is it?'

'That my lovely, is the finest meal you've ever had in your life. That I promise.'

Astra realised that she was very hungry and started spooning the delicious concoction into her mouth. 'Mn . . . Fantastic . . . Don't tell me you managed to smuggle unprocessed food aboard?'

'You bet, my lovely. I restocked the food lockers with food I sneaked out of the farm galleries. Angel Two saw me and wanted to know what I was doing.'

Astra looked worried. 'Did you tell him?'

Darv laughed. 'I assured him, my lovely, that it was food from the dispensers.'

'That's twice you've called me that.'

'Called you what?'

'My lovely,' said Astra.

'Do you mind?'

Astra shrugged. 'It just seems a funny thing to call anyone.'

'You, my lovely,' said Darv emphatically, 'are not anyone.'

'*Challenger* to shuttle,' said Telson's voice from a nearby speaker.

Darv had his mouth full. 'Go ahead, *Challenger*,' he mumbled.

'Last call before we're below the horizon. Anything to report?'

'Nothing to add to our last report,' Darv replied. 'The androids have excavated down twenty feet directly over the anomaly. They'll carry on through the night. The seismic monitors indicate that they've got about fifty feet to go before they reach the anomaly or whatever it is.'

'Very good, Darv,' said Telson. 'We'll be out of radio contact in fifteen minutes. We'll leave you to sleep and give you a call in the morning on our tenth orbit. Goodnight and out.' The speaker clicked silent.

Darv said nothing for a moment as he stared out of a side view port at the darkness. There was absolute silence apart from the hum of the air-conditioning, and the clang and rattle of the two androids busily digging some forty yards from the shuttle.

'I've just thought of something, Astra. Night and day controlled by the sun. For the first time in half a million years, we must be the first people in the solar system to be following the night and day of the sun.'

An hour later, Angel One and Two sounded an alarm that brought Telson and Sharna running into the *Challenger*'s galactic resources centre.

'A flying machine or some sort of spacecraft moving above the surface of Kyros,' reported Angel Two as Sharna scrambled onto the telescope's couch. Telson located the object on the radar display while Sharna touched out the co-ordinates that swung the telescope down until it was pointing at the planet.

'Got it,' said Telson. 'Course two-four-eight. Bearing eight-nine. Speed nine zero miles per hour. Height one thousand feet. What the hell is it?'

Sharna zeroed the objective lens on the moving dot that was racing across the face of the desert, heading towards the terminator and into the planet's dark side. She increased the telescope's gain but was unable to resolve the object into anything more tangible than two moving dots – one of which was the object's shadow chasing its parent body across the undulating dunes. The shadow occasionally plunged into deep rills before renewing its pursuit across the sands.

'Its present course will take it straight to the anomaly base,' Angel One announced. 'It will arrive in three hours if it holds its present speed.'

Telson swore. 'We've got to warn Darv and Astra. How long before we're above their radio horizon, Angel One?'

'Five hours and ten minutes, commander,' Angel One replied promptly.

'What about using the main drive?'

'Our acceleration would be too slow to make a significant improvement on that time. Also, of course, four are required in the control room.'

Telson swore again. Even if two could manage, the thrust exerted by the photonic drive could achieve only a very gradual rate of acceleration – the *Challenger*'s multi-billion ton mass was not designed for tight manoeuvering within the vicinity of a planet without many hours of preparation in the main control room.

Sharna took her eyes away from the telescope's visor. 'Surely there must be a way in which we can get a warning to them?'

'There is no way,' said Angel Two. 'Perhaps it is not a flying machine or a spacecraft although the crispness of the radar echoes we are receiving suggests a metallic object and therefore artificial.'

In sheer anger and frustration Telson drove a clenched fist into the palm on his hand.

The gesture did nothing to prevent the mysterious object from crossing the terminator and plunging into the dark side of Kyros. A few minutes later it dipped over the far curve of the planet and radar contact was lost.

The high-pitched tone lasted less than a quarter of a second but it woke Astra. She turned on a light, moved to Darv's bunk and shook him by the shoulder. He was awake immediately.

'What's the matter?'

'There was a sort of whistling sound just now,' said Astra, glancing fearfully at one of the black view ports.

Darv listened for a moment and frowned. 'That's odd – the androids have stopped work. We'd better go out and see what's happened.'

The idea didn't appeal to Astra. 'Do we have to? Couldn't we wait until sunrise?'

Darv was already pulling on a partial pressure suit. He paused and grinned at Astra. 'You don't have to come. Those stupid androids have probably come up against a problem that they don't know how to deal with. You stay and make me a hot drink or something.'

'No,' said Astra resolutely. 'I'm coming with you.'

Ten minutes later Darv settled the mask of his breathing set into a more comfortable position and opened the outer air-lock door. He shone the arc lantern's brilliant white beam on the aluminium steps for Astra's benefit and stepped onto the surface of Kyros.

'We should wear our PD weapons,' Astra muttered.

Darv chuckled 'And have you blasting my head off if I trip or something? No thanks.'

The beam of light picked out George standing stock-still beside the huge hole that he and the excavator android had been digging.

Darv and Astra approached him but he made no move and did not answer Darv's question concerning the androids' lack of activity.

'Odd,' said Darv, shining the lantern into the hole and illuminating the motionless excavator android. 'They've either switched themselves off or they've received a cease activity command. You didn't sleepwalk and use the radio did you?'

'No, I did not,' said Astra with some vehemence. She glanced anxiously around at the brooding shapes of the dunes crouching in the starlight. There was something very wrong with the silhouette of the nearest dune – something that caused her suddenly to clutch fearfully at Darv's arm and point.

When Darv was a boy one of his favourite occupations had been watching the terror videos in the *Challenger*'s generously stocked entertainment library. Whenever the background music and the lighting had been used in such a way as to heighten the tension – to suggest that something unspeakable was about to happen, he had always experienced a curious prickling sensation that started at the base of his spine and travelled up to the nape of his neck.

He experienced that same sensation as he brought the beam of the arc lantern up to illuminate the dune. But the beam of light never reached its objective. Inside the partially pressurised gauntlet, Darv's fingers went numb. He dropped the lantern to the ground. The powerful beam sprayed across the sand to where the three hideous creatures stood beneath a grotesque ship that was standing on six insect-like legs.

PART 4

The Solaric Empire

The soft landing instrument package fired its miniature retro-rockets and stirred up a cloud of sand as it dropped the last four feet. A pod on the top of the ungainly lander opened and a television camera mounted on a telescopic pedestal extended slowly upwards until it reached a height of ten feet above the surface of the desert. Sunlight flashed on the camera's lens as it panned slowly, taking in the abandoned space shuttle and the two immobile androids. A dish antenna on the lander beamed the television pictures up to the orbiting *Challenger*.

'George!' said Telson's voice from a speaker on the lander. 'What happened here last night?'

George remained silent. A telemetric radio signal stabbed out from the starship. The two androids immediately resumed work: the excavator clanked into life and commenced adding to the mountain of sand it had created with its rotating buckets, and George continued with his task of shovelling loose sand away from the edge of the hole.

'George!' Telson's voice repeated. 'What happened here last night?'

George stopped shovelling and trundled to the lander. This was the strangest android he had ever seen. His analysis was that it had no right to give him orders. Nevertheless, he answered the questions.

No . . . He didn't know or care what had happened to the two-legged androids . . .

He and his colleague had seen or heard nothing. They had been told to dig and that was exactly what they were doing despite what the sand was doing to their mechanisms and that it was no good expecting miracles . . .

Four thousand miles above Kyros, Telson calmed down and agreed with Sharna that there was little point in shouting at and heaping curses on an android.

'The only thing we can do now,' Sharna reasoned, 'is search the entire landing site with the television cameras.'

After two minutes they discovered several sets of footprints in the sand leading up the slopes of the dunes. Sharna used the remote controls to increase the height of the camera's pedestal. It was Telson who spotted something odd on the crest of the dune which was where the footprints led.

'Hold it there,' breathed Telson.

Sharna cancelled the camera's slow tilt.

'See those marks on the sand? Zoom in on them . . . That's it.'

The crest of the dune swelled until it filled the screen. Clearly visible in the sand were six regularly spaced saucer-shaped depressions. Angel Two broke in on their thoughts: 'Thermal wake monitors on the soft-landing instrument package are giving a positive reading. The area around the depressions has been exposed to a considerable amount of heat during the night.'

'Meaning that the ship we saw landed there, Angel Two?'

'The probability factor is extremely high, commander,' Angel Two replied.

'Higher,' said Angel One suddenly. 'I have located the ship in sector eight-four-zero.'

Telson operated the radar while Sharna swung the telescope to the new settings. They both located the ship at the same time. It was a point of light moving against the stars. Spectrum analysis showed that it was moving away from Kyros on a fast solar orbit.

'As its motion is on the zodiacal plane,' said Angel Two, 'we can make two predictions: either it does not have the power to move at an angle to the zodiac, or it is heading for one of the outer planets. We will be able to make a high status prediction of its destination in one hour.'

Telson slumped into the telescope's couch and stared at the moving point of light on the telescope's repeater screen. 'What the hell does it matter where it's going, Sharna? We're stuck here now – we can't go after it. And even if we could, what could we do? We're unarmed . . . I should never have let them go . . .' Sharna realised that Telson was near to tears. She had never known him cry, even when he was a child. She wished she could think of suitable words of comfort.

'Angel Two,' she called out after a few moments had passed. 'Is there a method we can devise so that two people can operate the main control room?'

'None,' said Angel Two. 'All four seats must be occupied. The appropriate commands must be keyed simultaneously into the four control desks.'

It was the answer Sharna had expected. 'But surely there must be some way!' she persisted.

Telson looked up and shook his head. 'There's no way, Sharna – you know that as well as anyone.' And then he turned quickly away so that she could not see his face.

Sharna shared his misery. It seemed impossible even to consider that she might not see Darv and Astra again, and that she and Telson would have to spend the rest of their lives orbiting Kyros in the *Challenger*.

She reached out a tentative hand, touched Telson on the shoulder and shook him gently. The practical side of her nature asserted itself. 'Come on, Telson. It's no good us sitting here. We might as well go to the excursion terminal and bring back those androids and the shuttle.'

'How?' said Telson dully.

'The excursion terminal is in an uncontrolled zone, of course,' Angel One's voice said. 'But there is certain to be a remote control flight desk.'

For the first time in her life Sharna felt vaguely irritated that everything she said or did in the *Challenger*'s controlled zones could be overheard or seen by the guardian angels.

'Telson! Look out!' screamed Sharna.

But her warning was too late. The excavator android disembarking from the shuttle in the excursion terminal misjudged the width of the ramp. Its track slipped off the edge. Telson leapt clear as the huge machine toppled, but not quickly enough to prevent one of the android's buckets ripping into the leg of his one-piece suit. The excavator android came to rest at a precarious angle while Telson lay on the floor moaning in pain, trying to staunch the blood flowing from the deep wound in his right leg.

Sharna ignored the danger from the swaying excavator and pulled Telson to safety before kneeling beside him and fashioning a makeshift tourniquet from the blood-soaked remains of his torn coveralls.

'I don't think it's as bad as it looks,' said Telson, grimacing in pain as he spoke.

'Told you sand bad for mechanisms,' grated George who had observed the incident with that dispassionate interest that only manual androids were capable of. 'Excavator android's steering now need attention.'

Despite her preoccupation with Telson's injury. Sharna managed to prefix her instructions to George with a selection of words that were particularly insulting to manual androids.

Grumbling to himself about sand, George went off to fetch the surgery androids.

An hour later, while Sharna was anxiously watching the two surgery androids deftly put the finishing touches to their meticulously careful treatment of Telson's injury, she had an idea that she considered nothing short of brilliant.

Astra turned and came face to face with one of the creatures that had kidnapped her and Darv.

She screamed.

Darv quickly pulled off the grotesque breathing mask and held it out apologetically for Astra's inspection. 'Sorry,' he said sheepishly.

'You stupid, crazy idiot!' she raged.

'I said, I'm sorry.'

Astra calmed down and looked curiously at the mask Darv was holding. It had two bulging eyepieces and a hideous proboscis instead of the simple exhaust outlet of their own breathing masks.

'No wonder they looked so frightening,' said Darv ruefully.

'Maybe they're just like us underneath?'

'Where did you find it?'

Darv gestured to an open locker. It was the only storage space in the cramped cabin that the creatures had bundled them into. Above the locker was a small wash basin with an outlet that ejected a thin stream of warm water when hands were placed under it. The toilet facilities, like the little they had seen so far of the alien ship's interior, were simple but efficient. Still trembling with anger rather than fear, Astra turned back to the view port while Darv opened the flap set into a bulkhead to see if their captors had provided them with more food. The compartment was empty. He sighed and fiddled with the breathing mask. Thirty hours had passed since the alien ship had taken off from Kyros. They had spent the entire time locked in the tiny cabin. Their initial shock at being frog-marched aboard the tiny ship by the creatures had worn off and now they were bored. In truth, Astra was more concerned about Sharna and Telson, trapped aboard the *Challenger* for eternity, than she was for her own safety.

'I suppose,' Darv mused, idly toying with the breathing mask, 'that they could be human – survivors of the Solaric Empire who weren't evacuated when the Earth left the solar system?'

'They didn't understand when you spoke to them,' Astra pointed out.

'They didn't *answer* when I spoke to them. It's not the same thing.'

Astra continued to stare out of the view port. Something caught her eye. She pressed her cheek against the clear plastic in an attempt to see sideways. 'Darv – come here a minute and look.'

Darv went to the view port and saw a giant planet emerging. The visible crescent of the massive oblate sphere was divided into a series of richly coloured bands that ran parallel to the equator. It was one of the most distinctive planets he had ever seen and one that he recognised immediately from the holograms in the *Challenger*'s library.

'It's Zelda isn't it?' Astra asked.

Darv nodded.

'Surely they can't be thinking of landing there. It's nothing but methane and ammonia.'

Darv continued to watch the outer planet for some minutes and realised that the ship was performing a series of intricate manoeuvres. Suddenly Zelda was eclipsed by a grey horizon embracing a barren, crater-scarred airless landscape less than a hundred miles beneath the ship. The terrain was similar to the moon but the ugly, gnarled mountain ranges were covered in a layer of frozen carbon dioxide.

'It's one of the moons of Zelda,' said Darv.

'Which one?'

Darv shrugged and continued gazing down at the bleak landscape that was racing towards the ship. The remains of what had been a remarkable multi-domed city came into view as the ship passed over a mountain range and turned. It continued to lose height and details of the city became clearer. At ten thousand feet it filled the view port. Darv and Astra could see the architectural similarities with First Footprint City on the moon. The difference was, that whereas the city on the moon was relatively undamaged, all the domes of this place had either collapsed or seemed to have been subjected to some sort of bombardment. Apart from a small cluster of domes that the ship was heading for, none were intact nor did it look as if any attempt had been made to repair them. Some of the domes on the outskirts of the once-proud city appeared to have been deliberately torn apart and the interconnecting trackways ripped up.

Darv and Astra simultaneously sensed that something was behind them. They wheeled around. One of the creatures was standing in the cabin's open doorway. Except that he wasn't a creature: he was tall and slender with finely chiselled features and humourless grey eyes that were watching them carefully. He was wearing a black skin-tight suit like the others had worn. It was made from the same material as the grotesque masks.

Darv tried to outstare the stranger but was deterred by the hard, unblinking grey eyes.

'So they are human,' he said to Astra.

The stranger spoke. His strange accent accentuated his vowels but Darv and Astra had no difficulty in understanding him. He beckoned them out of the cabin and said harshly:

'I am most certainly human. Exactly what you two are, and who taught you our language, is something that we intend to find out.'

Darv ignored the beckoning gesture. He caught hold of Astra's wrist and stood his ground. 'My name is Darv', he said, 'and this is Astra. Now that you know who we are, you might at least tell us who you are.' He hoped that his voice didn't betray his fear's for the expression now in the stranger's eyes was one of unbridled hatred.

'My name is Spegal. Commander of the Solaric Empire Space Corps. Come.'

'And this place?'

Spegal took a step forward. 'You insult my intelligence by pretending that you don't know?' he rasped.

It took all Darv's self-control to force himself to meet Spegal's stare. 'We genuinely don't know,' he said simply.

Spegal looked puzzled for a fleeting second and then the hatred was back. 'This is Zelda Five,' he said. 'The fifth moon of Zelda and the capital of the Solaric Empire.'

Unaware of what Telson and Sharna were planning with two of the surgical androids on the excursion terminal, the guardian angels were rethinking their entire strategy. Their conviction that they were the greatest intelligences in the Universe was in no way diminished by the series of unexpected events that had overtaken the *Challenger*; they still firmly believed that they could and would conquer the Earth. The problem was finding it – a problem that never be resolved so long as the *Challenger* was marooned in orbit around Kyros with insufficient crew members to man the starship's main control room. Therefore the first step they had to take was to increase the numbers of the crew.

The complex program was set in motion: the automated food processing centres, which had been working at a fraction of their capacity since the Great Meteoroid Strike and the ensuing depletion of the crew's numbers, were instructed to stop adding Biostatron to the food produced by the farm galleries. The chemical plant which produced the sexual retardant drug was closed down, and the galley androids which had been programed to prepare the crew's food in such a way that ensured the drug remained effective during cooking were reprogramed so that their culinary techniques would gradually revert to normal. The guardian angels decided against an immediate change-over to avoid arousing Telson's and Sharna's suspicions if the food suddenly tasted different. The entire dietary change would take place over a period of thirty days. After that, Sharna and Telson would develop rapidly to full sexual maturity and could be disposed of once there was a suitable number of their children in the care of the nursery androids.

Developing a fourth-generation crew, this time one totally subservient to the guardian angels, would take twenty years but they did not mind. Unlike humans they had a capacity for infinite patience.

The first thing that Darv noticed about Helan when he and Astra were thrust into her presence were the twin swellings on her chest. They were plainly visible despite her loose-fitting tunic. The videos and holograms in the library had shown that all women possessed such swellings but there had been one hologram that he vaguely remembered that had shown a naked woman . . . She had been standing on a planet.. Or was it a planet? The sky had been such a vivid shade of blue that it could not have been real . . . but there had been clouds – soft white clouds . . . The memory of the strange hologram was tenuous and elusive. Perhaps it had been a dream.

'These are the creatures, your excellency,' said Spegal respectfully.

Helan smiled at Darv and Astra across the polished bauxite slab that served as her desk. She was a slim, somewhat gaunt woman in her early forties. Her austere appearance was accentuated by her long, talon-like fingernails and her close-cropped hair. Her smile was as chilly as the dank, underground cavern that was her office. The only touches of luxury were a scarlet carpet with a deep pile, and a high-backed, richly-upholstered chair. The effect of these two items in contrast to the general bleakness of everything else suggested to Darv and Astra that they were in the domain of a ruthless woman who wielded immense power and, furthermore, enjoyed wielding it.

'I'll question the boy or whatever he is later, Spegal.'

Darv refused to budge and had to be dragged fighting and kicking from the office. Astra screamed and went to his assistance but was grabbed by two men who sat her forcibly in the hard chair in front of Helan's desk.

Helan smiled icily at Astra when the commotion was over. 'Good day to you, Astra. My name is Helan and I am the chief prosecutor of the Solaric Empire.' She smiled again. 'A somewhat frightening title, I fancy. You may call me Helan. Now . . . I have some questions I wish to ask you.'

'I'm not saying anything without Darv.'

'Then I shall have Darv brought back in here and destroyed while we both watch.' Helan's statement was more of a definite promise than a vague threat.

It was some seconds before Astra spoke. 'What do you want to know?'

Helan's smile became slightly less cold. She touched the controls that activated a tiny screen set flush into the surface of her stone desk. Astra could see a screen divided by a glowing red line.

'First I must warn you not to lie, Astra. Two cerebral analysers have focused their beams into your brain. Lying will modulate the beams and they will channel the modulation back into your brain. You will find it a most unpleasant experience which you are unlikely to survive.'

'I've nothing to hide and therefore no reason to lie,' said Astra defiantly.

The line on the screen remained steady. Helan frowned briefly and touched a control. A hologram of the *Challenger* swam briefly in the air above the desk.

'Is that your mothership?'

'Yes. The *Challenger*.'

'A formidable looking ship. Is it armed?'

'No.'

Helan dropped her eyes to the screen but the line remained steady.

'And where does it and you come from?'

'From Earth.' Astra leaned forward. 'Do you know what happened to the Earth, Helan?'

The question surprised Helan although she was careful not to show it. She was not accustomed to prisoners asking questions. 'And what is Earth? A city? If so, what planet and what system?'

'I don't understand. The Earth *is* a planet.'

'Where?'

'We don't know. It was a planet of this solar system but its people took it away to another sun half a million years ago.' Astra paused. 'Surely you've heard of Earth? You speak its language.'

Helan arched her eyebrows. 'You think that explains how *you* can speak our language, Astra?'

'Why not? My grandparents were born on Earth.'

The line on the screen did not flicker. 'Tell me what you know in your own words, Astra.'

Astra talked for five minutes and ended with the encounter with the Sentinel on the moon. At that Helan's fixed smile became a humourless laugh.

'You know about the Sentinel?' Astra inquired.

'The moon Sentinel – guarding the Shrine of the First Footprint? Oh yes, Astra – we know about the Sentinel. A romantic artifact dreaming about the golden age of the Solaric Empire and a golden planet that never existed.'

'Have you ever been there?'

Helan had a vague feeling that the interview was not going according to plan. 'No one is allowed to go there. The moon is dangerously close to the sun. Tell me Astra, if this world of yours was once part of our solar system, where was its orbit?'

'Where the moon is now.' said Astra. 'In fact the *Challenger*'s year is based on the time that the Earth took to complete one orbit of the sun.'

Helan's poise deserted her for an instant. Astra saw the fleeting surprised expression and noticed how she looked at the screen as if not believing the message of its unwavering line. 'The standard Solaric year is based on the moon's orbit,' said Helan doubtfully. And then she was smiling again. 'But then you would have carefully researched us before entering our solar system. But not carefully enough.'

'I don't understand.'

Helan chuckled. 'Do you consider yourself a human being. Astra?'

'Yes.'

'A human female – yes?'

'Yes.'

Suddenly Helan was no longer smiling. 'I am without a doubt a human female, Astra. And yet you must concede that there are considerable physical differences between us. How old are you?'

'Twenty-five.'

Helan nodded and seemed to come to a decision. 'Thank you, Astra. Just a few more answers to a few more questions and I think I will have enough for my report. Somehow I do not believe that the Grand Emperor will favour a trial in view of what you've told me.'

'A trial?' queried Astra, bewildered. 'What trial?'

'There won't be one, Astra. We are very particular about according human rights to even the worst criminals in the Solaric Empire,' Helan's voice was icy again. 'But I doubt if you and Darv will qualify to receive them.'

Grand Emperor Thorden, ruler of a handful of inhabited moons of the outer planets which were all that was left of the million-year-old Solaric Empire, loved medals and riotous parties. He was wearing many of the former and indulging in the latter when Helan entered the underground gallery and stood surveying the decadent scene with undisguised distaste.

Thorden had organised the revellers into two teams for one of his inevitable shooting contests and, judging by the row he was making, he and his team had been particularly successful at blasting the androids at the Eastern end of the gallery. Their task to was to invade the Western end of the gallery which was occupied by the partygoers armed with hand lasers.

'How's that then?' Thorden bellowed as he demolished a fast moving android that had managed to reach the long banqueting table and leap onto it. Pieces of the vanquished machine exploded in all directions, forcing laughing and shrieking girls to dive for cover.

'Inspired shooting, sir,' said Thale, a young man who wore the double circle insignia of a captain in the Space Corps.

The compliment enraged Thorden. 'Inspired! How the hell can it be inspired shooting if I'm the best shot in the empire?'

Helan approached the short, thick-set figure who was glowering at Thale. 'A word with you please, Thorden.'

'What?'

'I have an urgent matter that requires your attention.'

'But the party's only just begun, dammit.'

'I have two aliens outside. I would like you to see them.'

Thorden frowned. 'Aliens? Dammit, Helan – it was proved a hundred thousand years ago that there's no such thing. Humans are the only intelligent life-form in the galaxy and that's us. Me in particular.'

'They're aliens, Thorden.'

Thorden stared at Helan for a moment before turning to his guests and telling them to manage without him for a while. He took Helan to one side.

'We're talking about the pirate prospectors that Spegal picked up on Kyros?' he inquired.

Helan nodded.

'But Spegal said that they were human.'

'Humanoid,' Helan corrected. 'They're certainly not human but crude imitations. My guess is that they were copied from a couple of kidnapped human children – from a pirateer ship perhaps – and that the aliens didn't realise that they were duplicating children. Our prisoners' story is that they're from a planet called Earth.'

Thorden frowned. 'There was a legend when I was a kid about a planet called Earth.'

'If it exists, it means that there's a rich world somewhere for us to conquer,' said Helan. 'Their mothership is in orbit around Kyros. According to Spegal it's at least ten miles long.'

Thorden goggled at Helan. His success as an emperor was based on his sound military philosophy of never picking fights with enemies who were more powerful that he was. Ships ten miles long were best treated with respect rather than declarations of war, and he told Helan so.

'It's unarmed,' Helan countered.

'What?'

'I used the cerebral analysers on the aliens during their interrogation. There is no doubt that they were telling the truth when they said that it was unarmed. What is more interesting is that their mothership is unable to move from its orbit around Kyros unless there is a crew of four in its main control room. There are two aliens aboard at the moment,' Helan gave a mirthless smile. 'And we are holding the other two.'

'A world to conquer,' breathed Thorden softly. 'Just what we need, Helan. The empire is stagnating in what little there is left of its wealth. Let's take a look at our two aliens.'

Helan moved away to summons her captives while Thorden bellowed at the revellers for their attention.

'Why is it,' he demanded, 'that in twenty years not one commander in my Space Corps has discovered as much as a lump of rock which is worth the empire possessing? Well?'

Thale saw that Thorden was glaring at him. 'Because there's nothing in range of our ships, sir,' he said ineffectually.

'Nothing in range!' Thorden thundered, glaring round at the others and making them wish that they hadn't accepted his invitation. 'Well, let me tell you something,' he said, beating his chest. 'I have discovered a world that has the resources to build ships ten miles long! What have you got to say to that, eh?'

No one had anything specific to say, but Thorden's words did cause a buzz of comment among the younger officers.

'Okay. Bring 'em in, Helan.'

Two powerfully-built guards pushed Darv and Astra into the centre of the gallery while Helan moved to Thorden's side. Thorden held up a hand to quell the sudden swell of conversation that greeted the appearance of the two captives.

'These, my friends, are aliens from the planet Earth,' Thorden announced. He took a good look at Astra and Darv and frowned. 'Helan – why haven't they got two heads of whatever it is aliens have?'

'I explained that they were imitation humanoids,' was Helan's patient reply.

Thorden grunted. 'Look like a couple of twelve-year-olds to me.' He stumped across to Darv. 'What's your name, boy?'

Without flinching from the hostile glare, Darv said: 'My name is Darv and I am not an alien, and nor is Astra.'

'My name is Darv, SIR!' roared Thorden.

'Sir.' Darv amended.

'You know who I am, boy?'

'I think I can guess what you are . . . Sir.'

'I am Grand Emperor Thorden of the Solaric Empire. What have you got to say to that?'

Darv was determined not to show the fear that was twisting like a live creature in his stomach. 'If being a citizen of the Solaric Empire means having to live underground on a collection of cold worlds, then we don't think much of it or its emperor.'

Astra could hardly believe that Darv could be so stupid as to provoke Thorden. She waited for him to lash out at Darv but the expected retribution never came. Instead, Thorden turned his attention to her.

'I suppose your Earth is a warm planet with a breathable atmosphere, eh, alien?'

Astra nodded. 'But we've never seen it, sir. We were born on our ship.'

'We're not aliens,' said Darv emphatically. 'We're human beings like you.'

Helan moved into the circle of watching partygoers that had formed around Thorden and the two prisoners. 'Like us, Darv?' she asked mildly.

'Yes.'

'Dammit, Helan,' Thorden muttered. 'They're just a couple of kids.'

Ignoring Thorden, Helan said to Astra: 'How old are you both?'

'I'm twenty-five. And so is Darv.'

Astra's answer produced a wave of comment.

'You said that they were telling the truth, Helan,' growled Thorden.

'And so they are,' said Helan. 'I want a man and woman

in their mid-twenties.' She beckoned to the taller of the two guards. His name was Quin – a giant of a man. He was nearly seven feet tall with rippling muscles which, in addition to his other physical characteristics, made him a firm favourite with Helan when she felt so inclined.

Helan positioned Quin so that he was facing Astra.

Thorden guessed what Helan was planning and gleefully grabbed one of his own favourites, a generously rounded girl named Della, and pushed her in front of Darv.

'Now, Darv and Astra,' said Helan. 'I want you to release your gowns.'

Darv and Astra exchanged puzzled expressions but did as Helan requested. Their clothes slid to the cold stone floor. They stood naked before the assembly, staring back unflinchingly at the circle of gaping faces.

'Dammit,' Thorden choked. 'They are child – '

'Do you mind being naked before all these people, Darv and Astra?' Helan cut in.

Darv hesitated but Astra chipped in. 'No. Why should we?'

'Quin,' Helan commanded. 'Drop your tunic.'

The giant moved nearer to Astra and stood grinning down at her. The buckle on the belt around his waist was level with Astra's eyes. His huge fingers plucked at the buckle and his uniform fell to the floor. There was a silence in the gallery; all eyes were upon the giant naked guard – his supple skin gleaming in the poor lighting. He leaned back – proudly thrusting out his pelvis until it was nearly touching Astra's face.

'Well, Astra?' inquired Helan.

'I don't think I've ever seen anything so ugly,' said Astra truthfully. 'Are all the men like him?'

The guard looked faintly annoyed. Helan waved him aside and gave Della a curt instruction. The girl complied. She released her gown. It slid to the floor. She smiled encouragingly at Darv who was gazing in some bewilderment at her full breasts and puckered nipples.

'What do you think of Della?' asked Helan.

Darv didn't know what to think. The girl and the sight of her body seemed to awaken a yearning in him that troubled and puzzled him. He had seen Sharna and Astra naked often enough but he had never before felt such a strange emotion as he was now experiencing.

'Quin and Della are about the same age as you two,' said Helan coldly. Yet I am sure you will agree that there are significant differences between you and them.'

Astra and Darv remained silent, unable to think of anything to say that would detract from the truth of Helan's statement.

'Do your companions on the *Challenger* look like you, or like Della and Quin?' Helan pressed.

'Like us,' said Darv' tearing his gaze away from the beautiful girl standing before him. 'Just because we don't look exactly the same as you doesn't mean . . . I mean . . .' He groped for the right words. 'We're all different heights and different weights. It doesn't mean that we're not human beings.'

Helan gestured to Della and Quin to get dressed and leave the centre of the circle. The guard gave Astra a parting scowl before returning to his station near the entrance to the gallery.

Helan resumed her questioning. 'Do you know what babies are, Astra?'

Astra nodded. 'Of course. We have pictures of them and of ourselves. We were all babies once.'

'But how do you have them? How do they come about?'

Thorden was irritated by the way that Helan was running what was rightly his show, but he remained silent. Although he was careful never to show it, he was a little scared of his cold-blooded chief executive.

'No,' said Astra after a long pause. 'I don't know how babies happen. It's something I've always wanted to find out more than anything else, but so much information is missing from the *Challenger*'s library.' She looked hopefully at Helan. 'Do you know? Will you tell me?'

Helan broke the silence that followed. 'The mothership owned by these . . . creatures will be useful to us. It may contain clues as to the whereabouts of this wondrous planet Earth and give us the means of reaching it.'

'And conquering it,' Thorden added.

Helan moved closer to Darv and Astra and stared at them, her eyes burning with loathing. 'As for its owners . . . They no longer understand their ship for they cannot tell us where the Earth is. There can no longer be any doubt that they are not human. They must be dealt with accordingly.'

Astra was crying. There was nothing Darv could say to comfort her. They were sitting side by side on a wide bunk – the only fitting in the small, windowless cell apart from a television sensor and a ventilation grille.

'Perhaps we're not human after all,' she sobbed.

'Don't be silly. Of course we are.'

'We're some sort of creatures that the guardian angels made when the real humans on the *Challenger* died.'

Darv put his arm round Astra's shoulders and gently drew her to him. 'We're not creatures like that. We have blood. We can see, feel, walk, run.' He stroked her hair. 'And even cry . . .'

His words had a slight effect for Astra gradually quietened. She was trembling with cold and fear. She clung to Darv so that he had some difficulty in pulling a blanket around them both.

'There's not one video or hologram in the library that shows people without clothes.' said Astra miserably. 'The angels destroyed them. They knew we were different and didn't want us to find out.'

'I think I did once find a recording of a naked man and woman,' said Darv uncertainly.

Astra sat up and looked at him in surprise. 'When?'

'I'm not sure. Sometimes it seems just like a dream, but I keep getting this picture in my mind of a man and woman standing on a planet which had an intense blue sky . . . And there were clouds . . . And rich green grass. I can't remember the name of the planet but the woman was holding a baby and she had growths on her chest just like that Della.'

Astra pressed her temple against Darv's chest again and was silent for a moment. She reached down and stroked his stomach. 'There wasn't so much difference between you and that guard as there was between me and Della. You're growing hair all over your body now.'

'Yes,' said Darv quickly, embarrassed for no reason that he could think of. 'I had noticed.'

'Maybe you're human and I'm not.'

Darv held her tighter. 'You say some silly things, my lovely.'

Astra yawned. 'Why do you call me that?'

'Because I like to. Do you mind or would you like me to call you something else?' He laughed softly. 'Something nice and insulting like the names I used to call you when we were kids?'

There was no answer. He looked down and saw that Astra was asleep. Taking great care not to wake her, he eased her into a comfortable position on the bunk and stretched out beside her. He listened to Astra's steady breathing for a while until exhaustion overcame him and he surrendered to a sleep filled with dreams of blue skies, soft white clouds and rich green grass.

'Dammit,' Thorden muttered.

'What's the matter, Thorden?' inquired Helan, knowing perfectly what was troubling the Grand Emperor.

Thorden nodded to the screen that showed Darv and Astra asleep on the cell bunk with their arms around each other. 'They're just kids.'

'What do you expect? They were copied from children.'

Thorden stared at the red touch control pad on the prison control panel before him and looked at the screen again. 'Dammit, Helan. Men – yes. Hundreds of men when I was rooting out rebels. But never children.'

'They are *not* children.'

'You'll have to do it.'

'It's your job, Thorden,' said Helan coldly. 'You hold the seal of office. All you have to do is touch that pad and the gas will do the rest.'

Thorden looked uncertain.

Helan began to get exasperated. 'Listen, Thorden – when

we discover their planet, we're going to have to destroy millions of them, not just two. Do you want to go down in history as the grand emperor of the Solaric Empire who failed his people and denied them their rightful salvation? You of all people? No – of course you don't. So all you have to do is touch that pad . . .'

Thorden stared at the control pad for a moment and then touched it.

In the cell adjoining the prison control room, gas began hissing through the ventilation grille. The bright orange cloud pooled sluggishly across the floor towards the bunk where Darv and Astra lay asleep.

PART 5

The Pools of Time

The two reprogrammed surgery androids were an amazing success: they had quickly assimilated the functions of the control consoles normally manned by Darv and Astra, thus enabling Sharna and Telson to accelerate the *Challenger* and manoeuvre it into a transfer orbit around the sun that intersected the orbit of Zelda Five – the moon of Zelda which had been the destination of the mysterious ship that had kidnapped Darv and Astra.

Telson regarded the huge image of Zelda Five that filled the repeater screen in the galactic resources centre while Sharna called upon Angel One to provide information.

'Zelda Five,' Angel One intoned. 'A moon on the outer planet Zelda. Gravity one; atmosphere zero; geothermal energy and mineral resources excellent. It was occupied by a mining concern when the *Challenger* was under construction. Therefore, by the time the Solaric Empire was established, it would have become a thriving colony. Perhaps they were not all evacuated when the Earth left the solar system. Perhaps they did not wish to be evacuated.'

Telson strode up and down in front of the screen, simmering with impatience. 'So the people on Zelda Five now, if there are any people, are descendants of the original colonists?'

'It is the one projection that avoids the maximum number of improbables, Commander Telson,' Angel One replied.

'So if they are human,' said Sharna slowly, 'they'll have human values? They'll know that kidnapping Darv and Astra is wrong?'

'A false projection,' said Angel Two. 'It assumes that human values remain constant over a given time.'

'Maybe,' Telson interrupted sourly. 'Right now I'm not interested in any argument except the one we're going to have with that miserable little moon if they're holding Darv and Astra. Angel One – are we close enough to go into a sixty-minute orbit around it?'

'Within the next thirty minutes, commander,' Angel One answered and called Telson back as he and Sharna were about to leave for the main control room. 'It seems inconceivable that you should have forgotten, commander, but the *Challenger* is unarmed.'

Telson thought for a moment, choosing his words carefully before replying. 'Perhaps Darv is right after all when he says that you and Angel Two are nothing but part of the ship's control systems. For beings that are supposed to be all-seeing and all-powerful, it seems inconceivable that the pair of you should lack imagination on such a monumental scale.'

With that, Telson turned and walked out of the galactic resources centre.

'Dammit, Helan!' Thorden shouted, jabbing a stubby finger at the picture of the *Challenger* on the screen that Spegal had just relayed to him. 'Look at it! Look at the size of the thing!'

'Spegal did say that it was ten miles long–' Helan began.

'And *you* said that the two on board couldn't shift it from its orbit round Kyros without those kids! Well, now it's here and I for one doubt if it's here on a goodwill visit.'

Thorden frantically jabbed the buttons to reverse the flow of gas into the adjoining cell.

'What are you doing!' demanded Helan, her voice hard and dangerous.

'Shutting the gas off – I want those two to live.'

'We decided that they were aliens and that they had to die.'

'*You* decided that they were aliens, and *you* decided that they had to die. Well, I'm undeciding.' Thorden moved to the door and bawled for medical attendants. Two men appeared in the corridor from a room opposite and dived into the execution cell in response to Thorden's instructions. They emerged a minute later supporting Darv and Astra who looked half dead on their feet because they were.

'In here. In here,' said Thorden, waving the medical attendants into the prison control room. 'Are they all right? Will thy recover?'

'I think so, sir,' said the first medical attendant. 'The gas had only just reached up to the level of the bunk.'

'You must do everything you can for them!' said Thorden dancing up and down impatiently. 'Nothing must be too much trouble.'

'Thorden,' said Helan patiently. 'Spegal wants to launch the interceptor squadron.'

'What!' Thorden looked aghast at the screen and the display which indicated the *Challenger*'s orbital height and position above Zelda Five. He fumbled at the control console and opened the channel to Spegal's battle centre. 'Spegal – you listen to me. You do nothing to upset that ship, do you hear? You don't launch anything without my say so.'

'But, sir,' Spegal protested. 'Her excellency assured us that the *Challenger* is unarmed, and it's closing its orbit to one hundred miles.'

'You do nothing!' Thorden roared. He spun around to where the medical attendants who were working on Darv and Astra with oxygen capsules. He was immensely relieved to see that both his captives had their eyes open. Darv was gazing hypnotised at the *Challenger* on the screen.

'Out! Out!' said Thorden, shooing the medical attendants and their equipment from the room. He put on a beaming smile and, ignoring Helan who was watching him in some disbelief, clapped Darv and Astra on the shoulder. 'Well, well, well,' he boomed jovially. 'Never known anyone who could sleep like you two, have we, Helan?'

'*Challenger*,' croaked Darv. He turned to Astra. 'Telson's come for us, Astra.'

'It's unarmed, Thorden!' Helan snapped, losing her patience. 'Your duty is to launch the interceptors!'

'Unarmed, eh?' said Thorden sarcastically. 'And it couldn't move from its orbit around Kyros, you said. Well let me tell *you* something – no one would build a ship that size unless its purpose is to move a lot of grief and mischief around the galaxy.'

'Thorden,' said Helan emphatically. 'I don't know how they managed to manoeuvre the *Challenger*. Perhaps they found a way of overcoming the control room manning problem, but there is no way in which they could develop an armament system.'

A high-energy beam stabbed out from the *Challenger*. It struck the ruined city near the position of the external surveillance camera causing the picture on the screen to jump. A second later the shockwave rumbled through the underground corridors and caverns of Zelda Five.

Before Thorden had a chance to turn to Helan with an appropriately sulfureous observation, the *Challenger* struck again with a blast that vaporised a mountain and concentrated Thorden's mind.

'Spegal! I want a voice channel to that ship immediately.'

'Sir – you must let me launch the interceptors!'

'A voice channel!' Thorden howled as another beam pattern reverberated through Zelda Five.

'Go ahead, sir. All channels are open.'

'The great warrior chief of Zelda Five is frightened,' said Helan venomously. 'I never thought I'd see the day.'

'Frightened?' Thorden's voice was indignant. 'Of course I'm not.' He paused. 'Yes I am – I'm frightened of unknown odds.' He turned to his captives. 'Darv!' he said, smiling warmly. 'What was your commander's name? Quickly!'

'Telson,' said Darv groggily, uncertain of what was going on.

'Commander Telson–' Thorden began and got no further because a voice suddenly boomed over the speakers.

'People of Zelda Five,' said the voice. 'Your attention please. This is Commander Telson of the starship *Challenger*!'

Darv and Astra were suddenly wide-awake at the sound of the familiar tones.

'I have reason to believe that you are holding two of my crew prisoners,' Telson continued. 'Unless you release them in thirty minutes, your miserable little moon is going to be blasted to cosmic dust.'

'Speak to him, Darv,' pleaded Thorden, yanking Darv to his feet and pushing him to the control panel. 'Tell him how well you both are, and how you're being treated as our honoured guests.'

'But she wants us dead,' Darv protested, pointing at Helan.

'And nothing has changed,' said Helan icily.

Thorden despairingly pushed Darv away from the panel. 'Telson – listen. I am Thorden – Grand Emperor of the Solaric Empire. We have Astra and Darv and they're safe. I think that we ought to meet to talk things over. I mean, there's no need for either of us to do anything that we might regret.'

'I won't have any regrets about atomising Zelda Five,' Telson replied. 'It's an ugly, misbegotten little moon that no one will miss.'

'And what about Darv and Astra?' Thorden demanded.

'Do you have a shuttle?'

'Yes. My private ferry.'

'Unarmed?' Telson inquired.

'Of course, commander.'

'We will expect you in an hour.'

'Very well, commander.'

'With Darv and Astra.'

'Naturally, commander. You will, of course, find me a reasonable man to deal with.'

'I'll try,' Telson promised. 'But you might have to make do with me.'

Table manners were not Thorden's strongest point. He grimaced and spat out a mouthful of food on his plate.

'I realise that I'm a guest on your ship, Telson,' he said blithely. 'But I have to say it – your food is lousy. Half your trouble's your food, you know. I'm sure I'd go a bit weird if I had to eat stuff like this every day.'

'Meaning that you don't believe us,' said Telson, regarding Thorden with some hostility.

Thorden smiled at Astra and Sharna. Pretty little things, he thought. Large, serious blue eyes – characteristics that hadn't been seen in Solaric women in ten thousand years. Women? These two were a couple of skinny girls. 'Meaning,' said Thorden carefully, 'that the videos and holograms of the Earth you showed me are impressive. A magnificent planet.' he tried to sound non-committal. In truth, he had been overwhelmed by everything he had seen since he had boarded the *Challenger*. It was a fantastic ship and he could hardly contain his excitement at the thought that it would be his provided he played these four kids along for a while.

'Look, Thorden,' said Darv earnestly. 'Surely you accept that we're all descended from the same people? We even speak the same language.'

'But we don't look the same, eh?' Thorden objected. 'To me you're just children. Pretty smart children maybe. I don't suppose even my top commanders, given this ship, would have thought of coming in low and blasting us by switching your meteoroid annihilation shields on and off. Clever.' He loaded some food on to his fork and changed his mind before continuing. 'But you're still very odd. You've even admitted that you don't know how babies are born.'

'Do you know?' asked Astra eagerly.

Thorden roared with laughter, 'All I can say is that your two guardian angels have deliberately kept you ignorant.'

'That is not so, Thorden,' interrupted Angel Two's voice suddenly.

Thorden looked uneasily around the *Challenger*'s restaurant at the rows of deserted tables and chairs. 'Which one was that?'

'Angel Two,' said Darv, watching Thorden with great interest. 'Don't you like them?'

'Damned voices,' Thorden muttered. 'The Solaric Empire finally defeated all its computers during the Third Computer War. Took fifty years.'

Darv grinned at Telson and said: 'So they *are* computers?'

'Now they're limited to functions where their supervisor has a switch to shut them off,' Thorden added.

Telson's face tightened in suppressed anger. 'Our angels are more than computers.'

'All guardian angels like to think they are,' said Thorden easily. 'They like it even more if they can convince people that they are. They like two things: power and increasing their power. Your two angels won't be happy with power over your ship – they'll want power over an entire planet. Preferably an inhabited planet of course.'

'Why?' Telson demanded. 'What good will it do them?' He wondered if Angel One and Angel Two would enter the argument.

Thorden pushed his plate away. 'It seems to me that they're no different from the angels that led to the First Computer War a thousand years back. Our forefathers buried them all on Kyros in a vast steel tomb – thousands of them – just in case there were a few active circuits left. That's why we didn't like you messing about on Kyros – digging on their burial site.'

Telson did an unusual thing. He laughed, causing Darv, Astra and Sharna to look at him in surprise. 'So that was the cause of the gravitational anomaly.' he mused. His expression hardened. 'Tell us about your angels, Thorden.'

Thorden hesitated, sensing that he was moving on to sensitive ground as far as Telson was concerned. 'Well . . . Maybe your angels aren't the same as ours . . . You're aliens . . . A different – '

'We're the same!' Sharna blazed suddenly. 'Earth was once a part of this solar system The records we've shown you prove it!'

Thorden regarded Sharna carefully for a moment. Her extra height made her appear older than Astra. She rarely spoke therefore it was hard to gauge her personality which made him feel doubly uncomfortable. He liked to get the measure of people he was dealing with. So far he had failed with Sharna.

'You know,' said Thorden, watching Sharna carefully. 'I'm almost tempted to believe you. It's pleasant to think that somewhere there could be a planet as soft and as agreeable as your videos and holograms suggest. An outside atmosphere that doesn't have to be contained by domes, with sufficient density to burn up meteoroids; sufficient pressure to prevent your blood boiling in your veins if you go out on the surface; and sufficient oxygen so that you don't need breathing aids . . . Pretty incredible, eh?'

'We've proved to you that it exists, Thorden,' said Sharna.
'Have you? Then where is this paradise?'
'That's it!' shouted Darv. 'That was the name Commander Sinclair of the second generation crew gave to the planet they discovered! Paradise!'

Before any of the others could speak, Darv was on his feet and was heading towards the restaurant's entrance. 'There's a recording in the library!' he yelled over his shoulder before disappearing.

Darv almost wept with frustration as he sat at the hologram replicator. He had spent two hours calling up recordings from the library. 'I know it's here,' he fumed to Astra who was helping him go through the index. Savagely, he touched the controls and called up the final page. The columns of information contained no reference to a planet. Darv swore and sat back just as Telson and Sharna entered the library with Thorden in tow.

'Well?' inquired Telson.

Darv thumped the replicator's control panel. 'I *know* there's a Paradise recording. *I know there is!*'

'Have you asked the angels?'

Darv gave a sarcastic laugh.

'Angel One,' called Telson.

'Commander Telson?'

'Did the second-generation crew discover a planet which Commander Sinclair called Paradise?'

'No, commander. As usual, Darv is mistaken. He is confusing his dreams with reality.'

'She, or "it", as we ought to call Angel One, is lying,' said Darv.

Telson spun the replicator chair around so that Darv was facing him. He said in a dangerously quiet voice: 'I think you ought to apologise to Angel One, don't you, Darv?'

Thorden defused the expectant silence that followed. 'I will tell you something about your angels, Commander Telson. Once they were servants – control systems to run your ship. And then a third-generation crew came along . . .' Thorden broke off and chuckled. 'You say that you're a third-generation . . .'

Telson was about to transfer his anger to Thorden but Sharna touched his sleeve. 'Let him finish, Telson,' she said quietly. 'Go on, Thorden.'

Unabashed, Thorden grinned and said: 'You know how they got the name "angel"? In the Solaric Empire the word "Angel" was short for ancillary guardian of environment and life – A-N-G-E-L. Simple, eh? The chances are that Darv has seen the Paradise recording but your two friendly guardian angels have arranged for him to forget that he's see it. The chances are that it was an undeveloped planet. But the one thing your precious angels won't want is for you to settle on an undeveloped planet when there's a populated and developed Earth somewhere for them to conquer.' He looked quizzically at Darv. 'Was there a reference on the recording to where Paradise was? The number of a planetary system or a star reference?'

Darv thought for a moment and shook his head. 'If there was, I can't remember it now.'

'We would never have survived without our guardian angels,' Telson muttered. He looked appealingly at Sharna. 'They controlled the nursery androids that brought us up.'

Thorden nodded. 'The angels wanted you to live. Androids can't control a ship of this size and complexity, but humans can. And the angels can control the humans if the humans are kept sufficiently ignorant to let them.'

'So you now believe that we're human?' Darv inquired.

'Maybe.'

'Do you believe now that there was a planet called Earth that was once a part of this solar system half a million years age?' asked Telson.

'We'll see, my friends,' Thorden chuckled. 'Maybe I can help in your search for this mysterious planet Earth, but first I must go down to Zelda Five for a few days to discuss the matter with my advisors.'

'Thorden,' said Darv thoughtfully.

'Yes, my friend?'

'How could we end the angels' control over us?'

'Somewhere in the ten-mile length of this ship is the guardian angels' central switching room. Find that, my friends, and you will be able to control them or destroy them.' Thorden gave a deep rich laugh. 'But it won't be easy because they won't be that keen to tell you where it is.'

The guardian angels debated the problem of Thorden and decided that if he returned to the *Challenger*, they would attempt to harness his greed and ambition for their own purposes. If they failed then Thorden was sufficiently dangerous to warrant destroying.

'State your business,' grated the voice from the grille set into the wall of the cavern.

'I don't have to,' Thorden growled. 'I'm the Grand Emperor, dammit.'

A small platen emerged from the wall beneath the grille.

'Place you seal of office here,' said the voice.

Thorden lifted the heavy medallion from around his neck and dropped it on to the platen. He was pleased that the security system guarding the Custodian of Time was still in working order after all the intervening years since his last visit. He was in one of the deepest and remotest of the million-year-old mining galleries that had been driven into the mantle of Zelda Five by his forgotten ancestors.

There was the hum of hidden machinery and a section of the wall creaked slowly inward, moved by servo-motors that had not been operated for over half a century.

'Enter,' instructed the voice.

Thorden recovered his seal of office and walked hesitantly into the dark interior. He felt a sudden twist of fear as the massive door swung shut behind him and darkness closed in. And then a voice spoke and the fear left him. It was a sweet young voice – the voice of long-forgotten lives and remembered youth.

'Hallo, Thorden. I wondered when you would come to see me again.'

'I can't see, Custodian.'

There was soft laughter. A column of red light appeared in the centre of the cavern. It rose from the middle of a circular slab of black rock that appeared to be suspended a few inches above the cavern's uneven hewn floor.

'Why have you come to visit me. Thorden?' The intensity of the column of light rose and fell in harmony with the timbre of the gentle voice.

Thorden approached the suspended slab and stared up at the column. 'Do you remember the stories you told me when I was little, Custodian?'

'Now I know why you have come, Thorden.' There was a barely perceptible chiding note to the voice. 'I deal only in the history of this planet. The immutable past. All else is alien to me.'

'You told me stories of the golden age before the empire, Custodian.'

The voice laughed and the column of light rippled. 'I may have built on the curious remnants in my memory of the unknown days before the empire, Thorden. But those were stories told to a wide-eyed boy. Mere legends, Thorden.'

'I want you to tell me those stories again please, Custodian. I want you to pretend that I'm that wide-eyed boy once more.'

The light dimmed for a second and then brightened. Thorden edged forward and, uncertain how the Custodian would react, he sat on the edge of the slab. It felt warm and reassuring to his touch.

'I used to sit here at your foot, Custodian, and I used to stare down into the pools of time where you made pictures. Do you remember?'

The Custodian's laughter made the column of light tremble. 'Of course I remember, Thorden.'

'Tell me the story that you used to tell me about the beginning of time – when you used to make me stare down into the pools of time . . . Please . . . Custodian . . . Please.'

The intensity of the light rose and fell. 'Very well, Thorden,' said the voice that was like music. 'But you must understand that it is only a story. A story built on the strange elements of unproved knowledge I have in my memory . . . Look down Thorden . . . Look down into the pools of time.'

Thorden stared down, Space as deep and as wide as the Universe had opened before him but he felt no fear. In the centre of the great void was a slowly contracting cloud of incandescent hydrogen gas. The intense white light at the centre of the cloud appeared to be radiating from the core that Thorden could not look at for more than a second at a time.

'Look down into the pool, Thorden . . . Look down . . . Down . . . You are looking back in time to when our sun was a whirling cloud of condensing gas spinning much faster then it is now. And then the sun began to spin faster and faster as it collapsed on itself until suddenly it hurled vast clouds of matter into space . . .'

Childhood memories flooded back to Thorden as he gazed down at the birth of the solar system of the hours he had spent at the foot of the Custodian, listening to her enchanting voice.

'But the sun's gravity was too great for the clouds to escape,' continued the Custodian, 'so they orbited the sun. Countless billions of years passed and then a nearby star far bigger than the sun suddenly exploded and for millions of years the sun and the clouds of gas orbiting the sun were bombarded with huge meteoroids.'

The images were fading from the depths before Thorden. He was about to speak to the Custodian before he realised that she was moving the picture forward in time.

'The mighty bombardment ended four and a half thousand million years ago. And when it was over, instead of clouds of gas orbiting the sun, there were planets . . .'

Thorden clutched the edge of the slab. For the first time he was giddy with vertigo as the black pit suddenly tilted; distant stars dipped out of his field of view and new ones appeared, but it was the breathtaking splendour of the planets that had risen in the foreground that held his attention and made him forget the fleeting sensation of nausea.

'Many planets bear the marks of that terrible assault to this day,' said the Custodian. 'And there they are . . . Beautiful children of the sun moving serenely against the stars as they circle obediently around their mother. There's Malkara – the first of the sun's six children – orbiting so near that her rocks are now melting and making rivers of lava . . . Look closer for we now come to the second planet – the most beautiful of the children of the sun . . .'

Thorden's ability to appreciate beauty had never been fully developed and yet he could not help being captivated by the sight of the sparkling blue-green planet that shone before him like a priceless jewel.

'In those days,' said the Custodian, 'the moon orbited the beautiful planet, but not any more, for the beautiful planet, like the princess who nearly stayed too late at the ball, has gone.'

Thorden spoke for the first time since the images had appeared. 'What happened to the planet?' he whispered.

'The people who lived on it were very clever for it was they who spread across the solar system and plundered the moons of the other planets for the minerals that the people of the beautiful planet needed. The first men and women to set foot on Zelda Five – our home – were miners.'

'But what happened to the beautiful planet, Custodian?' Thorden persisted.

There was a pause before the Custodian resumed speaking. 'One day its people became afraid of the sun that had given them warmth and light. They studied the strange forces of gravity and magnetism that pervade the cosmos. They built several artificial suns to pour down energy on their planet, and when they had mastered the forces of gravity and magnetism, they took their beautiful planet out of the solar system and went in search of a sun that they were not afraid of.'

'How long ago was this, Custodian?'

The images in the pools of time were fading. 'Time doesn't matter,' said the Custodian, her voice sounding far away. 'It's only a legend.'

'But what was the name of the beautiful planet?'

'Earth,' came the faint reply.

*   *   *

'Dammit!' Thorden shouted. 'I'm not interested in your problems, old man! If you wish, I'll arrange for you to have all the research facilities you need. All I want are straight answers to my questions! Is it possible?'

The old man tried to tidy some papers while he thought. It was the first time that a grand emperor had visited his observatory and he fervently hoped that it was the last.

'Well?' Thorden demanded.

'Time is very strange, you must understand,' said the old man. 'It has a variable quality. The rate at which it flows is dependent of the speed of the observer. The mathematics involved is not diff – '

'I'm not interested in the mathematics of the problem!' Thorden bellowed, making the old man wince. 'If I built a ship that could travel at near the speed of light, would it be possible for me to leave Zelda Five, journey for what was one hundred and fifteen years to me, and return to discover that a million years had passed here?'

'Well, yes,' said the old man doubtfully. 'I suppose it would be possible assuming that you could build such an advanced ship.'

'Thank you! And live for one hundred and fifteen years?'

'Provided you didn't make too many enemies – yes.'

Astra propped herself more comfortably against the dwarf fruit tree and sunk her small white teeth appreciatively into an apple. She crunched noisily and held the apple in front of Darv's face for him. He was stretched out on the grass beside her wearing only a pair of shorts. He took a bite at the apple.

'Your chest is getting really hairy,' she teased. 'And you're losing your freckles.'

Darv said nothing, preferring to savour the warmth of the solar lighting that beat down from the inside of the farm gallery's roof. His hand strayed languidly on to Astra's leg and caressed her thigh through the thin material of her one-piece suit.

Astra bit into the apple again. 'What do you suppose is

done to the fruit we're given to make it taste so awful?' she asked.

'I thought there'd been a slight improvement,' said Darv sleepily, moving his hand further up Astra's leg.

'But why process it? There's nothing wrong with it the way it is?'

'Perhaps Angel One and Two do something special to it during processing.'

'Like what?'

Darv grinned up at her. 'I don't know. Something to keep you young and innocent.'

Astra retaliated by jabbing Darv in the stomach. Then she was laughing hysterically as Darv sat astride her and proceeded to tickle her ribs.

'No – Darv! Stop it!'

She felt his hands move to her chest and began fighting him off in earnest. Darv caught her flailing fists and pinned them together with one hand on the grass behind her head. Her long blonde hair was entangled across her face. Darv brushed it away. He was grinning down at her.

'Do you give in?'

For an answer she tried crashing her knees into the small of his back but he merely shifted his weight down until she could no longer move her legs.

'You're hurting me, you idiot!'

'You used to like wrestling.'

'Not now I don't.' She tried arching her body to dislodge him but he was too strong for her.

'Then you've changed.'

She began to panic when she felt Darv's free hand move to the top of the seam on her suit. She squirmed frantically. 'What are you doing!'

'I only want to look at you, Astra. We always used to play naked together in the reservoir.'

'No, Darv – please!' She struggled violently and very nearly succeeded in getting a hand free until he tightened his grip. She felt him hook a finger under the seam and made one last despairing attempt to wriggle free as he opened the seam from neck to stomach. She felt cool air on her skin and realised that there was no point in further struggle. She lay still, fighting to get her breath back, and opened her eyes. Darv had suddenly released his hold on her hands and was staring down at her breasts, his eyes round with shock.

'Astra,' he whispered. 'Astra . . . I'm sorry.'

She folded an arm across her eyes so that he would not see the tears that were coming.

Darv eased his weight on to the grass and guiltily tried to close the seam on Astra's suit, but she seized his hand and held it tightly. He misinterpreted the gesture and tried to reassure Astra that he wasn't going to touch her. She answered by pulling him down and holding his head hard against her chest. Darv did not know whether half a minute or half an hour passed with them both lying perfectly still, but it ended with Astra's body suddenly shaking with uncontrolled sobs.

Sharna regarded Thorden in surprise. 'But why, Thorden? You have an empire to run.'

Thorden grunted. 'A handful of sterile moons orbiting Zelda, and a collection of barren worked-out asteroids. There're no more pirates and no more fun. What I need is excitement, Sharna.'

'And you think that searching for Earth is going to be exciting? Well you're wrong. It's going to take several years to reach the nearest star cluster before we can even start searching.' Sharna resumed cleaning the telescope's set of camera lenses – a task that she would not let the service androids carry out because once they had managed to break one.

'Telson said that we'll spend the time in suspended animation,' Thorden pointed out. 'He told me that it's just like going to sleep and waking up the next morning except that you feel a bit stiffer.' He toyed with one of the lenses until Sharna took it from him.

'What did Telson say to you coming with us?' she asked.

'He said that it's fine by him if you're in agreement.'

Sharna considered. 'Would you take orders from me or Telson?'

Thorden gave an expansive grin. All was going according to plan. 'But of course.' He slipped an arm around Sharna's waist and chuckled. 'And we won't be searching for Earth all the time, will we?'

Sharna's instinctive reaction was to push Thorden away but she realised that she didn't object to his touch or his smell. Nor did she raise any objections when Thorden turned her round so that she was facing him. He cradled her face in his broad powerful hands and said: 'You know something, my aloof and mysterious little Sharna? You're going to be really quite something when you're a bit older.'

'Two Zelda Five shuttles approaching,' Telson's voice said from a speaker. 'Screen Three. Sharna – I'm busy in the main control room. Will you go to the excursion terminal and see to them?'

'Right away, Telson,' Sharna replied.

Thorden glanced at the repeater screen that showed the two approaching shuttles but made no attempt to take his hands away from Sharna's face. 'That's Helan's private ferry and Spegal bringing my private ferry,' he commented. 'Why not let your guardian angels look after them for a few minutes?'

Sharna smiled and disentangled herself from Thorden. 'The excursion terminal doesn't come under the angels' control,' she explained. 'Someone has to be there.'

Better and better, thought Thorden as he followed Sharna from the galactic resources centre.

The two diminutive spacecraft settled on the floor of the *Challenger*'s excursion terminal having first passed through the huge air-lock. The larger of the two ships was Thorden's personal ferry. Unlike Helan's craft, it was designed for atmospheric flight: its sleek, streamlined shape gave it an aggressive, businesslike look. Helan emerged from her craft and exchanged brisk greetings with Sharna and Thorden.

'A very smart shuttle, Thorden,' said Sharna as they waited

for Spegal to emerge from Thorden's ferry. 'Why didn't you use it when you returned to the *Challenger*?'

Thorden was saved from having to answer the embarrassing question by Spegal's appearance as the ferry's door slid open.

'Spegal!' Thorden boomed, clapping his officer across the shoulders as he stepped down. 'Brought her up in one piece I see. Excellent. Excellent.'

Spegal beamed. 'All completely refitted in accord-'

'Have you met Sharna?' Thorden interrupted, treating Spegal to a crushing glare that Sharna didn't see. 'Yes – of course you have. Helan will take you back in her ferry when I've handed her my seal of office.'

'So they've accepted you?' Helan inquired, eyeing Sharna.

'Of course they've accepted me,' Thorden laughed. 'Who would refuse my delightful company, eh? Now then, Sharna – if you would show Helan and me to my cabin, please, so that I can hand over my seal. It's a simple private ceremony that won't take more than a couple of minutes.'

The group moved out of the terminal leaving Spegal alone with Thorden's ferry. As soon as the door closed, he moved to Helan's ferry and opened the door.

'Fagor!' he called out nervously.

The android that appeared with great suddenness in the ferry's doorway was jet black and a little over eight feet tall although its actual height was nearer ten feet because of its ability to hover some two feet above the ground. Sprouting from the android's armoured body were six powerful manipulators – four of them terminating in wide-angle laser projectors and the other two ending in stubby fingers that looked capable of ripping steel plates in half. It was one of the latter that whipped out, seized Spegal by the collar of his uniform, and lifted him up until his face was level with the two optical sensors on the top of the android's body.

'Where is the master?' growled the android's voice. 'If anything has happened to him, Fagor kills.' With that the android shook the unfortunate Spegal until he was sure his head was about to fall off.

'He's all right, Fagor,' Spegal gasped. 'You're picking up his heartbeat, are you not?'

Fagor released his grip and Spegal fell in a sprawling heap. He staggered to his feet and decided that Fagor's simple program – that of ensuring Thorden's will-being – did not require testing.

'You know what you have to do.' said Spegal uneasily, backing off as Fagor drifted nearer. 'You're to keep yourself hidden until the master needs you.'

'And then Fagor kills,' the android announced with grim simplicity while giving Spegal a bad time by waving one of its laser projectors at him.

'But you must not worry if the master's heartbeat slows down,' Spegal stressed, 'because he may have to go into suspended animation. Do you understand?'

Fagor understood.

'Now hide, Fagor.'

Fagor concealed himself behind a chemical fuel storage tank.

Spegal began to feel better and wondered exactly what Fagor would do if anything happened to Thorden. He decided that it would most likely be extremely quick, noisy, and more than a little messy.

Thorden chuckled richly to himself when Helan finished outlining the details of the refit to his ferry: the weapon shops had served him well. 'And Fagor?' he inquired.

'He's been programmed to look after you,' Helan replied.

Thorden did not pry any deeper. Helan's attention to detail was legendary.

'What about the two computers.' Helan asked.

'The angels?' Thorden grinned. 'Probably listening to us at this minute.'

Helan flushed angrily. 'You mean you haven't screened this cabin?'

'I can handle a couple of angels,' said Thorden smoothly. 'It won't take me long to find their central switching room. You worry about your instructions. As soon as we discover

Earth, I take over the *Challenger* and return to lead the invasion fleet.'

'It could take years, Thorden.'

'But think of the prize, Helan! A rich, warm planet with a breathable atmosphere. Can you imagine it? Being able to walk in the open without some sort of spacesuit? Being able to swim in lakes and lie in the sun?'

Helan was silent for a moment as she tried to picture the inconceivable. She shook her head and moved to the doorway. 'Good luck then, Thorden. Till we meet again.'

'Till we meet again, Helan.'

The light polarised as Helan stepped across the threshold and she was gone.

Thorden stretched out on the surprisingly comfortable bed and hooked his hands together at the back of his neck. 'Did you hear that, my little angels?'

'We heard,' Angel One replied.

'We can control androids,' said Angel Two.

'You won't be able to control Fagor, my mischievous little ancillary guardians of environment and life. I have only to give the word and Fagor could either seize control of the *Challenger* or destroy it. And if he gets the idea into his remarkably small brain that something has happened to me, he might do just that.'

The guardian angels digested this. 'What do you want with us, Thorden?' Angel One asked.

Thorden settled himself comfortably on the bed and grinned up at the sensor set into the cabin's ceiling. 'You two want to find a developed planet pretty bad, I guess. Oh come on, angels – I'm Thorden – I know all about free-will computers and I know how you like power. You want power over something more than a survey ship, eh? A planet maybe? A planet like Earth?'

'That could be an accurate assessment,' Angel Two admitted.

'You're damned right it's an accurate assessment. As I see it, we're both after the same thing. So we might as well do a deal.'

* * *

Darv was sure that he could never tire of looking at Astra's lithe, naked body as she lay asleep on the grass beside him. Compared with the fullness of Della, it was obvious that the changes to Astra's body were still taking place, but to Darv she was the most beautiful thing he had ever seen.

The solar lights were dimming for the night period and there was a chill in the air. He removed Astra's arm which she had draped across his chest and gently shook her shoulder to wake her. She opened her eyes and smiled at him.

'I was awake all the time,' she said, sitting up and shaking out her hair. 'You were staring at me.'

Darv grinned and pulled her to her feet. 'Do you mind?'

Astra shook her head.'

'Did I hurt you?'

She thought for a moment. 'No. But it was a strange thing to do, don't you think?'

Darv nodded and helped her as she stepped into her suit and closed the seams. 'It was more than strange,' he said candidly, 'It was weird. And I can't for the life of me think why I did it.' He paused and added: 'Or why you let me.'

'Darv? Astra?' said Telson's voice. 'Can you hear me?'

'Yes Telson,' Darv replied. 'We can hear you.'

'You are both wanted in the main control room in one hour when we'll be starting preparations to leave the Zelda Five orbit.'

Darv suppressed a yawn. 'Where are we going, Telson?' he asked.

'Tersus Nine,' Telson replied. 'It's the nearest star cluster to the solar system and has over two thousand main sequence stars. Sharna and I consider it the best place to start the Earthsearch Mission.'

Astra stared at Darv in alarm; the colour had drained from his face and his eyes appeared to be glazed with shock. 'Darv?' she said anxiously. 'What's the matter?' She had to repeat the question twice.

'Tersus Nine . . .' Darv whispered.

'What about it? Darv – answer me!'

He focussed his eyes on her. 'The Paradise recording.' he

said hollowly. 'I *didn't* dream it, Astra! *I knew I didn't dream it*! Star Cluster – Tersus Nine was where Commander Sinclair of the second-generation crew said that they had found the planet that they called Paradise!

PART 6

Across the Abyss

For two years the mighty ship had plunged across the awesome void of interstellar space at three-quarters of the speed of light while its cargo of five human beings slept the death sleep of suspended animation, watched over by the guardian angels.

For two years Fagor had remained still and silent, hidden in the excursion terminal, listening to the slow heartbeat of his master who lay with the four members of the *Challenger*'s crew in suspended animation. For each minute of the two years Thorden's heart had beaten once, and for each minute of the two years Fagor had been reassured.

The surgical android moved slowly along the suspended animation tanks, carrying out its routine nutrient and oxygen supply checks. It stopped when it came to the tank in which Sharna's pale body floated. Following Angel Two's instructions, the android withdrew the plastic tubes from her body and, locating the correct spot with its delicate manipulators, carefully slid a hypodermic needle into a vein. The android waited until it noted the rapid eye movements beneath Sharna's closed eyelids before removing the needle and signalling a service android to lift her body from the tank on to the recovery grid.

While Sharna's respiration and pulse rate gradually returned to normal, the surgical android carried out tests which, like the recovery procedure just used, were not past of the normal revival routine. It eased Sharna on to her side and pushed her knees up to her chin before pushing a probe into her body to check the development of her ovaries. A whole series of minor tests followed that included measuring the fatty deposits on her hips, and even the volume of her breasts. The conclusion that the surgical android communicated to Angel Two was that Sharna was now sexually fully developed. Also, she was approaching full consciousness.

'Sharna,' said Angel Two softly. 'Can you hear me, Sharna?'

Sharna stirred on the recovery grid and mumbled something that the guardian angel could not distinguish.

'Listen carefully, Sharna. We are about to wake you. We are about to wake you. You and the others have been in suspended animation for two years . . . Can you hear me, Sharna?' The masculine voice was soothing and reassuring.

'Hear you, Angel Two . . .' escaped from Sharna's lips.

'The *Challenger* is halfway to the Tersus Nine Star Cluster, Sharna.'

'Going to wake us,' muttered Sharna.

'Only you, Sharna. We are waking you and no one else.'

Sharna moved her legs languidly and rolled onto her back. Her eyes remained closed.

'When you wake up, Sharna, you will discover that your body has changed, and you will accept those changes as being perfectly normal – which they are.'

'Don't understand . . .' Sharna muttered.

'Place your hands on your chest, Sharna . . .'

Sharna's hands encountered her breasts. The expression on her face gradually changed to one of anguish as he explored the unfamiliar contours. 'Ugly,' she said, rolling her head from side to side. 'Ugly. Ugly. Ugly!'

'No, Sharna,' said Angel Two's softly persuasive voice. 'You are now very beautiful. And when you wake up you will think of yourself as being perfectly normal because you are normal. And the others are normal . . . Normal . . . Do you understand, Sharna?'

'Normal,' Sharna mumbled calming down. 'I'm normal . . .'

'And beautiful.'

'And beautiful.'

The surgical android gave Sharna another injection in response to an instruction from Angel Two.

A minute passed.

Sharna opened her eyes and stared up at the lights.

She sat up.

For an instant she was puzzled by the unaccustomed weight of her breasts and the hair on her body.

'Good day, Sharna,' said Angel Two's voice brightly. 'Time to wake up.'

'Good day to you, Angel Two,' Sharna replied, gazing at the comatose forms of the other four. 'Hey? What's going on? Why am I the only one awake?'

'We need you in the galactic resources centre, Sharna.' said Angel Two smoothly. We're sorry that we had to wake you but we considered it important.'

'But why only me? Have we reached the star cluster?'

'Not yet. A service android is taking your post-suspended animation meal to the centre. We'll explain there.'

Sharna located the point of light from the co-ordinates that the guardian angels had given her. As soon as she transferred the data on the object to the spectrum analysers she knew it was not a star that she was examining through the optical telescope. For one thing it was moving against the stars and the light she was receiving from it was reflected starlight. Furthermore it was moving on approximately the same course as the *Challenger* but at a lower speed in relation to the *Challenger*.

'Range . . . Over a thousand million miles,' said Sharna, checking the data displays. 'We'll be overhauling it in thirty hours at our present convergent rate.' She thought for a moment. 'Nova debris?' she suggested. 'An asteroid?'

'Possible but unlikely,' commented Angel Two. 'This region is relatively clear of matter. The particle sweeps have hardly replenished the reservoirs.'

'We're okay for mass?'

'Yes.'

'Okay,' said Sharna. 'So what do you and Angel One think it is?'

'It might be a ship. We have signalled it on all bands and

allowed several time delays between each set of signals but there has been no response.'

Sharna touched the spectrum analyzer-controls and studied the new information. 'About the same size as the *Challenger*,' she observed. 'You were right to wake me. We'll carry out another observation in fifteen hours. There should be a fifty per cent improvement in resolution by then.'

Sharna got up from the telescope's couch and experienced a moment of surprise at the movement of her breasts.

The guardian angels decided that if the object was a ship, then it was certain that Sharna would insist that the others should be brought out of suspended animation.

Then there was the problem of Thorden.

They debated Thorden and decided that now was the time to move against him. Killing him would be a simple matter – they could easily account for his death to the others by saying that as a newcomer they did not know enough about his metabolism to sustain him during suspended animation. The big problem the guardian angels had was Fagor. They didn't know how powerful the android was – perhaps Thorden had been bluffing when he said that Fagor could destroy the *Challenger* – or maybe he had not. Assuming that Fagor was a force to be reckoned with, how did he know whether or not his master was dead or alive? The guardian angels decided to move with great caution. First they would lower Thorden's metabolic rate until his heart was beating once every two minutes . . .

Just to see what happened . . .

The radio pulses that relayed Thorden's heartbeats ceased.

Fagor stirred and flexed his manipulators. It was the first movement he had made in two years. His second action was internal – a systematic check of all the weaponry in his formidable arsenal. Two minutes passed. Thorden's heart gave a beat and Fagor relaxed.

* * *

Sharna centred the image in the telescope's objective lens. It was completely swamped by the light from the spiral galaxy in Ramedes. She corrected the aberration with a filter and switched the resulting picture to an image intensifier.

Everything else was forgotten as she gaped at the ship in astonishment.

Angel Two broke the silence in the galactic resources centre. 'The odds against such an encounter are–'

'I'm not interested!' Sharna snapped. 'I want the others revived immediately!'

The picture on the telescope's screen was that of another *Challenger*.

The post-revival method used for Darv, Astra and Telson was the same as that used on Sharna: the hypnotic, persuasive voices of the guardian angels assured them that they would look upon the bodily changes that had taken place as normal although in Sharna's and Astra's cases the changes had already started before they went into suspended animation.

Telson ignored Darv and Astra as they chased each other whooping and yelling round the tanks in the suspended animation chamber. He sat on the edge of the recovery grid and stared down at himself – baffled by the sight of the fine covering of dark hair on his torso and legs.

Darv knocked against Telson as he scrambled across the recovery grid and pinned Astra, laughing and shrieking, against the wall.

'For God's sake!' Telson snarled. 'Why can't you two act your age? You're not kids any more!'

Darv released Astra and turned to face Telson. He grinned amiably. 'Sorry, Telson. Maybe you'd be happier if I talked our beloved guardian angels into putting you under again?'

Telson regretted his boorish behaviour. 'I'm sorry, Darv – Astra . . . Forgive me.'

Astra and Darv stared at Telson in surprise: it was virtually unknown for him to apologise. Astra put a reassuring hand on Telson's knee and looked at him anxiously. 'That's all right, Telson,' she said. 'But what's the matter?'

As Telson looked into Astra's round blue eyes, he realised for some strange reason that he was ashamed of his nakedness and embarrassed by Astra's nakedness. It had never happened before and it worried him.

'Nothing,' he said, shaking his head as if to clear it. He caught sight of Thorden's form lying in its tank. Glad of the chance to change the subject, he said: 'Why hasn't Thorden been revived?'

'First thing I asked while you were coming round,' said Darv. 'The guardian angels don't think Sharna's discovery is any of his business.'

Telson peered closely at the telescope's repeater screen, hardly able to credit his eyes. He straightened up and glanced at Darv and Astra. They shrugged in reply to his raised eyebrows and continued to stare at the screen and the strange object that was now a million miles away.

'Could it be a reciprocal image of this ship that the telescope's generating Sharna?' he asked.

Sharna shook her head. 'I've checked and double-checked every system.'

'The Sentinel on the moon mentioned another *Challenger* that never returned,' reminded Astra. 'Can you increase the resolution?'

Sharna touched the telescope's controls. The fuzzy picture of the mysterious ship cleared slightly. It was possible to discern the appalling damage it had suffered. The entire ten-mile length of its hull was riddled with holes that varied from craters a few yards across to yawning fissures.

'My God,' breathed Telson. 'She has been in the wars.'

'I'd say the wars have been in her,' Darv corrected. 'Look at he edges of those holes or whatever they are. 'They're splayed outwards – not inward. Meteoroids could never have caused that sort of damage. Those wounds are self-inflicted. Thousands of them.'

Telson studied the picture and admitted that Darv was right.

'So what do we do now?' Sharna inquired.

'Simple,' said Telson. 'The first thing we do is find out how much time and propellant mass we need to match course and velocity with that thing.'

'To board it?' asked Darv hopefully, fully expecting Telson to veto the suggestion out of hand. But the anticipated rebuff did not come.

'We'll see,' said Telson.

Well, thought Darv, looking at Telson in surprise, you have changed.

After a week consisting of seven ten-hour sessions in the main control room, the crew finally completed the series of precision manoeuvres that ended with the *Challenger* lying five miles off the seemingly derelict hulk of its sister ship – their respective courses and velocities perfectly matched.

The crew were exhausted. Darv raised no objections to Telson's sensible suggestion that they all rest for two days before taking further action. In the meantime Angel One and Angel Two would keep the hulk under close surveillance and immediately report any signs of life or movement.

The guardian angels issued further instructions to the surgical android that was watching over Thorden's near lifeless body in the suspended animation chamber.

The machine reduced the operational working levels of the nutrient and oxygen feeds with the result that Thorden's pulse slowed to one heartbeat every five minutes.

In the excursion terminal on the opposite side of the ship, Fagor stirred and decided to familiarise himself with the *Challenger*'s layout.

* * *

Astra stopped combing her hair and gazed pensively across the waters of the reservoir. It was evening. The overhead lights were low and a mist was rising off the water.

'Do you want to know something?' she said to Darv who was sprawled on his stomach beside her. 'The reservoir is my favourite place in the whole ship.'

'You've never explored the whole ship so you don't know.'

'Do you suppose that there's still hundreds of lakes all over the Earth?'

'You've seen the holograms and videos.'

Astra leaned across Darv and kissed him between the shoulder-blades. 'But that was the Earth of a million years ago . . . If I ever have a baby I shall want to watch him playing with you in a real lake, under a real sun. Not like this.'

Darv yawned. 'First we have to discover how babies happen.'

Astra laughed softly. 'I think I know now.'

Her statement prompted Darv to propel himself on one elbow and stare at her, 'You *think* you know?'

'It's strange,' mused Astra, 'but when we came out of suspended animation, I suddenly realised that I knew that I knew . . . That I knew everything. Didn't you feel the same? As if you'd remembered something you'd forgotten?'

'All I wish I could remember are the details in the Paradise recording.'

'You never will,' said Astra. 'For the simple reason that there's no such recording.'

'But I'm telling you there is!'

Astra gave a sudden scream and pointed across the reservoir. 'Darv! Over there!'

Darv jumped to his feet and stared in the direction of Astra's outstretched finger. 'What's the matter?'

'I saw something moving!'

'Well there's nothing there now. Perhaps it was a service android?'

Astra's face was white and her hands were trembling. She shook her head. 'No, Darv – it was far too big, and none of the service androids are black.'

It took them thirty minutes to walk round the perimeter of the reservoir to the spot where Astra claimed to have seen the strange android.

She seized Darv's arm and pointed. 'There! Now do you believe me?'

A hole over ten feet high had been blasted through the bulkhead that separated the reservoir from one of the major ducts that conducted water vapour to the farming galleries. The melted edges of the hole were still warm to Darv's touch.

'Looks like it's finally happened,' he said ruefully. 'A service android's gone berserk. Either that or they've cut this hole to get some specialised machinery into the duct.'

Fagor's appearance when he entered the controlled zones caused Angel One and Angel Two considerable alarm. For one thing his armament matched up to Thorden's claims, and for another, the malignant machine seemed to sense that something was amiss with its master. But Fagor's presence did nothing to weaken the guardian angels in their resolve to destroy Thorden. They assumed that Fagor had a simple brain. From that false premise they also assumed that it would be easy to get Fagor to leave the *Challenger* on some pretext so that the meteoroid annihilation shields could deal with him.

'Not now,' said Telson, securing his PD weapon in its holster. 'The service androids are always carrying out structural work so I don't see what you're worried about.'

'Telson,' said Astra. 'This isn't structural work – it's an enormous hole.'

'Enormous,' emphasised Darv who was helping Sharna into a mobility suit.

Telson snapped his helmet into place and opened the visor.

'You're right to report it Darv. I'll look at it as soon as we get back.' He moved to the shuttle's steps. 'Ready Sharna?'

'Ready,' Sharna pulled on her gauntlets.

The four shook hands.

'Now don't worry about us,' said Sharna in reply to Astra's

anxious expression. 'I daresay Telson and I will do a better job of looking after ourselves than you and Darv did on Kyros.'

An hour later, when Darv and Astra had returned to the main control room, the space shuttle, with Sharna and Telson on board, separated from the *Challenger* and moved towards the derelict hulk. The narrow gap between the two ships meant that it was possible for Telson to move the shuttle by means of its directional thrusters rather than use the main engine.

Sharna switched on the shuttle's exterior lights when they were within five hundred yards of the drifting ship. 'No problem getting in by the look of it,' she commented, operating the controls that played the lights over the mass of holes and ruptures that covered the scarred outer skin.

Telson guided the shuttle towards the largest hole while continuing to send reports on their progress to Darv and Astra.

The ship loomed larger and larger in Telson's and Sharna's field of vision until they could no longer see the stars. The mighty fissure they were heading for yawned black and forbidding like the maw of a creature from the terror videos. Sharna aimed the hull searchlight into the black hole and illuminated a bulkhead that was set far enough in from the outer skin to provide room for the shuttle to manoeuvre once inside.

Telson positioned the shuttle in the exact centre of the hole with the aid of brief stabs from the thrusters. He gave Sharna an encouraging smile and opened up the thrusters that propelled the shuttle into the hull.

Radio contact with the shuttle was lost a few seconds after it entered the hull. It had been expected but that did not prevent Darv from swearing softly. He had hoped that the number of holes in the hulk would permit the passage of some radio signals.

He switched on two scanners and listened. There was nothing.

Unknown to him and Astra, the guardian angels decided that the moment had arrived to order the destruction of Thorden.

The fateful command was issued to the surgical android.

Five minutes later Thorden crossed the fine boundary line that separated suspended animation from death.

And five minutes after that Fagor went berserk.

The interior of the deserted ship was in much better condition than its exterior appearance suggested. Telson and Sharna were surprised to discover that most of the damage to the inner bulkheads had been repaired – albeit somewhat crudely in places. The only gravity was the natural but feeble force created by the ship's mass so that Telson had little trouble controlling the shuttle as it moved through the wide abandoned galleries.

Sharna's lights picked out a massive rust-encrusted bulkhead that blocked the gallery.

At that moment Sharna sensed that something was very wrong, 'Rust?' she said to Telson. 'How can there be rust if this place is in a permanent vacuum?'

'Could be some other form of corrosion,' Telson reasoned. 'Anyway we've seen enough and come far enough for our first inspection. 'We'd best be getting back.'

Telson operated the thrusters so that the shuttle pirouetted about its axis to face the way it had come.

'Oh please dear God – no,' said Sharna, her voice a horrified whisper when the shuttle had completed its turn. 'Tell me it's a dream.'

But there was nothing dreamlike about the steel bulkhead that was sliding closed in front of the shuttle so that Sharna and Telson were trapped.

Fagor blasted his way through several walls on his route to the *Challenger*'s main control room.

'Fagor! Listen to me!' said Angel One's voice.

Fagor stopped work on melting a passage through a bulkhead and glared around at the empty gallery. 'Who speaks to Fagor!' he roared. 'The killers of the Lord Thorden! Fagor will destroy them!'

'Fagor – listen.'

The giant android located the source of the sound and fired all of his lasers simultaneously.

'That merely destroys one voice terminal,' said Angel One. 'There are a million such terminals throughout the ship.'

'Then Fagor will destroy a million voice terminals!' And suiting actions to words, he annihilated four more. 'Fagor will avenge the death of the Grand Emperor by destroying his murderers!'

'We will help you, Fagor,' said Angel Two.

'Another voice,' growled Fagor. 'Fagor does not like voices. Fagor kills voices!' More voice terminals were wiped out.

Clearly Fagor wasn't fooling. The guardian angels formed the impression that he was going to be much more tricky to deal with than they had anticipated. Such single-mindedness in an android was outside their experience.

'Listen, Fagor!' said Angel One. 'Those who killed your master have left the ship and have entered the ship we are lying alongside. Go after them and we will guide you, but you will have to leave the *Challenger*!'

Fagor was unimpressed by the offer of help and said so. He resumed blasting his way through the bulkhead and announced that he intended to seize control of the *Challenger* and plunge it into a sun.

The guardian angels decided that they would have to rethink their relationship with Fagor.

Even before the door had finished closing, artificial gravity came on. Without Telson having a chance to compensate with the directional thrusters, the shuttle settled on its landing skids. Telson decided that he might as well conserve fuel so he shut the thrusters down, allowing the shuttle to remain where it was.

'You'd better switch the lights off, Sharna,' he said tiredly.

'God knows how long it's going to take us to think ourselves out of this mess.'

Sharna closed down the exterior lights and left one light on in the cabin. She was about to say something but cocked her head on one side.

'Hear anything?' she asked Telson.

Telson listened for a moment and then he heard the faint hissing sound. He and Sharna gaped at each other. 'Air!' Telson exclaimed. 'By God, Sharna – we're in a working air-lock!'

It was a guess but after ten minutes it began to look as if Telson had been correct: the shuttle's instruments were indicating that the ambient atmospheric pressure was ninety per cent, that the air was breathable, and the temperature tolerable.

'Okay,' said Sharna, making doubly certain that the instruments were giving correct readings. 'We might as well go out.'

'No,' Telson stated flatly, his innate caution prevailing.

Sharna sighed. 'Then tell me what good we're going to do sitting in here feeling sorry for ourselves?' She rapped playfully on the visor of Telson's helmet. 'We can keep our mobility suits on,' she said with her usual practical assurance. 'So we'll be okay if there is a serious leak. And in any case, we won't go far from the shuttle.'

Telson saw the sense in Sharna's reasoning and agreed.

A few minutes later the shuttle's outer door opened. Telson and Sharna emerged clutching arc lanterns and PD weapons. They set off in opposite directions to examine the bulkheads that formed their prison.

Sharna was the first to find something.

'Telson – over here.'

'What?'

Sharna pointed to a touch-control panel. 'Identical to the wall panels in the *Challenger* for operating the personnel air-lock doors,' she observed.

'Except that there's no door,' said Telson, training his arc lantern on the rust-streaked surface of the bulkhead.

Sharna rubbed her gauntlet on the corroded steel, releasing a fine shower of rust particles. 'There.' She pointed. 'A door.'

Telson looked closer and could make out a fine vertical line. Before he could raise an objection, Sharna had touched the control panel. The join that Sharna had exposed became the outline of a small door. It strained for a second to overcome the friction of neglected moving parts and then slid sideways.

The scene that greeted them was so unexpected, so unbelievable, that they both stepped through the doorway, refusing to credit the evidence presenting to them through the restricted field of their visors.

They were standing in a crowded marketplace which was thronged with men and women of all ages. They were swarming around gaily-painted but rickety stalls, shouting and bargaining at the tops of their voices.

The first thought that occurred simultaneously to Telson and Sharna was that they were viewing a huge hologram. But the reality and depth of the scene told them that this was not so.

'Monsters!' screamed a voice. 'Underpeople monsters!'

A hundred startled faces turned towards Telson and Sharna.

'Monsters!' the cry went up. Suddenly people were screaming and stalls were overturned.

'No!' cried Telson, taking several steps forward. 'We're not monsters! We're just like you!' He dropped his PD weapon and lantern and fumbled awkwardly in an attempt to open his visor.

Panic took hold of the crowd; more stalls were overturned and people were trampled underfoot as the great mass drove themselves into a blind, unthinking stampede. Those who fell, even the injured ones, jumped to their feet and, with fearful glances over their shoulders, threw themselves into the receding wake of the scattering, screaming mob. They disappeared down wide corridors that opened into the vast main gallery that formed the marketplace.

Telson and Sharna stood stock still, unable to think clearly or speak coherently. A vehicle with a howling siren and flashing lights on its roof came hurtling out of one of the corridors and charged across the marketplace. It moved on rubber-rimmed wheels that screeched loudly and released clouds of blue smoke as the vehicle skidded to a standstill within twenty yards of where Telson and Sharna were standing.

'The door!' Telson yelled. 'Let's get out of here!'

They spun round but the door had closed.

'Stay where you are and don't move!' barked a voice from the vehicle. 'One move from either of you and we open fire.'

It was the sort of voice that commanded instant attention and obedience. Telson and Sharna stood perfectly still.

'Drop your weapons!'

Sharna and Telson allowed their lanterns and PD weapon to clatter to the ground.

'Now turn around and walk slowly towards us with your hands above your heads.'

First Captain Praston Kroll, Deputy Chief Executive of Holocaust City, regarded Dren's captives and silently cursed all policemen – especially policemen who came between him and his hangover.

'Telson and Sharna, sir,' said Dren, dumping the two mobility suits he had removed from his prisoners in an untidy heap on Kroll's desk. 'The female is Sharna. They were wearing these, sir – obviously designed to cause panic.'

'Now look – ' began Telson.

'You will not speak unless you are spoken to!' Dren shouted. He noticed Kroll's pained expression and added: 'Sorry, sir.'

Kroll nodded. 'Thank you, Dren. A protracted party at the chief executive's house last night.'

Kroll managed a smile for the prisoners' benefit. 'My name is Kroll. I have the customary four other names which I won't bore you with but I would like to hear your full names please.'

'We don't have other names,' said Sharna. 'We're from the starship *Challenger* which is lying alongside – '

'You will confine yourself to answering questions!' Dren bellowed. He remembered Kroll's party and blurted out a hasty apology.

'Your citizens' number.'

'No numbers, sir,' said Dren. 'I've checked.'

Kroll's expression hardened. 'Now that is most interesting, Telson and Sharna.'

'Will you let me speak?' asked Telson.

Kroll shrugged and waved an expansive hand.

'We're from a starship,' said Telson. 'The sister ship to this one.'

'I'm very stupid, Telson. You must explain. What is a starship?'

Telson stared at Kroll in surprise. 'But you must know. You're living on one!'

'On one what?'

Telson felt Sharna's hand slide into his own. 'Well . . . A starship.'

'I see. And what does a starship do?'

'Well – it travels to the stars.'

Kroll nodded sagely. 'Ah, yes – of course. And where are these . . . stars? Perhaps you would like to tell me, Sharna?'

'The stars are in space,' said Sharna simply.

'All of them?'

'I don't think much of your sense of humour.'

'And I don't think much of underpeople terrorising the citizens of Holocaust City,' Kroll replied pointedly.

'What are underpeople?' asked Telson.

Kroll turned his attention to Telson. 'Or underpeople that insult my intelligence by telling me lies.'

There was a silence. Dren held up two PD weapons. 'These are their sidearms, sir. Similar to ours. We've tested them.'

Kroll nodded to Telson. 'Your technology is improving it seems. The time is fast approaching when another war with you will be required.'

'May I ask you a question?' Sharna inquired.

'By all means.'

'Do you know what space is?'

'But of course, my child. As deputy of Holocaust City, I'm entitled to more space than any other citizen, with the exception of the chief executive, of course.'

'So you don't know what is beyond Holocaust City?' Sharna persisted.

'The underpeople,' said Kroll distastefully. 'Filled with creatures such as yourselves.'

'Look,' said Telson. 'If you would let us take you to our space shuttle, we could show you our ship – and even your ship from the outside. We could show you space and the stars. We can show you the heavens – billions of stars and countless galaxies – the entire glory of the Creation!'

'It's no use,' said Sharna, breaking the silence that followed. 'They obviously don't want to know.'

'This concept of space you have,' said Kroll, leaning back in his chair. 'It is obviously very important to you?'

Telson looked scathingly at Kroll. 'Well of course space is important. It's where everything is.'

'Including the underworld?'

'Including the underworld; including Earth . . .'

Kroll looked surprised. 'Earth?' he said, allowing his chair to fall forward.

'Why, yes,' said Telson hopefully. 'Have you heard of Earth?'

'Yes . . . Yes – we've heard of Earth.' Kroll looked sharply at his captives. 'Is Earth important to you?'

'Yes,' said Telson. 'We're searching for it.'

Kroll raised his eyebrows but said nothing.

'We were born in space on the *Challenger*,' Telson continued, 'but the Earth is the home of our grandparents – our spiritual home if you like. And yours too because you are also descended from the people of Earth.'

Kroll thought for a moment and gave Telson and Sharna a broad, warm smile. 'If only you had said right at the beginning that you were searching for Earth – it would have saved so much misunderstanding all round.'

'Then we can go?' Sharna asked hopefully.

'But of course, my child. We'll send you on your way in the morning. But first you must dine with me as my guests of honour. Afterwards my servants will prepare a room for you. It's small but I'm sure you will find it most comfortable.' Kroll beamed at Telson and Sharna in turn and rose to his feet to shake hands with them.

* * *

Sharna lay awake, watching the early morning light edge across the ceiling of the tiny bedroom. She had not been able to sleep all night. There had been so much to think about – so many thoughts and questions that had followed close on the heels of the night's abandonment. Telson lay asleep beside her. As she looked at him, she realised with a start of surprise that it had taken her twenty-five years to discover that his brusque manner had been nothing more substantial than a flimsy camouflage for his shyness. Why had it taken so long? Why had they been children yesterday and adults today?

'Telson . . .'

'Mm?'

'It's getting light. I wonder how they do that?'

'Some form of diffused lighting radiated from inside the dome,' Telson replied, pulling a cover over his head. 'Probably controlled by computers that they don't even know exist. He sat up suddenly and stared at Sharna. 'I'm . . . I'm sorry,' he stammered. 'I'd forgotten about . . . about – '

Sharna laughed at his embarrassment. 'It doesn't matter, Telson. Really it doesn't.'

There was a loud banging on their door. 'Time to get up in there!' yelled a servant's voice. 'Big day today!'

'Earth,' said Sharna, falling back on the pillow. 'I can't really believe it, Telson.'

Telson wanted to slap her playfully as Darv would have slapped Astra. Instead he said: 'Come on – we'd better get dressed.'

Kroll marched into the room, all smiles and good cheer. 'Good morning, Sharna – Telson. How was the breakfast? If it fell even slightly short of perfect, I shall have my servants flogged.'

Sharna and Telson assured him that their breakfast had been beyond criticism.

'Splendid. Splendid,' said Kroll rubbing his hands. 'Are we ready?'

'Are we really on our way to Earth?' said Sharna.

'But of course, my child. Of course. There's no point in waiting any longer and there's a large crowd waiting to say goodbye to you.' Kroll chuckled. 'Your arrival yesterday created quite an impression you know. I think we'll walk. It's not far. Come.'

The silent crowd packed into the marketplace opened a path in front of Kroll as he strode towards the wooden platform. Telson and Sharna followed with Dren close behind. Kroll nodded and smiled to faces he knew in the crowd, but ignored outstretched hands that might slow his pace. He mounted the steps that led to the top of the railed platform and beckoned Telson and Sharna to follow.

Kroll shook hands with a masked man who was waiting on the platform and examined the two lengths of rope that the masked man held out for his inspection.

'Excellent. Excellent.' said Kroll, beaming around at the sea of expectant faces. 'Sharna. Telson. If you would stand over here please.'

'I think there's been some sort of mistake,' Telson said, moving to the indicated position. He pointed to the far bulkhead. 'Our space shuttle is on the other side of that wall.'

The masked man tossed the ropes over a heavy beam that was suspended above the platform.

'Now look,' said Sharna, exchanging a baffled look with Telson. 'How can you send us – '

'What religion are you?' Kroll inquired. 'Do you have religions in the underworld?'

Telson stared at him. 'Religion?'

Kroll smiled. 'The general prayers, I fancy, Dren. And the hoods as there are children present. I despair of some parents.'

Dren stepped forward to face Sharna and Telson. He found the place in the book he was hunting through and began to recite:

'Oh Mighty Power – Guardian of the Fusion Reactors of our beautiful Holocaust City – Giver of Light and Warmth – Sentinel of the Food Farms – we ask you to accept the spirits of these two creatures into your Kingdom of the Planet Earth where they will find life everlasting.'

'Excellent,' said Kroll, still beaming as he fastened the nooses around Telson's and Sharna's necks. 'I'll just make sure you're standing in exactly the right spots and you'll be on your way.'

PART 7

New Blood

It had been eight hours since Telson and Sharna had entered the hulk.

Darv decided that he could no longer bear the strain of doing nothing. He left his seat in the *Challenger*'s main control room, grabbed Astra by the wrist, and dragged her to the entrance.

'We're going after them,' he said in answer to Astra's protests.

'But we can't leave the ship while that android's on the loose, Darv. Not after what Angel One and Two warned us what it could do.'

'They created the problem by failing to maintain Thorden properly while he was in suspended animation – if you believe their story that they didn't have enough data on his metabolism. Let them worry about Fagor – we've got to do something about Telson and Sharna.'

'We don't have a shuttle,' Astra pointed out.

'There's Thorden's ferry.'

'Which we don't know how to operate.'

'Listen,' said Darv harshly. 'We didn't know how to operate the shuttle until we tried, so stop raising objections!'

The controls of Thorden's ferry were simple but different. Darv had little trouble steering it out of the *Challenger*'s excursion terminal and towards the drifting hulk. Guiding the ferry inside the narrow confines of the dark galleries was more difficult.

Astra's warning cry was too late and the impact with

the rusting bulkhead, despite the ferry's crawling pace, was enough to throw her against the blank control panel.

'Sorry,' said Darv, backing the ferry away from the obstruction. He peered ahead to where the gallery divided into two. 'Which one do we take? Left or right?'

Astra didn't answer. She was staring at the control panel before her that had unaccountably come to life as a mass of glowing touch-control areas and function identifications.

'Darv,' she said quietly. 'Take a look at this panel.'

Darv looked and his eyes widened. 'Plasma cannons . . .' he read aloud. 'Heat-seeking anti-personnel lasers . . . Infra-red followers . . . Wow!'

'Don't touch!' Astra warned, seeing Darv's finger moving to one of the touch-control zones.

There was a sudden blaze of intense white light outside the ferry's forward view ports. When the latent images stopped dancing on their retinas, Darv and Astra saw that an entire section of bulkhead ahead of them had disappeared.

'Wow!' said Darv again. 'If this was Thorden's idea of an unarmed ferry, I wonder what the armed ones are like?'

They moved on, threading their way slowly through the labyrinth of corridors and galleries, not worrying about the problem of finding their way back because the ferry's inertial navigation system was recording every twist and turn.

The figure picked out in the ferry's external lights waved to them. Darv set the ferry down hastily in the centre of the gallery and gaped through the view port. 'Now what do you suppose that is?' he said.

The strange figure was wearing a crude, ungainly mobility suit. It approached the ferry and pointed at the outer air-lock door. Darv tried to contact the figure by radio but without success; it continued to alternate its gestures between friendly waves and pointing at the air-lock door.

'It doesn't appear to be armed with a PD weapon or anything,' Astra observed. 'And it's obviously trying to tell us something . . .'

'Do we let it in?' Darv queried.

'Why not? We could keep our PDs trained on it.'

'Okay. I can always blame you if anything goes wrong.' With that, Darv touched the control to open the outer air-lock door.

The figure was lost to sight as it entered the air-lock, Darv closed the outer door and equalised the air-lock air pressure. He and Astra turned round in their seats and aimed their weapons at the inner door.

'Ready?' said Darv.

Astra nodded. Darv touched the control on the panel and the inner door hissed open. He could just make out the gleam of a pair of eyes inside the figure's helmet. The figure hesitated a second and them walked towards them.

'Hold it there,' Darv commanded, stretching our his arm and pointing his weapon at the creature's head in case it did not understand his language. The figure understood. It stopped.

'Take your helmet off.'

The figure's hands went up, released the helmet's catches and lifted it off its shoulders. Long black hair cascaded on to the figure's shoulders.

'Hallo,' said the girl brightly, giving Darv and Astra a friendly smile. 'Universe – am I glad to see you! *And* you speak our language! We were all desperately worried in case the first couple were the only people from your ship. I say, are those things awfully dangerous? It's just that I'm about to be licensed for child-bearing and it would be awful if anything happened to me. I'd never get another chance—'

'Hold on. Hold on,' said Darv, more than slightly confused by this unexpected turn of events. 'First things first. Who are you?'

'Oh Universe! You must think I'm rude. My name's Lenart.' She began divesting herself of the clumsy mobility suit. What emerged caused Astra to scowl and Darv to stare. 'You know,' Lenart said cheerfully, unconcerned that Darv was gaping at her exposed breasts, 'we heard that the first couple spoke our language but we refused to believe the reports. There's so few of us left that we have to send half-trained observers into Holocaust City.' She giggled. 'Oh sorry. I always talk too much when I'm nervous. I suppose you want to know about your friends? They were arrested yesterday in the marketplace.'

'I think I'm going insane,' Darv muttered to Astra. 'Lenart. What marketplace? Who arrested them?'

'Can this spacecraft function in an atmosphere?' Lenart asked excitedly.

'I don't see why not,' said Darv.

'Is it armed?'

'Yes it is,' Astra said hotly. 'And if you don't-'

'Just a minute,' Darv intervened. 'Lenart – are our friends in danger?'

Lenart nodded. 'But we can rescue them if we're quick. Let's get moving and I'll explain.'

'You'll explain now!' said Astra.

'No – please. There isn't enough time. We must get this spacecraft through the gallery air-locks as quickly as possible.'

Darv followed Lenart's complex directions through a series of corridors that were barely wide enough for the ferry to negotiate. After five minutes they emerged into an open space lined with rusting bulkheads that bore signs of hasty repairs in some places.

'We're back near the hull's outer skin.' Lenart explained. 'We're in the air-lock where your friends left their shuttle yesterday. We must wait for the air pressure to build up.'

'Where's this marketplace?' Darv demanded.

Lenart pointed at the ancient-looking bulkhead that lay ahead. 'On the other side of that.' She leaned forward and looked at the weapons panel in front of Astra. 'Universe!' she exclaimed. 'Laser cannons! Just what we need for blasting through.'

'Do you know how to use them?' Darv asked.

'I'm sure I do,' said Lenart enthusiastically.

'Astra – let Lenart sit there.'

Astra surrendered her seat to Lenart with a scowl but without argument.

'Pressure's up to one atmosphere,' Darv reported. 'Now what?'

Lenart gave a whoop and hit the laser cannon controls. The air-lock filled with blinding white light that was painful to look at. Lenart discovered how to swing the murderous beams of energy from side to side. 'Forward!' she yelled. 'Death to Holocaust City!'

Unable to see where he was going, Darv drove the ferry forwards fully expecting it to collide with the bulkhead. Instead they emerged into a huge open space that was as vast as the farming galleries on the *Challenger*. Below them were hundreds of people crowded around a raised platform.

'Lower!' screamed Lenart, her face flushed with excitement.

Darv pushed the ferry's nose down and Lenart immediately opened fire again with the laser cannons, sending raw energy blazing into the crowd. She added to the uproar with a continuous stream of bloodthirsty yells that chilled Darv's blood and made it difficult for him to concentrate.

The crowd scattered before the onslaught. When his retinas cleared after one particularly sustained blast Darv saw that the beams had cut a swath of death right through the crowd. The nightmare scene she had created had no effect on Lenart's aim for she continued to fire off random blasts at anything that moved.

'The scaffold!' she yelled. 'Get over to the scaffold!'

Darv presumed that she was referring to the raised platform in the centre of the emptying marketplace. There were some figures standing on the platform.

'Telson and Sharna!' Astra suddenly screamed in Darv's ear.

'There they are! Lenart – for God's sake stop firing!'

'It's all right!' whooped Lenart. 'I'm keeping my fire away from them! Death to Holocaust City!'

Darv swept low over the heads of the fleeing crowd as he swung the ferry towards the platform. He could see Sharna and Telson frantically waving. Two figures who were trying to restrain them jumped to the ground and ran when they saw the ferry alter course towards them. A beam fired by Lenart passed dangerously close to the platform and tore into the ground ahead of the two fleeing figures.

'Missed!' Lenart howled.

'Lenart! For God's sake stop firing!' Darv yelled. 'Astra! Drag her away and get back to the air-lock doors. I'm going to open both of them!'

Astra dragged Lenart's head back by her magnificent long hair and informed Lenart that she ran the risk of having her throat cut unless she stopped the insane massacre. Lenart took the hint and ceased firing.

She grinned at Darv, her breasts heaving and gleaming with

perspiration. 'Universe! That was much more fun than the sex competitions!'

Under normal circumstances Darv would have wanted to know more about the sex competitions but he was concentrating on bringing the ferry down to a low hover over the platform. He opened the air-lock doors and heard the distant screams of the receding crowd. Astra called out urgently to Sharna and Telson. A few seconds later the ferry dipped under their weight as they scrambled aboard.

Telson sank on to a seat when the hurried greetings were over. He shook his head disbelievingly. 'Those idiots were going to hang us.'

Darv grinned as he eased the ferry up to a safe height. 'Don't blame them if you started ordering them about. By the way, this is Lenart. We know as much about her as you do except that she's a bit bloodthirsty.'

'Hallo,' said Lenart cheerfully, shaking hands with Telson and Sharna. 'It's them or us with the Earth Worshippers, and for once it was them.'

'Earth Worshippers?' queried Astra.

'A long story,' said Sharna.

Lenart folded her arms around Darv, giving him an exultant hug. 'You'd best turn the ferry around, Darv,' she said. 'and I'll show you back to our regions of the ship. Tandor will want to meet you. She's our leader.'

'And who exactly are you?' inquired Darv.

Lenart laughed. 'I'm one of the underpeople.'

Two girls, dark and very pretty like Lenart, ushered Telson into Tandor's presence and withdrew.

Tandor rose from her couch and smiled warmly at Telson. 'Commander Telson. Please come and sit beside me.' She took Telson by the hand and sat him on the long couch, 'Lenart has told me all about you, of course. The Earth Worshippers do have the most curious ideas about hospitality.' She smiled again, revealing perfectly formed white teeth.

Telson watched Tandor carefully as she sat beside him. She was a tall, regal figure with dark skin and long hair that was startlingly black. He guessed her to be in her mid-forties. As she leaned back and regarded him, he saw that her flimsy white dress was transparent and that it was all she was wearing.

'Was the meal to your satisfaction, commander?'

'It was fine . . . Fine . . .'

'Please, Commander Telson. There are two things you must do. First you must call me Tandor. Promise?'

Telson nodded and gave a cautious smile. 'Promise.'

'And I have to decide what to do with you,' Tandor continued. 'Because you are an enemy of the Earth Worshippers, it does not follow that you are a friend of my underpeople. I hope my logic is clear.'

'We're no one's enemy. Show us the way out of this hulk and we'll be on our way.'

Tandor held up her hand. The sleeve of her dress fell to her elbow revealing flawless skin. 'Please tell your story, Commander Telson. Right from the beginning.'

Telson marshalled his thoughts and provided Tandor with a detailed account that started with the *Challenger*'s origin and ended with his and Sharna's recent rescue. Tandor listened attentively, nodding her head occasionally, not speaking until Telson had finished.

'So you have never seen Earth?' she inquired.

'No. We were born on the *Challenger*.'

One of the dark, pretty girls entered the room bearing a tray and two drinks which she set on a low table in front of the couch. She flashed Telson a brief smile and left the room.

'Try your drink, Commander Telson. You will find it most refreshing after all that talking.'

Telson sipped his drink appreciatively. The taste was strange but most pleasant. He drained the glass and placed it on the table.

'The *Challenger* is also the name of this ship,' said Tandor.

Telson nodded. 'We're descended from the same people, Tandor. This ship of yours – or what's left of it – is the sister of our ship.'

'That I guessed.'

'We thought it was a derelict hulk.'

'A hulk, but not derelict,' Tandor corrected. The fusion reactors are still working. They provide us with light, warmth, energy – and will continue to do so for many millions of years – just as yours will.'

'What happened to your ship?'

Tandor's smile faded. 'What little there is left of the ancient records tells us that our ancestors set out from Earth. The second-generation crew divided into two factions over the way the ship ought to be run. One side believed in equality and community effort, and the other side believed in individual endeavour and reward. The difference of opinion became an argument with the third-generation crew; a feud with fourth-generation; and a war with the fifth-generation . . . A very bitter and bloody war . . .'

'Which your people lost?'

Tandor shrugged. 'We have our independence and they have theirs. We believe that life on the ship represents the sum of our total existence and that we had better make the most of it. We have seen space and the stars and try to understand them. The Earth Worshippers believe that life on the ship is one step to an eternal life outside time and space on their marvellous, mythical Earth.'

'But surely they know that this ship is . . . is . . .' Telson was lost for words for a moment.

'Floating in space?' Tandor suggested.

'Well, yes.'

'We've taken prisoners to the observation dome and they've either gone insane or accused us of trying to warp their minds with optical illusions.'

Telson stared at her. 'How can anyone reject space?'

'Why not? Sealing one's mind against the truth is something that people excel at. Over the generations the Earth Worshippers have gradually sealed off their minds and their Holocaust City from reality. To them the ship is their universe, and their universe is the ship.'

'We told them that the Earth was a real place, and that we were searching for it,' said Telson.

'Which is why they were going to hang you . . . You blasphemed against their beliefs.'

Tandor swung her long legs on to the couch giving Telson a tantalising glimpse of more than slender thighs.

'Look, Tandor, your ship could join our ship in the search

for the planet Earth. We're on our way to the Tersus Nine star cluster where there are many main-sequence suns – all within a few light-years of each other. Also it's the nearest star cluster to the Earth's original solar system. We're certain that's where we'll find Earth.'

'No, commander.' said Tandor firmly.

'But you know that the Earth exists, Tandor. And if you visit our ship, we can show you the holograms and videos in our library. It's a planet – an entire planet. Lakes; hills; forests. Your people would become free! They would know what it was like to be outdoors under a blue sky – to feel a warm sun on their backs and a fresh breeze on their faces.'

Tandor's rippling laugher cut into Telson's enthusiasm like a knife.

'And you know about these things, commander?'

'Well, no,' said Telson. 'But we do have the holograms.'

'Dream machines,' said Tandor contemptuously. 'And you think that I should offer my people a beautiful future in which all my dreams come true? Well, I will tell you something, commander. They have had many generations of rulers who have promised them the Earth – that better times were just around the corner – and they became bitterly disillusioned. There was a revolution and my dynasty came to power and has held on to that power because we have always spoken the truth of the unchanging present. We conserve; we recycle; we maintain a fixed population level. We are not happy all the time but we are content for most of the time.'

'It sounds depressing.' Telson muttered.

Tandor shook her head.

'Not as depressing as dreams that can never be fulfilled,' she said. 'And so long as the Elixir of Life banks can be replenished every so often, then there are rare moments of joy in our community.'

'The Elixir of Life?'

Tandor rose from the couch and smiled down at Telson. 'You must return to your friends and rest before the special celebration I'm planning in honour of you and Darv.'

'But there are four of us,' Telson protested, rising to his feet. 'What about Sharna and Astra?'

Tandor nodded thoughtfully. 'They will be most welcome to attend of course. Most welcome.'

Her tone made Telson uneasy. 'Thank you, Tandor. Naturally, we're very grateful for being rescued, and for your kind hospitality, but we would like to be on our way.'

'But I must insist that you stay for the celebration.'

Telson stared at Tandor, perplexed. 'But I don't understand. What is there to celebrate?'

'That you and Darv are different. You both have different colour hair and eyes from everyone else on this ship – different from us and the Earth Worshippers.' Tandor chuckled at Telson's bewildered expression. 'You're new blood, Telson. New blood!'

'New blood?' Darv queried.

'That's what she said,' Telson answered.

'But she must've said what she meant,' said Sharna.

'No.'

'Well, I don't mind giving blood,' Astra commented. 'But they don't know what blood groups we are or anything – they haven't tested us.'

'Maybe she was speaking figuratively?' Darv suggested.

Telson looked sharply at Darv. 'What's that supposed to mean?'

Darv looked as if he was about to say something. He changed his mind and shrugged. 'I don't know. I'm sorry.'

'Then why say it?'

'I said I'm sorry.'

Telson paced the length of the large room that the four of them had been provided with. 'You should never have allowed them to take your PD weapons away from you,' he said irritably.

'You and Sharna lost yours,' Darv pointed out.

'We were captured by the Earth Worshippers!' Telson snapped.

'There's no point in arguing,' said Sharna, always the practical voice.

'What else is there to do?' Astra muttered. 'We don't know if we're with friends or enemies. We don't know where the shuttle is and we don't know where the ferry is. We don't even know what Fagor is up to on the *Challenger*. For all we know, he could be wrecking the ship.'

Telson swore. 'Our first task is to find the shuttle or the ferry. It doesn't matter which.'

'How?' Darv inquired.

Telson gestured irritably. 'We just walk out of here and look for them. The door's not locked.'

'You go ahead and try it,' said Darv grimly. 'You walk out of that door and you'll be joined by two or three pretty girls who'll look just like Lenart and who will beg you to return to this room.'

'We tried it while you were seeing Tandor,' said Sharna. 'Twice. All smiles and apologies. Worried about our safety in case the Earth Worshippers launched a retaliatory attack, they said.'

Telson's experience at the hands of the Earth Worshippers made him uneasy. 'What the hell do they want with us?' he muttered.

'We're the new blood, remember,' Sharna replied. 'So when does this so-called celebration or whatever start?'

'Two hours after the beginning of the night period,' Telson replied.

'You!' roared Fagor. 'You halt or Fagor destroys!'

The surgical android halted. Like all such units on the *Challenger*, it was programed to spend long hours carrying out delicate operations on the human members of the crew without mechanical or electronic failure therefore it had a built-in responsibility to maintain itself in first-class working order. That responsibility manifested itself as a self-preservation instinct which was why it skittered to an abrupt standstill when the appalling black android that it had been trying to avoid bellowed at it.

It watched with mounting apprehension as Fagor skimmed along the corridor towards it and noted in alarm that two of its fellow surgical units were obediently following Fagor at a discreet distance.

Fagor stopped near the surgical android and glared down at it. 'You will help Fagor control the ship.'

The surgical android agreed that it would help Fagor control the ship.

The guardian angels observed the unlikely quartet moving through the corridors to the main control room but remained silent, having learned that Fagor did not like the sound of their voices. They decided that they would have to evolve another method of dealing with the fearsome black android.

Darv nearly choked on the barbecued rib that Lenart was holding for him to chew. He sat up and laughingly pushed the girl's hands away. 'No, Lenart, please- I can feed myself.'

Lenart pulled his head back on to her lap. 'Don't you like me feeding you?' she pouted. 'Fresh meat specially for you.'

Darv grinned up at her. 'It's the most delicious thing I've ever tasted,' he admitted as she carefully wiped the rich sauce from around his mouth with a napkin. He turned his head and looked sheepishly at his companions who were seated on cushions around the huge banquet that had been spread out on the floor of the garden. 'What can I do with her?' he appealed.

Astra pointedly ignored him. She was sitting apart from the rest and had steadfastly refused all offers of food from the dark, smiling girls who periodically helped themselves to selections from the glistening mountains of fruit before rejoining their companions clustered laughing and chattering around the small, heated swimming pool. Some of the partygoers were dancing some were listening to the music, and some were waiting in an orderly if gossipy line at the barbecue where ribs were spitting and hissing over an induction grill.

'God, they're good,' said Sharna appreciatively, tearing meat off the bone with her teeth and licking her fingers. She and Telson had their backs propped against each other having discovered that it was the most comfortable way of eating.

'What's the matter with Astra?' asked Telson.

'Oh really, Telson. Can't you guess?'

Telson glanced across at Darv who was trying to push a ripe fruit into Lenart's mouth. Then Lenart was giggling and squirming as Darv used his tongue to catch the rivulets of juice that were trickling down her neck.

'You ought to speak to him, Telson,' said Sharna. 'It's not right that he should carry on like that in front of Astra.'

Telson didn't want to get involved, nor did he consider that Darv and Lenart were misbehaving. If Astra wanted to sulk at nothing, that was her affair. Instead he remarked: 'Have you noticed that there are no men here?'

Sharna gave a sudden laugh. 'You're impossible, Telson. I wondered when you'd notice.'

'I noticed right away,' said Telson defensively. 'I thought that maybe they had a custom in which the girls get the party going and the men join later.'

'We haven't seen one male among the underpeople.' Sharna pointed out, sinking her teeth into her rib.

'Another rib?' offered a girl, holding out a plate to Sharna and Telson. 'As our guests of honour, you're entitled to two each.'

'I didn't know the food was rationed,' said Telson, accepting the offer.

The girl's cheeks dimpled as she smiled. 'Only the ribs.'

'What are they?' Sharna asked.

'Ribs,' the girl replied simply.

'Real ribs? You mean we're not eating artificial meat?'

'Real ribs,' the girl affirmed. She looked at Telson and giggled at a private joke.

There was a disturbance at the far end of the garden when Tandor swept in. She was wearing a flowing dress that moved like smoke.

Sharna watched the leader of the underpeople as she moved among the girls, exchanging kisses and greetings. 'She is very beautiful, isn't she?'

Telson's reply was a non-committal grunt.

Tandor spotted her guests and moved towards them, arms outstretched and smiling. 'Hallo, everyone. I see they've been looking after you. I'm so glad. No. No. Please don't get up.

This is a very special occasion and I want you all to enjoy yourselves.'

She saw Astra sitting apart and went to her side. 'Astra. It is Astra, isn't it? Why aren't you eating?'

'I'm not hungry.'

'But, my child, we've gone to so much trouble. I even authorised the – '

'I said, I'm not hungry!' Astra cut in.

'Tandor!' said Lenart excitedly, pulling Darv to his feet. '*Please* can I leave the party for a few minutes with Darv?'

Tandor frowned. 'Now you know that's out of the quest – '

'*Please*, Tandor,' Lenart pleaded. 'Nothing can happen – I haven't been licensed yet. It was me that found them. And Darv wants to. It's his idea.'

'Well . . .' said Tandor doubtfully. 'It doesn't look as if Astra likes the idea . . . but then she'll soon have to get used to it.'

'I don't give a damn what they do!' Astra declared vehemently, her eyes spitting hatred at Lenart.

'Darv,' said Sharna casually, 'I think you should stay with us, don't you?'

'Oh let them have their fun,' said Tandor, smiling around at everyone in turn. 'On your way, Lenart, but no longer than thirty minutes.'

Lenart gave a whoop of triumph and hauled Darv across the garden to the entrance.

Astra bowed her head so that her long hair hid her tears.

Darv closed the gap and bought Lenart down in a flying tackle that ended on the floor of the corridor in a tangle of naked limbs.

'Universe!' Lenart laughingly protested as she tried to get up. 'I can't breathe!'

'So who's the fastest runner?' Darv panted as he grinned down at his captured quarry.

Lenart giggled. 'I didn't know that men were so fast.' Her eyes became serious. 'We'd better be getting back now.'

Darv shook his head. 'There's no hurry,' he said, no longer smiling. 'We've another ten minutes.'

'It'll take us that to walk back to the party.'

'But there's so much that I want to find out.'

'Well, let me get up then.'

Darv caught hold of Lenart's wrist and lifted her to her feet, shifting his grip to her forearm as he did so.

'Well,' Lenart began. 'I was born twenty years – '

'About why there aren't any men among the underpeople,' said Darv quietly.

Lenart stared at him and laughed. 'Universe – you do ask funny questions. Of course there are men. We've got a collection of at least fifty . . .' She smiled and touched his face with her free hand.

'None of them are like you though, Darv.' She felt his grip on her arm tighten and saw that the laughter had gone from his eyes,

'I'd like to meet them, Lenart.'

'We must get back . . . Please, Darv you're hurting my arm.'

'I said I'd like to meet them.'

'Well, you can't.'

Darv thrust Lenart's face against the wall and twisted her arm up into the small of her back. She gave a cry of pain and struggled to break loose. When that failed she screamed.

'No one will hear you,' said Darv evenly. 'You said yourself that everyone was at the party. Now.. My little tease, do you show me your collection of men or do I break your pretty little arm in several places?'

Lenart sobbed on pain and terror as Darv began pushing her arm higher into the small of her back.

'Yes! All right!' she cried out when she could bear the pain no more.

Darv stepped back and took hold of Lenart's wrist.

'Which way?'

Her finger trembled as she pointed along the corridor.

'How far?'

'About five minutes – if that.'

Darv pushed Lenart in front of him. They stumbled along the corridor. After a few minutes they came to a reinforced door that looked similar to the door to the suspended animation chamber on the *Challenger*. It slid open in response to Lenart's touch and closed behind them when they had entered.

Lenart looked embarrassed as Darv gaped in amazement at the neat rows of clear plastic pods. Under each cover lay a sleeping, naked man. Connected to each man were a tangle of nutrient and body waste tubes.

'Not unlike our suspended animation chamber on the *Challenger*,' said Darv at length.

'It's one of the few original systems of the ship still in working order,' said Lenart, not meeting Darv's eyes. 'The lead shielding was added after the first nuclear war with Holocaust City to keep out radiation.'

Darv said nothing. He counted the men. He noticed that only a quarter of the pods were occupied.

'There's fifty-one,' said Lenart.

Darv turned slowly to face her. 'But the whole point of suspended animation is that the entire population is made unconscious during interstellar travel – not just the men.'

Lenart shrugged. 'It is better that they are that way.'

'Why?'

'So that there is peace; so that they do not dominate us. Please, Darv – we must go now. If Tandor were to find out. No, Darv! You mustn't touch!' She snatched Darv's hand from the master control panel. 'You could damage them!'

Darv pushed her into the seat in front of the control panel. 'All right then – operate it.'

'No, Darv – I mustn't!'

Darv glanced at the numbers on the pods. 'Touch out the data on forty-one.'

'Darv . . .' said Lenart tearfully.

'Do as I say!'

As Lenart operated the controls and looked up at him for reassurance Darv began to appreciate why the men were as they were. But he suspected that there was another more fundamental but sinister reason. A hologram of a good-looking smiling young man appeared above the control panel.

'Hallo.' said the young man speaking in a pleasant voice. 'My name is Forty-One. I was born during the seventh generation and I was last activated during the hundred and tenth generation when I helped provide Karina of the Velos family with a daughter. Here is a steriograph of the baby.'

A three-dimensional image of a dark-haired baby appeared momentarily alongside the hologram.

'She grew into a beautiful woman' continued Forty-One. 'I am an accomplished player of many musical instruments and I have a fund of amusing and witty stories. Please touch out your genetic identity code and the bio-analysis system will display a steriograph of what our daughter will look like. I do hope that you will select me, and I am sure that we will spend a most enjoyable month together.'

The hologram wavered and vanished.

'That's the real reason,' Lenart said after a pause. Their elixir is pure which is why we look after them very carefully. Nearly all the babies born to the Earth Worshippers are mutations and have to be destroyed.'

Darv moved to the nearest pod and stared down at the unconscious occupant. 'Even in suspended animation one ages.' he said slowly. 'But very slowly.'

Lenart nodded. 'Their numbers are gradually decreasing . . . Several lost their fertility during the past few days and were destroyed a few hours ago.'

'What happens to their bodies?'

'I don't know.'

'And Telson and I are to be replacements . . .'

There was an awkward silence.

'Darv, would you believe me if I said that I didn't want this to happen to you?'

Darv considered. He turned Lenart's chin towards him. 'That depends on whether or not you are willing to tell me where our PD weapons are and where the shuttle and ferry are.'

Lenart looked away from him. 'We heard from the observers that the Earth Worshippers discovered the shuttle and destroyed it. They considered it a profanity.'

'And the ferry?'

'Safe. It's in an outer gallery air-lock next to the garden where the party's being held.'

Darv nodded. 'And what about our PD weapons?'

'Darv! Lenart!' said Tandor warmly when they reappeared in the garden. 'I was about to send out a search party to bring you back.'

Darv grinned at Tandor. 'Don't be too hard on her, Tandor. It was my fault.'

Tandor looked Darv up and down. For an unpleasant moment Darv thought that she had spotted the bulge under his one-piece suit near the armpit. She smiled. 'I can't say I blame Lenart so I'll overlook it on this occasion, Darv.' She turned to the crowd and clapped her hands for silence. 'The girls of the Wenlo family have organised a special entertainment,' she announced. 'A delightful dance routine which they've been rehearsing all afternoon. So I want everyone to sit down and be quiet.'

There was a sudden hush in the garden. The lights dimmed except those trained on the wide parapet around the edge of the swimming pool. Darv sat down beside Telson and tried to ignore the infuriated glares that Astra was blasting in his direction. Lenart moved discreetly to a position near the entrance to the garden and sat down.

Three girls stepped on to the parapet and began a strange dance that was barely in time with the music.

'Enjoy yourselves?' Telson inquired sarcastically.

'She gave me something,' Darv replied, keeping his voice low.

'I'm sure she did.'

Darv made certain no one was looking his way and opened the seam on his one-piece suit. Without making any overt movement, he carefully slid the PD weapon into Telson's hand. He gave it an astonished glance and quickly concealed it. 'Have you got one?'

Darv nodded. 'Lenart's sitting near the entrance. She'll lead us to the ferry and operate the gallery air-lock. You'd better explain to Astra and Sharna.'

Telson shifted his position and talked in low tones to Sharna and Astra. Darv noticed that Astra shook her head several times and that Telson appeared to be remonstrating with her.

'All set,' Telson whispered when he had returned to Darv's side. 'But you're going to have to do some explaining to Astra when we're out of this mess.'

'The only reason I left the party with Lenart – '

'Save it for Astra,' Telson cut in. 'Ready?'

Telson and Darv rose to their feet holding their PD weapons. It was the signal for Astra and Sharna to move quickly to the wall. Some girls near the barbecue screamed. Telson loosed off two bolts that blasted a crater in the floor in front of the dancers. One over-balanced and fell into the pool. Suddenly there was pandemonium as girls fought and screamed to get clear of the blasters.

'No one is to move!' Darv yelled.

The partygoers froze with the exception of a girl who made a dive for the entrance. She was pulled up by a shouted warning from Tandor who saw Darv swing his PD weapon towards her as he and Telson backed up to the wall.

'Next time I won't hesitate,' Darv threatened.

Tandor's laughter broke the silence that followed. 'And where do you four think you're going?' she inquired.

Telson gestured to the others to leave. Lenart had already slipped out of the garden when the shooting started.

'I'm sorry we can't stay for the end of the party, Tandor,' said Telson evenly, moving sideways towards the entrance.

Tandor laughed again. 'I won't stop you leaving for a while, commander. The party goes on for another four hours therefore you won't have missed much by the time you return.'

'Don't try to follow us,' Telson warned.

'I promise you that we won't.'

Telson disappeared. A number of girls started after him but Tandor called them back.

'They'll be back,' was Tandor's confident prediction. She waved an imperious hand. 'Continue with the party.'

In the corridor, Telson found Sharna waiting for him. Together they raced to the end of the long passageway where Lenart was frantically beckoning him.

'First turning on the right,' she said breathlessly.

Telson grabbed her hand and pulled her along with him. 'You're coming with us.' he growled in answer to her protests. 'They'll tear you apart for helping us if you stay.'

'No!' Lenart pleaded. 'I've got to work the gallery air-lock for you.'

They rounded a corner and saw Thorden's ferry in the middle of the gallery resting on its landing skids. Darv and Astra had opened the outer door and had disappeared into the cabin. Sharna took the folding boarding steps in one leap and Telson followed pushing Lenart in front of him. She tripped on the steps as Telson thrust her into the cramped cabin.

'Please,' she implored. 'I have to operate the air-lock,'

'Darv!' Telson yelled. 'Can this thing blast its way out?'

'No trouble.' Darv answered.

'If she's coming then I'm staying,' Astra declared.

'Oh for God's sake, Astra, stop behaving like a child!' Sharna snapped with an uncharacteristic display of temper. 'Telson explained to you why Darv left the party.'

'I've not heard it from Darv!' Astra shot back. She saw Lenart put her arms around Darv and kiss him. She was about to lunge at the girl but Sharna restrained her.

'Goodbye, Darv.' said Lenart. She moved to the ferry's air-lock, gave a cheerful wave and wished them all good luck before going down the steps. She ran across the gallery without looking back and the door closed behind her.

Darv dropped into the ferry pilot's seat and closed the air-lock doors. He said nothing to Astra as she took her seat beside him. He activated the control panel and watched the displays that indicated the falling external gravity and atmospheric pressure. At one tenth gravity the reaction from the directional thrusters was sufficient to lift the ferry off the floor.

The main gallery door in front of the ferry began sliding open before the atmospheric pressure had reached zero. The resulting surge of air helped sweep the ferry through the slowly widening gap. Telson and Sharna were virtually thrown into their seats as Darv slewed the ferry round in a tight turn to avoid a bulkhead that suddenly loomed up in the lights.

'Which way!' he yelled, slamming on full braking thrust as the lights bathed another wall of solid steel.

'They upset the inertial setting when they moved the ferry!' Astra yelled back.

From the slight curvature of the main structural bulkheads, it was possible to determine which direction led to the outer hull. Darv wasted no more time charging along blind galleries; he swung the ferry's nose round until it was pointing at an outer wall and opened fire with all the laser cannons. All four were momentarily blinded as the energy beams sliced into steel and vaporised it. Darv charged the ferry through the resulting hole and stabbed the laser cannon controls to demolish the next bulkhead. It was thicker than the previous one and required a continuous blaze of energy before it began to collapse. The forward thrust generated by the plasma-spitting cannons tended to push the ferry backwards. Darv found that he had to open up to full directional power in order to keep the ferry's nose close to the bulkhead so that the energy pouring from the cannons was concentrated on one spot. Suddenly the steel wall collapsed under the terrible onslaught. Darv stopped firing and the ferry shot forward. He started firing again to deal with the next bulkhead and ceased when he realised that the ferry was in free space.

Telson was about to congratulate Darv but the words of praise never came. 'Swing her round!' he barked at Darv.

Not believing the evidence of his eyes and deaf to cries of dismay from Sharna and Astra, Darv pulled the ferry around in a turn that circumnavigated the battle-scarred starship.

'Oh no,' breathed Telson, too shocked to think of anything more original to say.

The drifting hulk was alone in space. The *Challenger* had vanished.

PART 8

Marooned

Astra finished her calculations and shut down the ferry's computer to conserve power.

'Well,' Telson prompted.

Astra glanced at Darv who was concentrating on a painstaking radar search for the *Challenger* while Sharna hunted with the ferry's optical telescope. 'I'd like Darv or Sharna to check them first.'

Telson grunted in annoyance. 'Stop being so wet, Astra. We can check them afterwards.'

'Leave her alone,' Darv muttered, not looking up from the radar display.

'Well,' said Astra. 'Assuming that Fagor seized control of the *Challenger*, and assuming he did it within thirty minutes of Darv and I leaving the ship, *and* assuming maximum acceleration . . . Then the *Challenger* must be within one million miles.'

'It's a lot of assumptions,' Telson complained.

'That's why I want the figures checked.'

'But *how* did he seize control?'

'I've got an echo!' cried Darv. All three crowded around the pilot's seat and stared at the display. Darv switched in the discriminators so that only one point of light was showing on the screen. 'Bearing two- seven-six decimal eight-five. Range three-nine-two-zero-zero miles!'

'Which means that her recessional velocity will be constant,' Telson mused.

'Okay,' said Darv. 'So let's get after her!'

Telson put a restraining hand on Darv's arm. 'Wait. We need a lot more data.'

'Oh come on, Telson,' said Darv impatiently. 'If we sit around here scratching for data, that four hundred thousand mile gap's going to become half a million miles.'

'The problem isn't so much distance as time.' Telson snapped. 'How long it will take us to catch up with the *Challenger*, and how long our air supply will last! Before we do anything, we put the computer to work on some calculations.'

'Telson's right, Darv,' said Sharna reasonably. 'We'd better totalize all our fuel and liquid oxygen and compressed-air reserves.'

It took thirty minutes for the answers to emerge: the ferry had enough fuel for a two hundred second engine burn at maximum thrust. This would provide the necessary velocity for the ferry to reach the *Challenger* in about 210 hours. The ferry's total air supply including the supplies in the mobility suits, was enough to last four adults 173 hours.

'There's your answer.' said Telson bitterly, 'By the time we catch up with the *Challenger* we will all have been dead thirty-seven hours.'

'So we do nothing?' inquired Darv, his voice tinged with sarcasm.

'Argue with me as much as you like' said Telson. 'But it's no good you arguing with those figures.'

'So what do you suggest?' Darv demanded. 'That we all take a bioterm and lie down on the floor?'

Telson pointed through a view port to the hulk of the starship that was lying some ten miles from the ferry. 'We go back into that thing and join one of its societies.'

Darv gave a hollow laugh. 'You can, Telson.'

'We don't have any choice!'

'Well, it just so happens that the people who live in that wreck do have a choice if they get their hands on us,' Darv said. 'Whether we live or whether we die. We're not too popular with them at the moment, so I have the feeling that if we showed our noses in there, they'd opt for the latter.'

Astra stared forlornly at the distant pinpricks of the stars. 'I suppose I always knew that we had no hope of ever finding Earth. But there was that tiny ray of hope that maybe . . .' She broke off, unable to summon up the words that best expressed her feelings.

'I'm sorry, Astra, said Telson. 'For what little comfort it is, at least we can say we tried.'

Darv stood over Telson, his face pale with anger. 'You call this trying? Sitting here doing nothing except feeling sorry for ourselves?'

'Who is going to help me put a meal together?' said Sharna suddenly. 'I don't know about you three but I'm starving.'

'I'll help,' Darv volunteered.

The meal consisted of reconstituted fruit. It was hardly palatable but everyone had their minds on other problems.

'What about taking over the hulk by force?' Astra suggested as the four of them ate at the folding table. 'Maybe we could repair its main drive and continue the search?'

Telson shook his head. 'Taking over by force is a possibility . . . But . . .'

The others waited for him to continue.

'Yes, Telson?' inquired Astra.

There was a curious glazed looked in Telson's eyes when he replied. '. . . Never repair the main drive. Only got to look at it . . .'

'At least we're okay for food and power,' said Sharna. 'We won't freeze or starve to death.' She yawned.

'We ought to think about . . . About it . . .' mumbled Telson.

'About what?' asked Astra. 'Telson – are you all right?'

'Wouldn't want to really . . . Go back,' said Sharna, slurring her words. Her fork fell from her fingers. Darv caught her body as it fell sideways.

Astra gave a cry of concern and jumped up to help Darv. At that moment Telson slumped forward.

'Help me get them on to the bunks,' Darv commanded.

'What's happening?' cried Astra in bewilderment.

'Grab her feet – that's it.'

They lowered Sharna's unconscious body onto the nearest bunk. Astra knelt down to attend to her while Darv turned his attention to Telson.

'Darv – she's asleep!'

'So would you be if you'd swallowed two grains of morphon.'

'But – '

'Just give me a hand and stop arguing!'

Astra helped Darv shift Telson's heavier body onto the opposite bunk. 'Why?' she asked when they made certain that the unconscious forms were breathing regularly.

'Because,' said Darv, kneeling to study the fasteners that fixed the seats to the floor, 'sleeping bodies don't use so much oxygen and they don't argue. Hand me that toolbox.'

'What are you going to do?'

'What *we* are going to do,' Darv corrected, 'is strip this ferry of everything – every item of mass that isn't essential. And after that, we're going after the *Challenger*.'

An hour later Darv overrode the safety interlocks and opened the ferry's outer door without first de-pressurising the airlock. The sudden rush of air into the vacuum of space swept out everything that had been stacked in the airlock: cooking equipment, cushions tools and even the toilet door – all formed a strange cloud of surrealist debris moving away from the ferry.

Darv noted with satisfaction that the reaction from the ejected mass had provided the ferry with a speed of thirty miles per hour in the direction of the *Challenger*; a laughable amount but every little bit counted.

'Ready?' he asked.

Astra sat beside him and loaded the inertial navigation system. 'Your arrogance alarms me,' she remarked. 'Thinking that you know better than a computer.'

Darv turned on the fuel feeds to the main rocket engine and set the ignition controls.

'You can't argue with the figures,' Astra persisted well aware that Darv was ignoring her.

'Orientation?'

'Set.' said Astra. '*Challenger*'s range now five-zero-one treble zero. Over half a million miles. We'll have been dead thirty-nine hours by the time we reach the *Challenger*.'

Darv grinned. 'It would have been thirty-seven hours if Telson had got on with it.' He opened the power controls so that the engine would burn at maximum thrust as soon as it was ignited. 'What we can't know,' he continued, 'is the error factor in the displays. We might get a ten per cent error in our favour giving us a two hundred and twenty second burn instead of two hundred seconds.'

'And we might get ten per cent less,' Astra retorted.

'Stand by. Maximum thrust three seconds from now.'

Darv tried to discern the faint point of reflected starlight that would be the *Challenger*. There was nothing. Only the radar display told him it was there. The three seconds ended. He fired the main engine.

The thrust pushed them back into their seats. Under normal circumstances Darv would have enjoyed operating the powerful little fighter but all he was concerned about at that moment was how long the rocket motor would burn for.

A hundred seconds passed. The fuel reading display winked with depressing monotony as the digital values fell.

One hundred and fifty seconds. The rate of acceleration increased in proportion to the decrease in the ferry's mass as it burned its fuel.

Two hundred seconds after ignition and the rocket was still firing.

Darv gave Astra a look of triumph. A low fuel warning gong sounded and then the fuel reading display was showing a row of bleak zeroes.

The engine ceased its burn 211 seconds after ignition.

'Eleven seconds over the top!' Darv yelled ecstatically. 'Didn't I tell you, Astra! Didn't I tell you?'

Astra made no reply as she worked on the revised figures. She looked up at Darv and announced that they would all have been dead for nine hours by the time the ferry reached the *Challenger*.

Darv gave a whoop of joy.

'I fail to see what the is to be so pleased about,' said Astra primly.

'But it's an improvement!'

'Your logic is crazy!' Astra declared. 'Nine hours – nine hundred hours – what does it matter? We'll still be dead!'

Darv calmed down. Astra moved aft to make certain that Telson and Sharna were comfortable.

'Maybe I'll think of something,' said Darv morosely.

'You'll think us into messes – never out of them.'

Darv was about to argue the point but Astra cut him short.

'We've got to conserve oxygen, remember,' she pointed out.

'We'd better lie down on some cushions.'

'We ejected all the cushions,' said Astra tartly.

'So we'll lie on the floor then!'

The guardian angels detected the ferry's departure from the vicinity of the hulk. It gave them hope. It meant that at least one member of the crew had left the drifting starship and was attempting to get back to them.

They decided against trying to contact the ferry by radio because Fagor, who was occupying the control room, would be certain to hear the transmissions. The major problem was to persuade the formidable android to leave the ship so that the meteoroid annihilation shields could be used against it. The problem was that Fagor appeared to have no intention of leaving the main control room. It was clear that he had every intention of carrying out his threat to crash the *Challenger* into the sun in revenge for the killing of Thorden.

'Okay, okay,' said Telson impatiently. 'No more recriminations. You thought that you were acting in the best interests of us all.'

'Some more water please, Astra,' said Sharna weakly. 'My tongue's stuck to the roof of my mouth.'

Astra supported Sharna as she sipped from a plastic cup that had escaped Darv's jettisoning policy.

Telson focused his eyes on the figures that Astra had given him. It would take another hour for the effects of the drug to clear. 'I can't read these,' he said irritably. 'So what's our air supply shortfall now?'

'Nine hours.'

Telson realised that he was having difficulty in breathing. His first reaction was that it was caused by the drug but he noticed that Astra was also having trouble.

'I've reduced the oxygen content of the atmosphere by five per cent,' said Darv in answer to Telson's query. 'And the carbon dioxide level's up two points.'

'Aren't the purifiers coping?'

Darv shook his head.

'Why not? You can replace the absorption pads.'

'It needs a special tool which I jettisoned.'

'Spare me the details,' Telson groaned.

'How much thrust do we need to reach the *Challenger* in time?' asked Sharna, examining the control panel displays.

'Anything that'll give us a thirty per cent increase in velocity,' said Darv. 'Why?'

'What about the directional thrusters if we set them to aft thrust? Wouldn't they give us a bit of a push?'

'It's worth a try,' said Darv, moving to the pilot's seat. It was something he wished he had thought of rather than wait for Sharna's streak of practicality to assert itself. He set the thrusters to deliver aft thrust for sixty seconds. This would leave adequate fuel for course corrections and manoeuvering if they ever managed to reach the *Challenger* – which even to Darv, always the optimistic, was beginning to look most unlikely.

The slight increase in velocity enabled Astra to calculate that their air supply shortfall had decreased by thirty minutes to eight and a half hours.

'Something, I suppose,' muttered Telson. 'What are you up to, Sharna?'

Sharna was using one of the display screens to call up schematic diagrams of the ferry's subsystems. 'Just looking,' she replied non-committally.

'What for?'

'I don't know yet,' Sharna replied touching the control keys. 'Ah. This looks interesting. Emergency drill for a fire in the main engine.'

'I shouldn't worry about it,' said Darv. 'We haven't got any fuel left to light a fire.'

Sharna looked up at the controls that were above the pilot's head. She pointed to a small red cover that was marked DANGER.

'See that?' she said.

'What about it?'

'Opening the cover and pulling the handle detonates thirty explosive bolts that jettison the main engine back along our flight path.'

'What!' shouted Darv, almost pushing Sharna over in his eagerness to read the screen. 'My God – she's right! Listen to this: "In the event of a serious malfunction during a burn, program one-zero-two will be automatically activated unless cancelled by the pilot"! And the program reads: "Ejection of main engine *and* fuel reservoirs"!'

Telson and Astra crowded around the screen. Sharna called up a simulation which showed the engines and fuel tank at the rear of the ferry being blasted backwards. The simulation ended and up came the simple sentence:

THE SUBSEQUENT VELOCITY INCREASE AS A RESULT OF THE JETTISON CAN BE CANCELLED BY THE PILOT BY MEANS OF THE DIRECTIONAL THRUSTERS.

'Increase in velocity,' said Darv weakly. 'I think everyone should sit down on the floor . . . It might be quite a jolt.'

As soon as everyone was in a safe position, Darv opened the red cover above his head and pulled the handle.

It was as if a giant with an unimaginable sledgehammer had struck the ferry a mighty blow from behind. Darv's head jerked back and hit the restraint cushion. The boom from thirty simultaneously exploding bolts was deafening.

'Wow,' said Darv weakly. 'Now we know why they put the handle in a little box. I wouldn't like to work that sort of control by accident.'

They all waited patiently while Astra worked on a revised set of figures. The computer tones bleeping occasionally when she touched the calculating functions.

'There's still a shortfall,' she announced when she had finished. 'Five hours.'

The news was a blow. They had hoped that the shortfall would be eliminated.

'Is there any chance that we could hang on for the extra five hours?' Telson asked. 'Even the faintest chance?'

'None,' said Astra. 'We've got another fifty hours to go and already I've got a splitting headache. It may be that that five hours is on the optimistic side. It could be nearer seven.'

'Fagor,' said Angel One.

The android whirled around and glared in turn at each voice terminal in the *Challenger*'s galactic resources centre. It had already learned the uselessness of destroying the voice terminals, nevertheless it lifted one of its arms and wiped out three of them because it made him feel better.

'We have decided to help you avenge the murder of the Lord Thorden,' said Angel One.

'Fagor will avenge him by plunging this ship into a sun!' grated Fagor.

'But it won't avenge him, Fagor. Already they are coming after you. They are returning to the ship to destroy you.'

'Fagor doesn't listen to lies!'

'Go to the telescope and you will see that we are telling the truth, Fagor. The picture of their ship is displayed on the repeater screen. Look at it, Fagor – look upon those who slew your master!'

His brain racked with suspicious impulses, Fagor crossed to the telescope and glared at the screen. The ferry was in the exact centre of the picture.

'That's them, Fagor,' continued Angel One's persuasive voice. 'They are coming to destroy you just as they destroyed your master.'

'That is the Lord Thorden's space ferry – Fagor recognises it.'

'They stole it Fagor. They stole it so that they could use it against you. Go out to them, Fagor. They will not be expecting you to do that. They think that you will remain in the ship because they believe that you are frightened of them!'

'Fagor is frightened of no one!' the android roared, glaring round the centre as if expecting to find someone who might contradict him.

'Then go out to them, Fagor. Take them by surprise! It is your only hope of avenging the Lord Thorden's death!'

The black android spun round and shot through the entrance to the centre. The guardian angels followed his progress through the ship, trying to determine whether or not their ploy had been successful. Fagor reached a corridor that joined the outer hull and began blasting away at the skin. Minor sophistications in spacecraft design such as air-locks were of little interest to him when he wished to move in a straight line. The result was that the guardian angels had to alert several squads of service androids to seal the corridor from the rest of the ship once the hull had been breached.

A minute later Fagor plunged through the hole into space helped by the tremendous out-rush of air. The meteoroid annihilation shields fired – spewing energy from their turrets impotently into Fagor's wake. The trouble with the shields was that they were designed to destroy incoming targets. Fagor was travelling the wrong way which caused hopeless confusion in the guidance system computers.

Alarmed by the failure of yet another ploy, the guardian angels plotted the course of Fagor's dwindling black shape and calculated that he would reach the ferry when it was within ten thousand miles of the *Challenger*.

Somehow they would have to warn it. At least with Fagor no longer aboard they could break their radio silence.

Astra had been the first one to succumb to the effects of the oxygen-depleted, carbon-dioxide-charged atmosphere in the ferry. She had lost consciousness and only been revived when Darv and Telson struggled to get her into a mobility suit and had turned on the air supply. The exertion left both men weak and dizzy, their lungs labouring painfully for clean, fresh air that wasn't there.

'Close her helmet,' said Telson.

Sharna shook her head. 'Not if she's going to vomit again . . . She's sleeping now . . . We'll take turns to watch her . . .'

Telson sank to the floor opposite Darv and looked up at Sharna.

'You'd best . . . best take a rest . . . No point . . .' He didn't have the energy to finish the sentence. After a minute his racing heart eased up. 'No point in trying to contact the *Challenger* by radio?'

Darv shook his head. 'Not with Fagor in control . . . Might alert him to where we are . . .' Darv subsided into silence. The only sound the two men made was the rasp of their laboured breathing.

Astra made a soft moaning sound in her throat and turned her head from side to side. Sharna had slipped to the floor close by. She lifted herself slowly on to an elbow and looked at Astra in concern.

'Nightmare,' said Darv. 'Lucky . . . Can't be any worse then the real one.'

Sharna nodded and lay back. She allowed her eyes to close and tried to ignore the pounding headache and the sheer physical effort of drawing breath.

Astra was drifting in the unreal world that lay halfway between sleep and consciousness. Dreamlike, mist-shrouded images crowded in on her, jostling for attention. She felt the cold touch of a nursery android and saw its solitary staring eye as it turned her in her crib. She relived the screaming fights with the other three children over disputed toys, and she heard the warm, friendly voice of Angel Two, her guardian angel coming to her defence when she was in the right. And later she listened as Angel Two answered her endless questions with infinite patience and understanding.

'Air . . .' she moaned fitfully. 'Why isn't there enough air, Angel Two?'

'The food farms produce all the oxygen we need, Astra.'

'But there isn't enough . . . Is there air on Earth, Angel Two?'

'Enough for millions of people.'

'Millions of people . . .' Images of people crowded on a lakeside beach swam into her mind. 'Millions of people,' she said in wonder. 'Tell me about Earth, Angel Two. Is it really like the hologram and the videos? Fields and lakes and mountains? Mountains so high that reach up and touch the clouds? Will there still be soft white clouds on Earth? They won't have used them up?'

'There will be soft white clouds, Astra. I promise.'

'*Astra!* Can you hear me! I can hear you!'

'And beaches by the lakes?'

'And beaches by the lakes, Astra.'

'*Astra!* This is Angel Two. Can you hear me?'

'I can hear you, Angel Two. It must be a truly wonderful place. And there will be babies, won't there? And there'll be one for me because you said that there would be one day.'

'*Fagor is coming, Astra!* You must warn the others!'

'Fagor?'

'*He's coming!* Tell the others, Astra! You must warn the others! Are they with you?'

'Fagor!' Astra screamed. 'Fagor!'

'Easy . . . Easy, Astra,' said Sharna gently, reaching into the open helmet with a moist cloth to wipe Astra's lips.

Astra's eyes snapped open. She stared up at Sharna and suddenly gripped her arm with a strength that Sharna was too weak to resist.

'Sharna! Fagor's coming!'

'You were having a dream,' said Sharna soothingly, turning on the suit's breathing system to flush poisoned air from Astra's helmet.

'No, Sharna! It wasn't a dream! I heard Angel Two telling me!'

'Sharna!' said a thin, reedy voice from inside the helmet. 'Sharna! Can you hear me? This is Angel Two!'

Astonished, Sharna bent her head nearer the open helmet. Angel Two spoke again. She broke Astra's grip on her arm and turned to Darv and Telson who were staring at her with lustreless eyes. 'Astra's helmet radio has been switched on!' she cried. 'Angel Two is trying to contact us!'

Telson and Darv continued gazing at Sharna. It was some moments before the import of what she had said sank in. They stumbled to their feet. Telson switched on the ferry's main radio.

'Angel Two? Come in Angel Two. This is Telson calling the *Challenger*.'

There was a delay of a few seconds due to the distance between the two craft. Then Angel Two's voice boomed out over the speaker.

'Hallo, Telson! This is Angel Two. Listen carefully. Thorden's android is coming for you and will destroy you. Set your radar co-ordinates to eight-nine-zero-four.'

Darv dragged himself to the radar display and set the co-ordinates. He picked up the tiny point of light that was Fagor's echo. According to the navigation computer, the ferry and the echo would meet in just under an hour.

'Can you take evasive action?' Angel Two asked when the information had been supplied to him.

Telson briefly outlined their hopeless predicament: although they had the weapons to deal with Fagor, they had no fuel, and just enough air for three hours whereas it would take another five hours after that to reach the *Challenger*.

In reply, Angel Two said that there was no way of braking the *Challenger* because, without Fagor, there were only three androids in the main control room.

'Pretty hopeless situation all round,' said Telson, hardly able to hear his own voice because of the pounding blood in his ears.

'So what will you do?' asked Angel Two.

Telson struggled to collect his thoughts. 'S'easy, Angel Two . . . If Fagor doesn't blow us apart . . . We . . . We'll leave the air-lock doors open . . . Make it easy for you to send in service androids to collect our bodies when we reach the *Challenger*.'

Forty minutes of listless silence passed in the ferry. No one spoke or wanted to speak – the effort was too painful and there didn't seem any point.

Darv watched the hardening point of light on the radar screen that was Fagor. He lifted his aching eyes to one of the forward view ports and saw, for the first time with the naked eye, the faint, illusive smudge of light that could only be the *Challenger*. The thought that they would reach their goal only in death angered him. And it angered him even more to think that a machine was seeking to deny them their last two hours of life.

He pulled himself to his feet and stood, swaying, trying to focus his brain. He kicked at Telson, reached down and helped drag him to his feet.

'Telson,' he panted, pointing to the radar display '. . . We fight . . .'

Telson regarded Darv unsteadily. He nodded. 'We fight . . . How?'

'Mobility suits.'

'Want them for the end.'

'That's what this is now unless we fight.'

Telson shook his head. 'Last twenty minutes' air in suits . . . Need it for the end.'

Darv dragged three mobility suits from their doorless locker. 'Sharna . . . Sharna!'

Sharna woke up.

Darv dropped the suit on top of her. 'On,' he commanded. 'And close the helmet and turn on air.'

Sharna thought the final minutes had arrived and began pushing her legs into the mobility suit.

'*Challenger* to ferry,' said the speaker abruptly. 'This is Angel Two. Fagor will be within six miles of you in ten minutes.'

Telson was undecided whether or not to take the mobility suit from Darv. Angel Two's voice seemed to make up his mind for him. 'We fight,' he decided with grim simplicity, and took the suit.

Darv knelt beside Astra. He closed the visor on her helmet and turned on her air supply. The effect of the cool, fresh draughts flooding into her tortured and starving lungs was instantaneous. She opened her eyes and smiled up at him.

'Is it the end?'

Darv kissed the inside of her palm before pulling her mobility suit gauntlets on to her hands and closing the pressure seals. 'Not yet, my lovely,' he said softly. 'Not just yet.'

It took Darv less than a minute to climb into a suit and turn on its air supply. The speed at which his head cleared was miraculous. The effect on Sharna and Telson had been the same. They were both alert and watching the radar screen intently. But it would be for only twenty minutes.

'He's five minutes away,' said Telson as Darv sat in the pilot's seat. 'I've got the radar to give us continuous ranging.'

'Angel Two,' said Darv crisply. 'Do you know the range of Fagor's lasers?'

'No precise information is available,' Angel Two replied. 'They're wide beam, so they're possibly short range unless he can narrow the beam.'

Darv acknowledged. 'We'd better play safe and try hitting him at a range of two miles,' he said to Telson.

'Can you do it?'

'I've no idea.'

'He's four minutes away,' said Sharna, watching the radar screen. 'God – he's coming in fast.'

Darv concentrated on zeroing the laser cannons so that their beams would converge to a single point of focus exactly two miles ahead of the ferry. He took great care with the directional thrusters, using delicate touches on the controls to align the ferry until the laser sights were orientated precisely on Fagor's radar image.

'One minute,' said Sharna.

'I can see him through the viewport,' said Telson quietly. He followed with a sharp intake of breath. 'Thorden brought that thing aboard? I was an idiot to have trusted him.'

'The angels didn't,' said Darv, not raising his eyes from the displays. He noticed that the point of light on the radar screen was no longer circular but an irregular shape. The digits on the radar ranging display became a blur as the distance between the ferry and Fagor decreased. When they reached zero, Fagor would be in the focal point where the laser cannons were concentrated. At the speed the android was moving, Darv knew that he would have to anticipate the zero reading by milliseconds to allow for Fagor's incredible approach velocity before opening fire on the android.

'Thirty seconds,' said Sharna.

Sweat trickled into Darv's eyes as he stared fixedly at the display.

'Twenty seconds.' Darv's gauntlet went automatically to his eyes to wipe them and encountered the closed visor of his mobility suit helmet.

A serpent of fear knotted and twisted in his bowels as the radar ranging display became a sweat-distorted blur.

'Five seconds.'

Darv tried rolling his eyes upwards to clear them and saw

Fagor's squat, malignant body hurtling straight at him. In that fleeting glimpse, it was the android's optical sensors, like two glowing eyes, that became permanently printed on his mind.

Light flashed from the end of Fagor's manipulators. The android had opened fire. Darv fired back.

'Missed!' Telson yelled. 'By God – you missed!' Telson threw himself at Sharna and dragged her to the floor just as Fagor's blast struck the side of the ferry. Darv fired again but the impact had pitched the tiny craft sideways – sending his firing wide of a target he could no longer see.

The next few seconds were a confused whirl of sound and uproar. The ferry's hull had been holed by Fagor's lasers; everything loose in the cabin was suddenly sucked up through a gaping hole in the roof where the ferry's poisonous atmosphere was geysering into space. The hurricane-like surge of air would have ripped Darv's body through the hole had he not jammed his knees under the control panel and clung to his seat with his hands. Something had happened to the ferry when he fired all the cannons but the chaos around him prevented him from thinking clearly.

Another crash shook the ferry. Darv stared unable to credit his senses as a huge steel arm, complete with powerful fingers smashed through the side of the ferry and into the cabin. Someone screamed over his helmet radio. Another steel arm slammed through the hull with terrifying force. The massive fingers closed around the edges of the torn metal – buckling the hull's frames and crushing reinforcing struts. The two steel arms suddenly flexed. An entire section of the ferry's hull was ripped away and Darv came face to face with the monstrous creation that was Fagor.

The hellish android rammed the upper half of his body through the hole he had made and reached for Darv who was too paralysed with shock to make a move to save himself.

The cabin suddenly filled with light. One of the arms lunged forward. The fingers which Darv knew were going to rip through his mobility suit and tear out his throat struck him on the chest throwing him backwards, There was another blast of intense white light . . . Fagor vanished, leaving the remains of a severed manipulator lying on the floor of the cabin near Darv's feet.

Astra lowered the PD weapon she had fired twice. For a moment she thought that she was going to vomit into her helmet but the wave of nausea passed. She stared at the other three in turn and then began laughing hysterically. It was not hard to see why; they had lost all their cabin atmosphere, such as it was. The only air they had left was the fifteen minutes' supply left in the reserves of their mobility suits. Her destruction of Fagor had in no way affected the inevitable fate that was about to overtake them.

Darv stared through the view port at the moving point of light that was the *Challenger* some ten thousand miles away. In that moment he remembered what had happened just before Fagor had smashed his way into the ferry. His hands went to the control panel. He thumbed the fire button and the laser cannons blazed energy at the stars.

'He's gone,' Telson muttered. 'So what the hell do you think you're doing?'

'Thrust,' said Darv weakly, forcing himself to speak. 'The forward thrust from the cannons decelerated the ferry when I fired them.' And then he was shouting. 'If the cannons can slow us down, they can also speed us up!'

Without waiting for Telson's reaction, Darv spun the ferry through one hundred and eighty degrees until it was pointing back along their flight path. He fired a long burst. The drastically lightened ferry, without the damping mass of its main engine, lurched in response to the thrust from the lasers and began accelerating. Darv fired continuously and the ferry accelerated continuously.

'Thrust!' Darv yelled, almost jumping up and down in his seat in jubilation. 'Lots and lots of lovely thrust!'

'Angel Two,' said Sharna. 'Can you hear me?'

'Go ahead, Sharna.'

'We're coming home.'

*   *   *

One by one, Telson, Sharna, Astra and Darv sank into the timeless death sleep of suspended animation. The surgical androids completed their detailed examination of the four near-lifeless bodies and lowered them into the tanks where they would remain for six years. The guardian angels were well pleased; not only were the crew safe and unharmed, but the start on the building of a new crew, who would be subservient to their ambitions, had been made. The surgical android had reported its findings to the angels.

Astra was pregnant.

PART 9

Star Cluster – Tersus Nine

The original plan of the guardian angels had been to wake the crew when the *Challenger* was at least two light-years into the spiral arm on the fringe of the galaxy's 100,000 light-year diameter wheel. That way, there would have been no danger of the *Challenger* being anywhere near the C-5 planetary system in Star Cluster – Tersus Nine after deceleration was complete.

They reckoned without Astra's baby. The six years in suspended animation had advanced the foetus to the age of two months. It was a routine examination of Astra's unconscious body by a surgical android that revealed the baby to be in distress.

It was a problem the guardian angels had experienced with the babies born to the first and second-generation crews and one that they thought they had solved with the frequent turning and massaging of the mother's body while she slept. It did not work in Astra's case: her child was one of those that needed something more than a warm, dark nutrient-providing organic incubator; it needed to develop inside a normal healthy living breathing moving woman who was leading a normal life.

To avoid arousing the suspicions of the crew, the guardian angels had no choice but to bring all four of them out of suspended animation and hope that they were not sufficiently intrigued by the C-5 planetary system to insist on a close look at it . . .

* * *

The storm raging in the atmosphere was nearly as old as the planet itself and provided one of the most fascinating spectacles that the crew had ever seen.

All four were gathered around the hologram replicator in the *Challenger*'s galactic resources centre, watching in rapt silence as the astonishing three-dimensional pictures from the instrument probe were displayed before them.

'The fifth planet in this solar system,' intoned Angel One. 'Its density is less than that of water and its atmosphere consists of hydrogen, helium, methane and ammonia. The exact percentages are on screen six.'

'And the fourth planet?' asked Telson.

'Very little information. The soft-landing instrument package was badly affected by the intense radiation from this solar system's sun. What data we did collect before the lander failed, indicated that it is a virtually airless planet very similar to Kyros in our home system.'

'What about the third planet, Angel One?' Darv inquired, guessing what the answer would be. He was not satisfied with the reasons why the guardian angels had been firmly opposed the to the *Challenger* going into orbit around the sun of this system. Telson had supported the angels but agreed on a compromise to avoid a confrontation with Darv. He agreed to the *Challenger* going into a circular orbit around the sun of this system but at the huge distance of one thousand million miles – a distance that was within the orbits of cold outer planets but well clear of the more interesting inner planets.

'As Angel Two and myself have already explained to Commander Telson,' said Angel One. 'It would be a waste of our resources to investigate the inner planets of C-5, Darv. This solar system is swamped with radiation from its sun. We have no more long-range probes, and it would be a waste to send in another soft-landing instrument package.'

Darv turned to Sharna. 'So what are the exact radiation levels?'

'I can't obtain readings from the monitors just yet, Darv.'

'Why not?'

Sharna was about to explain but Angel One intervened. 'The malfunction is regretted, Darv,' she said. 'Unfortunately the *Challenger* passed through a severe meteoroid shower a week before we brought you out of suspended animation. There was considerable damage to many of our external sensors which the service androids are still working on.'

Astra frowned. 'What happened to the meteoroid shields? Couldn't they have coped?'

'They were switched off at the time for routine maintenance,' was Angel One's bland reply.

Darv chuckled. 'Now that's what I call unfortunate; the same thing happened when the second-generation crew – including our parents – were wiped out in the Great Meteoroid Strike. Amazing that it should happen twice.'

'The shields must be serviced regularly, Darv,' said Angel One.

'Okay – so let's take the *Challenger* into a closer orbit around the sun and use the portable radiation monitors. There's plenty in stores.'

Telson shook his head. 'It would be too dangerous.'

Darv looked exasperated. 'We've only got the word of the angels that it is dangerous.'

'Commander Telson has been happy to accept our guidance on this matter,' said Angel One – a hint of acidity in her voice.

Darv turned away from the replicator in disgust and dropped on to the telescope's couch. 'Do you know why I would like to look at the third planet, Angel One?'

'It most certainly is not this so-called Paradise planet that has become such an unhealthy obsession with you,' Angel One answered.

'All right. All right,' Sharna cut in anxious to prevent another rift between Darv and the guardian angels. 'What I'd like to know is why did you bring us out of suspended animation if this system isn't worth looking at? Why not let us sleep on for another three years or whatever until we reached the next solar system?'

Angel Two chimed in with his warm, reasoning voice. 'We thought that you would like to see the first planetary system in the Tersus Nine star cluster.'

'But we're *not* seeing it, are we, Angel Two?' Darv pointed out. 'And how can we see it if you insist that we orbit its sun at a range of a thousand million miles?'

Angel Two had another excuse ready. 'Of course, Darv, you will appreciate that occasional activation of the suspended animation chamber is necessary to enable the service androids to check the life-support systems thoroughly.'

Darv grinned broadly at that one. 'Not true, Angel Two. I once read on the library that the systems were designed to be maintained and tested while they were in use.' Think your way round that, he thought, pleased with himself for having got the guardian angels rattled and on the defensive.

'The library data relates to the time when the *Challenger* was in pristine condition, Darv,' Angel Two chided. 'It has now spent over a hundred years being occupied by human beings whose attitudes to it have ranged from the indifferent to the arrogant.'

'All right,' Telson interrupted, feeling that the sterile argument had gone on long enough. 'We'll spend a few days studying the outer planets before deciding which system to move onto next.'

'Listen,' said Astra fiercely to Darv when she had stopped laughing. 'You do that once more and I'll do it to you, then I'll get an android to throw you out of my room!'

Darv stretched out on the bed beside Astra. 'Try it,' he invited, grinning. 'It has no effect on me.'

'Course it does.'

'I tell you it doesn't!'

'But it must do! Your fingers drive me mad when you do it to me.'

'Try for yourself.'

Astra tentatively tickled Darv under the ribs. He continued to grin amiably up at her. 'It's odd,' she admitted when she realised nothing she did had any effect.

Darv suddenly grabbed her and tickled her in the same place. Astra immediately went into a paroxysm of protesting laughter. She doubled up as she tried to fight off Darv's fingers.

'See what I mean?' he said when he stopped. 'Now why is that, I wonder?'

'Does it matter,' said Astra, flushed and breathless after her ordeal.

'Maybe not. But it does show how little we know about our own bodies.'

'I know all that I need to know about my own body.'

'Then you'll know that you're getting fat.'

'I am not!' Astra retorted indignantly. 'I think I will call that android.'

Darv cupped his hand against Astra's stomach and shook her playfully. 'You ought to look at yourself now and again . . . You see? You're getting fat. There must've been an error in your nutrient diet while you were in suspended animation.'

Astra touched her stomach and a look of wonder rather than alarm spread across her face. 'It's starting to show already? I didn't know . . .'

'Just as well we were woken up,' Darv commented, not noticing Astra's expression. 'A few more weeks and the androids would've needed reinforcements to lift you out of your tank and we would've had to roll you everywhere.'

Astra responded by cuffing Darv fairly hard. He retaliated by tickling her again. She rolled up into a tight, protective ball while laughing and trying to bite Darv's hands at the same time. Darv was about to give her spine the same treatment but she suddenly gave a loud gasp of pain and pressed both hands against her abdomen.

'Hey – Astra,' said Darv anxiously. 'What's the matter?'

Astra rolled on to her side and drew her knees up to her chin. Her face was twisted into an ugly grimace and she seemed to be holding her breath.

Darv placed an uncertain hand on her shoulder, completely at a loss as to what to do. 'Astra – do you want me to call a surgical android?'

Astra shook her head emphatically. After a few seconds the tension drained from her face and her body relaxed. 'Wow,' she muttered, rolling on to her back and stretching cautiously. 'I hope it wont be like that too often.'

'Like what?'

Astra smiled at his worried expression. 'Well . . . A sort of stabbing pain.'

Darv made a move to the entrance. 'I'd better fetch a surgical unit.'

'No, Darv. Please don't.'

'But – '

'I'm all right now. There's no need to fuss.'

'Well . . . Is there anything I can do?'

Astra nodded. 'If you don't mind leaving me now, please, Darv. I'm feeling tired.'

Darv gave her a kiss and left. He returned to his room and sat on the bed, nursing a vivid memory of Astra's pain-twisted face.

It was rare for Sharna's traditional phlegmatic attitude to be sufficiently disturbed for her to utter even a moderate curse but she did so when she discovered that the telescope was not working. Telson tried switching in a standby repeater system for her but the screen remained blank.

'Angel Two. Why isn't the telescope working?'

'The objective lens guard was damaged by a meteoroid,' Angel Two replied. 'Two service androids are making a replacement. In the meantime a temporary cover has been fitted over the lens to protect its surface from the cosmic dust.'

Telson frowned at Sharna, first making certain that his back was turned on the nearest of the guardian angels' sensors. 'Unfortunate, Angel Two,' he commented.

'It happened during the meteoroid shower that damaged so much of our external instrumentation, but the telescope should be back in service in four hundred hours.'

'Four hundred hours!' Sharna echoed in amazement.

'The androids are making excellent progress with the new guard, but it takes time,' Angel Two explained.

'Let's go and see for ourselves,' said Sharna practically. 'Maybe we can help? There's little else to do.'

'They're working in an unpressurized gallery.'

'All right then – we pressurise it,' said Sharna, determined not to be thwarted. She gave Telson a baffled glance.

Angel Two sounded apologetic when he said: 'One of the galleries that was badly holed during the Great Meteoroid Strike.'

Telson was beginning to feel uneasy. 'We could wear mobility suits,' he suggested.

'I'm sorry, Commander Telson, but it would not be safe for you. The gallery is a mass of torn and jagged metal that could damage a mobility suit. Also, the androids are using dynamic laser handtools.'

'It would seem, Angel Two,' said Sharna choosing her words with care, 'that we're having an unusual run of bad luck recently. A planetary system that's swamped with radiation even though its sun looks normal to the naked eye, and a number of instruments knocked out by meteoroids when the shields were switched off. One can't help wondering what is going to happen next.'

The surgical android moved silently into Astra's room while she was asleep and crossed to her bedside. The low level of illumination in the room was sufficient for it to work by without switching on the light. It extended a delicate manipulator and carefully drew back Astra's cover. It noted with satisfaction that she was naked and that one arm was flung across the bed in a convenient position although something would have to be done about the fact that she was lying on her stomach.

The android tested the needle to ensure that it was clear of air and pushed it into a vein in Astra's arm. It injected just enough of the drug to ensure that she would be co-operative but continue to remain unconscious.

'Astra,' said Angel Two gently. 'Turn on to your back please, Astra.'

Astra stirred. Angel Two repeated the request. Astra obediently turned on to her back without waking up.

The android's supple manipulator pads smeared ointment

on to Astra's abdomen and worked it into her skin until it glistened. It rubbed some of the ointment on to a small disc and spent two minutes passing the disc back and forth across Astra's stomach taking great care to ensure that every square inch of skin was covered.

Once the sonic scan was complete, the android reported its findings to the guardian angels. It was certain that Astra was expecting twins and that they were now out of danger. There was a high probability that one baby would be a girl and the other a boy. It concluded with the opinion that there was no reason why Astra could not be returned to a state of suspended animation.

The guardian angels were well pleased: twins meant that their plans for a fourth-generation crew were off to a good start. If a method could be evolved in which babies were developed and delivered while their mothers were in suspended animation, it would be possible to keep the third-generation crew in ignorance of the fourth-generation crew that they had given birth to. There were so many options available to the guardian angels and all of them were favourable. They felt that they had a right to be pleased after such a long catalogue of setbacks.

The surgical android pulled the cover back into place over Astra and noticed that her eyes were wide open.

'Baby?' she said questioningly. 'What about my baby? What's happening to me?'

'Sleep, Astra,' Angel Two soothed. 'Sleep . . . In the morning you will remember nothing . . . Nothing . . .'

Astra's eyes closed. Her head moved from side to side on the pillow. 'My baby,' she said fitfully. 'What do you want with my baby?'

'You will remember nothing,' Angel Two's voice repeated hypnotically. 'Remember nothing . . . Nothing . . .'

Astra stopped moving her head. 'Remember nothing,' she mumbled.

'Nothing,' Angel Two repeated.

Astra slept.

The guardian angels were well pleased.

* * *

When Astra took her customary shower the following morning she noticed that the water droplets clung to her stomach in an unusual manner. Puzzled, she ran a finger across her abdomen. There was a strange, greasy texture to her skin – it felt alien to the touch – as if something had been rubbed into it.

Vague recollections of an inexplicable dream came back to her: a surgical android at her side . . . The voice of Angel Two . . .

Perhaps it hadn't been a dream?

'It's crazy,' said Sharna to the others as they ate their breakfast in the restaurant, 'but the truth is that the *Challenger*'s blind. The telescope's not working; the spectrum analysers aren't working, and we've no more probes.'

Darv put down his cup and leaned his elbows on the table. 'Why don't we take the *Challenger* into a sling-shot orbit about that sun for a fast look at the inner planets? The *Challenger* must have been designed to cope with brief exposure to radiation' He looked hopefully at Telson, fully expecting a bombastic dismissal of his suggestion. Instead Telson merely shook his head. It seemed to Darv that Telson's attitudes were changing – especially his attitude to the guardian angels. Much of his lifelong respect had gone.

'It's difficult,' said Telson. 'The angels have got about a hundred androids working outside the ship on urgent repairs.'

'How urgent, I wonder?' Astra mused. She added: 'I had a dream about a surgical android last night. It came into my room . . . It had a long needle in one of its manipulators.' She gave a flippant gesture when she realised that no one was particularly interested in her odd dreams.

The four were finishing their meal when Angel Two made an announcement: 'The service androids have reported that they will now require two thousand hours to repair the telescope. In view of that we see no point in delaying our departure from this planetary system. We suggest that the *Challenger* is set on course for planetary system C-6 in Tersus Nine and that you then go into suspended animation.'

The news about the telescope caused Sharna considerable disquiet, and Astra was not happy about the prospect of going into suspended animation so soon.

'C-6 is the nearest solar system to this one, Angel Two?' asked Telson.

'That is correct, commander. Its distance is four point five light-years. The journey will take eight years.'

'Oh no!' said Astra suddenly. 'With an ageing rate of a day for every month while we're in suspended animation, that'll be several months off our lives.'

'I'm sorry Astra,' Angel Two answered, 'but it's no good blaming us for the size of the Universe.'

'We will have spent half our lives in suspended animation at the rate we're going,' Darv grumbled. 'And I would like to find a way of checking the inner planets of this system.'

'It would be a waste of time and resources, Darv,' Angel Two admonished.

Darv looked questioningly at Telson, willing him to ignore the guardian angels. Instead Telson merely nodded his head and said:

'We'll have to accept that Angel One and Angel Two are right . . . Angel Two – when do you suggest we commence acceleration?'

'In twelve hours, Commander Telson.'

Darv spread the tools on the floor of Astra's cabin and selected a large screwdriver.

'Where did you get them?' asked Astra.

'Stores.' Darv chuckled. 'Had an argument with a particularly dense android storekeeper. In the end I helped myself while he complained to the guardian angels.'

He inserted the screwdriver under the edge of the plastic wall panel and prised upward. Astra pushed a smaller screwdriver into the gap Darv had made while he worked the large screwdriver around the edge of the panel until it could be lifted away from the wall.

They studied the complex mass of fibre optic tracks that the panel had canceled and identified the guardian angels' control circuits to Astra's room by the simple expedient of reading the labels on the various connectors. It took Darv less than a minute to disable the appropriate optical tracks with a pair of wire-cutters. He sat back on his haunches to admire his handiwork and grinned at Astra.

'No more bad dreams, my lovely.'

'Are you sure that it'll work?'

'Angel One!' Darv called out. 'Angel Two!'

There was no reply. Not even after Darv had called several times.

'I also had an odd dream last night,' he commented as Astra helped him collect the tools together. 'I think I'll do the same in my room.'

A service android clutching a large toolbox appeared in the doorway. It trundled in without waiting for an invitation. 'An environmental control fault in this room has been reported,' it announced. I have come to make repairs.'

'Go away,' said Darv.

The android saw the exposed section of wall. 'It is forbidden for the crew to interfere – '

'Go away!'

The android stood his ground. It had a job to do and it intended to do it. 'It is necessary for me – '

'You see this?' Darv held a heavy hammer in front of the android's optical sensor. 'If you don't go away, I shall smash you into small pieces and drop them down a recycling chute.'

The android considered the problem: namely that it would have great difficulty in carrying out its allotted task if it consisted of small pieces dropped down a recycling chute. It decided to go away and rethink the issue or request further instructions.

'I'll leave you the wire-cutters,' said Darv when the android had gone. 'Whenever you see that the tracks have been repaired, you can cut them out again. So what was it you wanted to tell me?'

'I'm not going into suspended animation again ever,' Astra declared with a vehemence that surprised Darv.

'I see. You want to grow into an old woman while we remain young and beautiful?'

'I'm serious, Darv.'

'I don't doubt it. But why?'

'If I go into suspended animation again, I know that something terrible will happen to me.'

'Like what?'

Astra shook her head. 'I don't know what and I don't know how, but I do know that something will happen.' She hesitated. 'No – that's wrong . . . Perhaps I do know.'

'Do you want to tell me?'

Astra was silent for a moment. 'At first I thought of telling Sharna . . . She's understanding. I'm sure that she wouldn't laugh at me . . . And then I realised that the one person I really wanted to tell was you.' She took hold of Darv's hand. 'Maybe I'm mistaken, Darv, but I'm absolutely certain that I'm going to have a baby. Your baby . . . I mean – our baby.'

Darv gaped at Astra in disbelief. 'What!'

Astra nodded. 'It's true, Darv. That time in the orchard.'

'How do you know?'

'Because I do.'

Darv could think of nothing to say.

And then Astra poured out her suspicions and fears that arose from her dream. As she talked, they were unaware of what was going on in the adjoining disused room where, in accordance with instructions from the guardian angels, the android that Darv had thrown out of Astra's room was increasing the gain of the audio sensors.

It was not a particularly successful move from the guardian angels' point of view: even with the gain at maximum, they could distinguish was the difference between Darv's voice and Astra's voice, but not what they were saying.

After a few minutes, Darv and Astra fell silent. And then the guardian angels heard Darv moving to Astra's doorway where he was just in range of a corridor sensor.

Darv paused in the doorway, gave Astra an encouraging smile, and said: 'Do you remember what Thorden once told me about the guardian angels? He said that if I could find their central switching room, that I could either control them or destroy them . . . When I do find it, I shall destroy them.'

The guardian angels heard Darv's final statement. As far as they were concerned it amounted to a declaration of war.

'Anything?' Sharna asked when Telson entered Astra's room.

Telson sat down on the bed and stared moodily at the exposed wall panel. 'Nothing,' he said shortly. 'Just a note on his screen saying that they would be all right and not to go looking for them. Anything in here?'

Sharna gestured to the open closet. 'She's taken her favourite outfit, and her PD weapon with a clip of capsules.'

'Damn them.' muttered Telson. 'Damn the pair of them.'

Sharna sat beside him. 'It's just something they're going through. They can't survive for long by themselves.'

Telson looked bitterly at her. 'Can't they? Darv knows this ship better than any of us. He knows his way around the farm galleries and he knows whole regions in the uncontrolled zones from his exploring trips when he was a kid. And he probably knows more forbidden zones than he's ever had the guts to tell us about.'

'You're being too harsh on him.'

'It won't be my harshness that he'll have to worry about when he gets back,' was Telson's grim response.

'So what happens now?'

'Well that's obvious, isn't it? We have to delay the acceleration until they're found. There are fifty service androids out hunting for them.'

'Fifty!' Sharna looked shocked.

'It was the guardian angels' idea,' said Telson defensively. 'Anyway they've got to be found.'

'Even so – fifty androids . . .' Sharna stood. 'Perhaps we could help look for them?'

'No,' said Telson firmly. 'Angel Two said that it would be best if we kept well out of the way – in the main control room or somewhere. Most of the androids they've pressed into the hunt don't have the ability to recognise individual humans.'

'Is "hunt" your choice of words or the angels?' Sharna inquired. 'I would have thought "search" was more appropriate.'

Telson looked uncomfortable, 'It was the word Angel Two used,' he admitted.

The tranquillizer dart smacked into the bulkhead above Astra's head.

'Darv!' she yelled. 'Two of them!'

They threw themselves down behind a torn bulkhead and fired simultaneously at two androids that appeared at the far end of the gloomy gallery. The useful working lives of the two machines ended in a crash of plasma bolts that hurled them backwards in a tangle of partly severed manipulators.

'That's six we've knocked out,' laughed Astra, who was beginning to enjoy the hunt now that her initial fear had gone.

Darv fired at another android armed with a dart gun that was foolish enough to venture into the corridor without a preliminary check.

'Seven,' Darv amended. 'Come on.'

They moved silently through the dark regions of the uncontrolled zone for another thirty minutes without trouble. It was when they were skirting the galleries that housed the air-conditioning and rainmaking plant of a farm that they came up against organised opposition: thirty androids under the skilled command of a hull inspector unit who had radio facilities to co-ordinate all the androids in his team.

Astra and Darv discovered that they were trapped: no matter which way they went from the T junction where they were cornered, so they encountered a determined hail of tranquillizer darts by androids that kept under cover.

Darv swore softly when he discovered that the androids down one turning had taken up closer positions.

'Now what do we do?' Astra demanded.

'We don't surrender – that's for sure.' Darv looked up at a massive air duct that traversed the junction. It was at least six feet in diameter. He guessed that its purpose was to purge carbon-dioxide gas from the farm. 'If we could find a way of getting into that, Astra . . .' He pointed to the huge pipe.

Astra studied the duct for a moment. 'It's an idea,' she

said. 'We could cut a hole into it with our PDs if it's thin enough.'

'No – that way they'd know where we've gone.'

'Not if we cut the hole from the top.'

Darv grinned. 'Good thinking, my lovely.'

There was a renewed burst of firing which sounded dangerously close. Darv used a coolant pipe as a foothold and climbed on to the top of the duct, pulling Astra up behind him. They ran along the top of the giant duct, pausing to make certain that they were not being followed. In the poor light, Darv tripped on an obstruction and nearly dragged Astra down with him. He recovered his balance. They examined the strange blister protruding from the top of the duct. Astra ran her fingers around its periphery. There was a brief whir. The blister hinged open of its own accord. Lights came on automatically inside the duct, illuminating a ladder designed for androids which was perfectly acceptable for humans. The fact that the lights had been out when the hatch opened indicated that the duct was most likely unoccupied. Darv and Astra scrambled down into the duct and the hatch closed automatically behind them.

'Which way?' Astra's voice reverberated into the distant reaches of the tunnel-like duct.

Darv's sense of direction told him that right led away from the controlled regions of the ship. They raced along the inside of the duct for twenty minutes. Sometimes it swung in a slow curve to the left and sometimes to the right but mostly the duct was climbing – so steeply in places that their feet slipped on the smooth lining.

'We must have climbed five levels,' said Astra when they paused for a rest.

Darv lifted a finger to his lips and turned his head, listening intently. Then Astra heard the faint roaring sound that was coming from the direction they were leaving.

'What is it, Darv?'

He took her hand. 'I don't know. Come on, let's keep going.'

They turned their backs on the strange sound and jogged side by side for another ten minutes then stopped again and listened. It was louder. Something was hurtling towards them with incredible speed. They broke into a run. Suddenly Darv realised what the sound was.

'It's the daily purge!' he yelled. 'Trust us to choose this time!'

Astra was about to reply but the hurricane was suddenly upon them. It swept Astra off her feet and threw her to the side of the duct with cruel force before blasting her body, arms and legs wildly flailing, along the duct. Several times Astra clung with terror-induced strength to the occasional handhold but each time the unbelievable force of the shrieking, howling gale was enough to prise her fingers open and send her body tumbling along the tunnel. She screamed for Darv but she could not even hear her own words above the hellish thunder. Something snatched at her arm and held it. It was Darv – clinging to an inspection ladder with one hand and to her with the other.

She made a superhuman effort and forced her other hand against the gale to grab the ladder. Darv pushed her in front of him and slowly, every step requiring intense strength and concentration, they began climbing the ladder. Oblivious of the hurricane screaming through the duct, the inspection hatch above their heads opened automatically. Astra helped Darv climb through the hatch. They lay on the floor, chests heaving, eyes red-rimmed and staring, hardly daring to believe that the terrible ordeal was over. The hatch closed, reducing the sound of the piped hurricane to a dull rumble.

'I think,' Astra panted in answer to Darv's query, 'that I am one giant bruise with bits of me in odd places that could be something else.'

Darv laughed weakly and climbed to his feet. They were in the widest corridor he had ever see. His heart sank when he realised that the main lights were on. It meant that they were in a controlled zone.

'The lights aren't on further down the corridor,' Astra pointed out, reading his mind. 'They're not on in either direction – just where we're sitting.'

'Angel One!' Darv yelled. 'Angel Two!'

His voice echoed into silence.

'Angel One! Angel Two! This is Darv and Astra! Can you hear me or see me?'

The echoes died away. Astra shivered. 'Maybe they're just playing games with us,' she complained bitterly.

They walked for five minutes among the unfamiliar spacious corridor and noticed that the lights came on in front of them and went off behind them.

'It's an automatic system,' said Darv in wonder. 'We're in an area that's in working order that isn't under the control of the guardian angels! It means that we could live here in perfect safety!'

'Are you sure?'

'Well of course I'm sure. There're whole regions of the ship that the guardian angels have lost control over or forgotten about. I found that out when I was a kid because they always used to question me about where I'd been when I came back from one of my explorations. That's why I always suspected right from the beginning that they weren't an outside force as they wanted us to think.'

Astra glanced fearfully around as if suspecting that the guardian angels were watching them, planning some new treachery aimed at taking her baby from her. She shivered. 'It would be so lovely to be free of them,' she said.

Darv put his arm around her waist. 'We are, my lovely – I promise.'

'No, Darv. We can never be completely free of them as long as we have to live on the *Challenger*.'

The corridor ended in two doors that slid apart at their approach. They produced their PD weapons, flattened themselves against a bulkhead and waited.

Nothing happened.

The softly-lit interior of the strange gallery beyond the doors beckoned to them. Darv eased himself forward with great caution until he had a clear view in the gallery. His eyes widened and he signalled for Astra to join him. They entered the gallery together and gazed around in wonder at the gleaming control console and the swivel chairs fixed to the floor in front of each of the smart desks.

'It's just like another main control room!' Astra exclaimed, knowing that it could not be.

Three of the walls were lined with racks of equipment. The fourth wall consisted of a floor-to-ceiling expanse of uninterrupted plastic glass. They approached one of the control desks and gaped at it. The desk was similar to those in the main control room inasmuch as it was a mass of touch pads, but the similarity ended with the designation legends that identified the purpose of each control.

'"Earthquake release, system A,"' Darv recited, peering at a control panel. '"Rain seeding – systems A to E; photosynthesis control; atmospheric balance levels . . ."' His voice trailed away in disbelief.

'This one's much the same,' said Astra, moving to another control desk. 'All the controls relate to humidity balancing. Everything you need for planetary engineering on a massive scale by the look of it.'

Darv came near to smacking his forehead when realised where they were. 'This is the terra-forming centre, Astra!'

'It can't be – it was destroyed in the Great Meteoroid Strike.'

'*But it is!*' Darv insisted. 'The guardian angels were wrong! It wasn't destroyed! What else can this place be?'

It was when they moved to the glass wall and looked down at the huge expanse of an excursion terminal that Astra was forced to accept that Darv was right. Spread out below them was a bewildering variety of heavy machines: earth-movers, graders, bulldozers, tunnelling shields and huge transportable water purifiers. But most important of all were the six gleaming space shuttles parked in a neat row facing the excursion terminal's outer bulkhead. Each shuttle was sitting on skids in front of its own freight air-lock door.

'Wow,' breathed Darv.

Darv was anxious to go down to inspect the shuttles but Astra insisted that they complete their examination of the terra-forming centre before they did anything else.

They came to a hologram replicator that was not unlike the machine in the library.

'You know,' said Darv, sitting at the machine and gazing at the blank replication field, 'it was on a machine virtually identical to this that I saw the Paradise recording.'

'You're not going to start on about that again?' Astra complained. 'It must've been a dream that you've confused with reality.'

Darv shook his head. 'I haven't, Astra. I know I haven't. It was a recording of a planet in Star Cluster – Tersus Nine. This star cluster. And Thorden believed me.'

'Yes – but which planetary system? There'll be thousands in a star cluster.'

Darv frowned. 'The recording said . . .' He hesitated and shook his head. 'I can't remember. But the planet had hills, and green grass, and clear blue skies . . . I didn't dream that. I'm sure I found the disk in Commander Sinclair's cabin. I took it to the library and played it on one of the machines.'

'You've never been able to find the recording,' Astra pointed out.

Darv's face creased in concentration. 'I sat at the machine just as I'm sitting at this one. I pushed the recording disk into the play slot and touched the start control.' Suiting his actions to his words, Darv touched the hologram replicators start control.

'Then what?'

'Then the Paradise recording was played,' said Darv simply.

'All right then,' said Astra practically. 'If there was a Paradise recording, what happened to it?'

'Can I be of any assistance?'

Darv and Astra whirled round and goggled at the android that was regarding them.

'Can I be of any assistance?' the machine repeated. 'If you are working late, perhaps you would like me to serve your meal here? You can eat where you like provided you don't make a mess for me to clear up.'

Darv was the first to recover from their shock. 'Who controls you?'

'You do.' was the android's simple reply.

'What about the ancillary guardians of environment and life?' Astra demanded.

If it was possible for the android to sniff it would have done so. 'The guardian angels abandoned me many years ago at the same time as the people did. I've had to struggle on by myself trying to keep the place clean for when the people came back.'

'And a splendid job you've done too,' said Darv solemnly.

'Would you like me to serve your meal here?'

'Yes please.'

The android turned and pointed to one of the control consoles. 'You can call up the menu for today on that screen, sir. Just touch out – '

'Just bring us something of everything,' Astra interrupted. 'We're ravenous.'

The machine turned to the entrance and glided out of the centre leaving Astra and Darv gaping after it.

'When we've eaten, we'll have to tell the others about this place,' said Darv.

'No.'

'But they've got a right to know.'

'We're not going back,' said Astra angrily. 'We're not going back ever – you promised.'

'I know, Astra, but that was before – '

'You promised!'

'All right,' said Darv. 'But we ought to talk over what we're going to do about this place.'

Astra sank gratefully into a swivel chair. 'When we've eaten and had some sleep,' she pleaded. 'I'm dead on my feet.'

Darv grinned. 'Sure. We've got to look after the two of you, eh?'

'Could be twins for all we know.' Astra lifted her tired feet on to the console and stretched. 'Hey – where are you going?'

Darv was moving to the entrance. He stopped. 'I'm going to find my way down to the excursion terminal to see if there are bunks in those shuttles. We can't sleep here.'

Astra climbed to her feet. 'I'm coming with you.'

'There's no need, Astra. And besides – you said that you were dead on your feet.'

'I don't care what I said – I'm coming with you. From now on we never let each other out of our sight.'

* * *

The guardian angels were not pleased.

The reports from their androids all told the same story: Darv and Astra had disappeared. Their primary concern was that the two fugitives were searching for their central switching room. Their original confidence that it could never be found by a member of the crew had been shaken. They accepted that they had underestimated Darv on a number of occasions, therefore it would be best to generate nightmare and hallucinatory barriers across all the approaches to their central switching room.

It was decidedly chilly in the excursion terminal so Darv and Astra shifted a large number of cushions from one of the space shuttles and spread them out on the floor of the terra-forming centre near the hologram replicator. They were assisted by the android who had served them an excellent meal earlier. The only problem with the machine was that the years of being alone had instilled in it a strong sense of order and tidiness. Although co-operative, it nevertheless made a great fuss about having to clean up the mess Darv and Astra had made on the floor during their meal. Nor did it approve of the makeshift bed. They decided to call the android "Tidy" – a name which it seemed happy to accept.

Darv and Astra were settling down on the cushions when Tidy glided into the centre and started cleaning the consoles. One of the machine's manipulator motors was emitting an irritating whine.

Astra sat up on her elbows. 'Leave them alone please, Tidy.'

'I always clean the consoles at this time.'

'And I always sleep at this time so I'd appreciate it if you cleaned them some other time.'

'How can you sleep surrounded by such squalor?'

'How will you be able to keep everything clean if I rip off your manipulators one by one?' Astra countered.

The android considered its options and moved to the door, muttering to itself.

'Tidy,' Astra called after the machine.

The android paused. Darv groaned and tried to cover his ears will a cushion.

'When do the lights go out?' Astra inquired.

'They don't go out,' said Tidy. 'I have to turn them out. I have to do everything since the guardian angels abandoned me.'

'Well, we'd like them out now, Tidy,' said Darv.

'Too early,' said Tidy.

Darv gave an exclamation of annoyance and rolled off the cushions. He crossed to the android and regarded it with unbridled contempt. 'Listen Tidy, we're your guardian angels now. Understand?'

'All right,' Tidy conceded. 'That means that it's your job to turn the lights out. And don't go leaving greasy human fingerprints everywhere.'

Shortly after she managed to doze off to sleep, Astra was woken by a light in the terra-forming centre. Her first thought that Tidy was being awkward again until she realised that the light was flickering. Moreover, it was coming from the hologram replicator. She rose to her knees on the cushions and stared at the three-dimensional image in amazement. She shook Darv.

'Darv – have you just switched the replicator on?'

Darv sat up and blinked at the replicated image in surprise. 'No, I've been asleep.' He jumped to his feet and stood in front of the machine. The image being replicated depicted rolling grasslands and distant hills. The sky was a deep blue filled with fluffy white clouds.

'Looks like a hologram of Earth,' Astra commented.

'Looks like it,' Darv agreed. He bent forward and examined the replicator. 'And yet there's no recording disk in the play slot . . . How can a replicator play a recording without a recording to play? It doesn't make sense.'

An animal appeared in the distance. With no comparative scale Darv and Astra could not judge its size. Also it was running away from them at high speed, raising a cloud of dust. A strange squealing sound was heard and then silence.

'Astra,' said Darv slowly. 'It's not a hologram of Earth. I know what all the large animals of Earth look like and none of them looked like that thing.'

Astra looked at Darv and saw that his eyes seemed to be glazed with shock. 'It's another Paradise, isn't it?' she whispered, clutching Darv's arm.

Darv could only nod.

'None of the Earth videos and holograms I've seen ever had skies as blue as that,' said Astra in wonder. 'And it looks so beautiful.'

'Tidy!' Darv yelled without taking his eyes off the replicator. 'Tidy!'

The android came gliding across the floor from the entrance.

'Did you switch this machine on, Tidy?' Darv demanded.

'I never switch any machine on except cooking burners and cleaners,' Tidy replied. 'I only clean machines in here.'

'This machine seems to be a repeater because it's playing a recording without a recording disk. Where's the master replicator?'

'I don't know what any of these machines are. I only clean them.'

Darv dismissed the android. He studied the curious image for some moments and switched the replicator off. 'It doesn't make sense,' he muttered.

'It does,' said Astra vehemently. 'It's Angel One and Angel Two playing games with us!'

'Now don't be silly. You know that's not possible,'

'I'm not being silly!' Astra began to get hysterical. 'They're playing a vicious game with us! Watching us! Laughing at us!'

Darv took Astra in his arms to comfort her.

'We can never escape from them,' she sobbed. 'All the time they're planning how they'll be able to take my baby from me!' She pushed Darv away and stumbled blindly to the entrance. Darv started after her but she beat wildly at him with her fists and struggled to break free. 'I want to get away from here!' she screamed. 'I must get away!'

'Listen to me!' Darv shouted, shaking her. 'I swear that the guardian angels have no control over this region!'

'You're lying! Everyone's lying! Our lives are one big lie and we can never, never escape! Never!'

Darv steeled himself and slapped her across the face. Her head jerked back. She stopped struggling and sank to her knees, tears streaming down her cheeks. 'I want to get out of the ship. I want to get a million miles from those things.'

Darv knelt beside her and took her hands in his. 'Astra my lovely, listen to me, please. We can't leave the *Challenger*.'

Astra turned her face to Darv. Her blonde hair was matted against her tear-streaked cheeks and there was an expression of abject despair in her eyes. 'There's those shuttles down there.'

'And how long could we survive for in one? Two weeks? Three weeks?'

Astra calmed down and pulled her hair away from her eyes.

'Four weeks at the most,' Darv continued putting an arm around her and holding her tightly. 'And after that . . . Not only us but the baby as well . . . Is that what you want?'

'I just want to get out of the ship,' said Astra miserably.

'I give you my solemn word that the angels have no control over this region. And if I could find their central switching room, then I would end their control over the entire ship.'

After a few minutes Astra had calmed down sufficiently for Darv to guide her back to the makeshift bed, He held her close until exhaustion and sleep claimed her.

The recording was still playing the following morning when Darv switched the machine on.

He shook his head, perplexed by the same hologram panorama of savannah and undulating hills. A sun, blood-red and swollen by atmospheric distortion, was sinking behind the hills so that a lone tree in the foreground threw a long shadow across the ground.

'How long does a hologram normally play for?' asked Astra.

'About two hours,' was Darv's reply.

'This one's been playing at least four hours now without a recording disk,' said Astra slowly. 'If I were to say that the angels were playing some sort of game with us, would you still laugh at me?'

'I never laugh at you, Astra. I said that the guardian angels have no control over this part of the ship. I still say that.'

'Then how do you account for that!'

Darv looked unhappily at the hologram. 'I don't know,' he admitted. 'I just don't know.'

'Then I suggest that you check this machine inside out by taking it apart!'

'Don't be silly – '

'I'm not being silly!' Astra snapped. 'That hologram replicator is doing the impossible and yet you refuse to admit that the guardian angels are playing tricks with us!'

Astra saw a strange expression enter Darv's eyes as he stared past her at the replicator. She spun round. 'Oh, no,' she said weakly when she saw the spectacle. 'Please tell me it isn't true.'

A herd of the most grotesque animals that it was possible to imagine were crossing the plain, They had strange mottled markings and their rear legs were about a third shorter than their front legs. There were about two hundred of them – raising a huge cloud of dust in the wake of their ungainly gallop. But it was not their misshapen legs that caused Astra and Darv to gape at the creatures in paralysed disbelief: it was the fact that the length of necks was twice the height of their bodies.

After a few seconds all the weird, ungainly creatures, including the stragglers, had passed out of the replication field's picture.

Darv was the first to break the silence that followed: 'You know, Astra . . . You could be right after all. Maybe this place *is* still under the control of the angels.'

* * *

Darv and Astra spent three hours checking the hologram replicator. They ignored Tidy's anguished complaints about the mess they were making and removed the machine's inspection cover. They knew very little about the workings of the complex hologram replicators but they were able to satisfy themselves that the signals were being fed into the machine by a fibre optic track from an outside source, The supply track disappeared into a bulkhead and was therefore impossible to trace.

'So I was right all along,' was Astra's grim comment when they pushed the machine back into place. 'The angels are feeding the hologram into this replicator. If they've no control over this machine, there's no reason why they shouldn't have control over all of them . . . We're not staying here a moment longer.'

'You've scratched my floor!' Tidy moaned as he carefully lined-up the replicator with the other machines.

Darv studied the machine thoughtfully and touched the start control. Nothing happened – the replication field remained dark. He touched the control again to ensure that he had operated it correctly and turned to Astra, grinning. 'You see? The recording has ended.'

'So?'

'Well . . . It means – '

'It means that the guardian angels see no point in continuing with the recording now that we've discovered what they're up to,' Astra pointed out.

At that moment there was a shrill scream, so sudden, so intense, that the colour drained from Astra's and Darv's faces. The terrible cry of agony came from the replicator. It dragged on for half a minute and ended with a chilling, sobbing moan. The merciful silence that followed was broken by the sound of powerful teeth crunching into bone.

Astra and Darv stood transfixed. Eventually Astra said in a low voice: 'The hologram didn't work so now they're trying to frighten us with sounds.'

The chilling crunching noises were replaced by the sound of heavy breathing and deep, menacing growls.

'Not just sounds,' said Darv weakly. 'Not if you look closely.'

The darkened replication field had cleared slightly. Astra realised that the recording was still running: she could discern the familiar outline of the hills with myriad points of light shining above them.

'Night,' said Darv simply. 'It was stupid of me not to have realised. The recording is now showing night.'

There was an outburst of snapping and growling from the replication field.

'Tidy!' said Darv urgently. 'Turn down the lights in here.'

'Not time.'

'Just do as I say!'

Muttering to itself, the android did as it was told.

The lights in the terra-formed centre dimmed, making it possible to see the two creatures in the replication field foreground that were conducting a dispute over a savagely mauled carcass. The larger of the two creatures seemed to have established ownership over the mass of gored flesh and was employing an intimidating repertoire of snarls and growls to discourage a smaller animal with similar ideas.

'Astra,' said Darv thoughtfully. 'When we came in here for the first time last night, can you remember everything that we did?'

'All that matters is what we're going to do next,' said Astra shortly. 'And that's to get out of this place now.'

Darv pointed. 'The first thing we did was look at the control desks. Right?'

'What does it matter?'

'And then we looked down into the new excursion terminal and then we examined all the various machines in here and I sat down at this replicator. Right?'

Astra shrugged. 'I suppose so.'

'Then I touched the start control. Nothing happened at the time. But three hours later you were woken up by a hologram playing in the machine's replication field.'

'So?'

There was an excited light in Darv's eye. 'We're a thousand million miles from the third planet of this solar system. Light travels at six hundred and seventy million miles per hour – so that's an hour and a half for the command signal to travel from this machine to the third planet. The signal switches on the instrument probe that the second-generation crew left behind on the planet, and the information from the probe takes another hour and a half to reach us! Making a total of three hours! Astra – that isn't a recording we're watching! It's a live transmission from the third planet! We've found Paradise!'

The great carnivore, having gorged itself senseless on the succulent viscera of its kill, allowed a host of circling smaller creatures to close in for a share while it settled down for a long sleep that would see it through until the following noon.

PART 10

Earthfall

'And this desk?' Telson inquired.
'Rain propagation,' said Darv. He pointed to another desk in the terra-forming centre. 'And that's the master console as far as I can make out. It provides for total weather control.'
Telson sat his stocky frame in one of the swivel chairs and thoughtfully eyed the control desk in front of him. 'I've got to give you credit, Darv,' he conceded. 'This place is quite a find.'
'But you haven't seen anything yet!' Darv enthused. 'With the resources of this centre it's possible to re-engineer an entire planet.'
'First find your planet.'
'That's the whole point about Paradise.' said Darv. 'When the second-generation crew discovered it, they decided that there was nothing that they need do to it because it was already perfect. Look – I'll show you.'
Telson allowed Darv to drag him from his chair and push him across to the vast window. Darv pointed excitedly down at the row of terra-forming machines. Sharna and Astra were emerging from the nearest shuttle. They waved up at the window.
'We've checked the inventories,' Darv continued. 'None of the machines are missing. No equipment was left behind on Paradise apart from the probe that's sending that hologram. No excavators. No androids. Nothing.'
'Because the second-generation crew didn't consider it worthwhile,' Telson reasoned.
'But you've seen the hologram transmissions from the surface, Telson! Animals, grass, trees!'

'One set of holograms from *one* probe in *one* location.'

'But it's enough!' argued Darv, resisting the temptation to bang Telson's head against the glass. 'And it proves that the angels are lying when they say that inner planets of this solar system are swamped with radiation.'

Telson turned to face Darv. For once one of Darv's attacks on the guardian angels left him more puzzled than angry. 'But why would they lie?'

Darv felt that at last he was getting somewhere in undermining Telson's confidence in the guardian angels. 'Because they don't want us to take the *Challenger* into a close orbit around this system's sun. They're frightened that we might like the look of Paradise and decide to settle on it. They want to find Earth because they want to rule a developed world.'

Telson gave a dismissive gesture. He was about to speak but Darv pressed on with his argument: 'Look, Telson – originally they wanted to find a developed planet because they wanted to rule it or dominate it in some way. That's why they made you extend the voyage. When they calculated the improbability of finding such a planet, they instructed you to return the *Challenger* to Earth. With their crazy logic, they thought that Earth would have reverted enough for its peoples to accept them as gods – there are enough theories in the library on the subject.'

'That's crazy,' muttered Telson.

'Is it? We virtually accepted the guardian angels as gods, remember. Having discovered that the Earth had vanished they naturally were keen enough for us to find it. For once, our aims were the same as theirs, but not for the same reasons. But they're not anymore.'

'Now you're being stupid,' said Telson dismissively. 'We all want to find Earth.'

'I don't!' The two words rang out across the terra–forming centre with a deathly finality that even unnerved Darv but not enough to make him hesitate. 'Astra and I wish to leave the *Challenger* for good if Paradise is suitable.'

'I won't insult you by asking if you've given this careful thought.'

'We have, Telson.'

Telson shook his head. 'I can't risk taking the ship into a closer orbit around this sun. 'I'm sorry, Darv.'

'But this orbit is useless! How can we possibly survey Paradise from a thousand million miles with surveillance equipment that's been sabotaged by our precious angels?'

'We don't know that they have sabotaged it,' said Telson stubbornly.

'Isn't it obvious?' Darv countered. 'Surely even you must've thought it odd that meteoroids should've knocked out our telescope and spectrum analysers just when we needed them?'

Telson had thought about little else but he remained silent.

'Which means,' Darv continued, 'that the only way of surveying Paradise is to go into a close orbit – either around the sun or, better still, around Paradise.'

Telson turned away from the window and sat down to give himself time to think. 'Darv – I'm sorry, but it's a risk I can't take. I can't go against the advice of the angels. If it was just your life and my life maybe it wouldn't matter – but there's Sharna and Astra to consider – '

'Astra's expecting a baby,' Darv interrupted. 'She wants to get off the ship as soon as possible because she suspects that Angel One and Two will try to seize control of the child.'

There was a pause before Telson answered. 'So Sharna guessed correctly. She told me that she thought Astra was pregnant . . . But how could the angels possibly control a baby?'

'The same way that they controlled us when we were babies – through the nursery androids,' was Darv's bitter reply. 'They planned it right from the beginning. I've always said that the Great Meteoroid Strike wasn't an accident. Now I'm convinced that I was right.'

Telson's customary irritation returned. 'Don't be so damned stupid. You've seen the holograms of Sinclair's address. How the hell could the angels manufacture a meteoroid?'

'They didn't – they took advantage of it.'

'How?'

'Look. The angels wanted control of the ship. They couldn't get control of the second-generation crew simply because there were too many of them so they waited until the first four children of the third generation had been born – us four. They switched off the meteoroid shields at the right moment and ensured that all the second generation were destroyed. Their plan was that we would grow up subservient to them. That we would navigate and manoeuvre the *Challenger* in accordance with their wishes.'

'All this is speculation,' Telson cut in impatiently.

'Two things went wrong for them,' Darv continued, ignoring the interruption. 'Firstly, they underestimated the amount of damage that a major meteoroid strike would cause with the result that they lost control over whole regions of the ship. Secondly, they didn't realise that even people brought up from babies by them might one day reject their influence.'

Telson considered for a moment and shook his head. 'I have never accepted their influence Darv. But I do accept their advice.'

The conversation was beginning to bore Darv. 'We're just going round in circles,' he said, adding in a reasoning tone: 'Look, Telson – let's compromise. We close in to a five hundred million mile orbit and take a close look at Paradise with one of the space shuttles. Their controls are identical to the old shuttle – we'd have no problems.'

'No,' said Telson resolutely.

Darv stared hard at him for some seconds. 'You know something Telson? For a few minutes just now I very nearly revised my opinion of you. I stupidly thought that I had misjudged you all these years and that maybe you were prepared to listen to reason.'

Telson refused to allow Darv to slacken his grip on his temper. 'I'm sorry that you should think that Darv. Especially as I am thinking of your safety and Astra's safety. The answer is still no.'

Darv turned away and gazed down into the excursion terminal. 'In that case, Astra and I will load one of those shuttles with supplies and leave the *Challenger*. He turned to face Telson. 'And there's nothing you can do to stop us.'

'You've got to stop them,' Sharna declared emphatically.

'You tell me how and I will,' said Telson moodily. 'Do I

stand in front of the shuttle they're trying to load and threaten them with a PD weapon?'

'It seems to me that you managed to brilliantly mishandle the situation.'

'You think that you could've done better?'

Sharna saw no point in aggravating Telson with the obvious answer. Instead she said: 'Surely Darv would consider some sort of compromise?'

Telson sat on Sharna's bed and glowered at the far wall. 'It's not a question of what Darv will consider – it's a question of what *I'm* prepared to consider. I'm not prepared to endanger the ship.'

'Yet you're prepared to see them embark on a thousand million mile journey in a space shuttle?'

'What the hell am I supposed to do!' Telson expostulated, much aggrieved at the notion that even dependable Sharna wasn't on his side. 'I don't have the power to hold Astra and Darv on the *Challenger* against their will!'

'Then take the *Challenger* into a closer orbit.'

'No.'

Sharna sighed. 'You really can be the most incredibly stubborn man, Telson.'

'How you can possibly defy my wish to ensure our safety and the safety of the ship as stubbornness is beyond me,' Telson retaliated. 'I would've thought that you of all people would see reason.'

Sharna sat on the bed beside Telson. She took his hand in a rare gesture of affection. 'Look at me, Telson.'

Telson looked into Sharna's wise eyes and turned away.

'Ever since we were five or six years old, I can remember having to keep the peace between you and Darv. For the best part of twenty years you two have been at war and for the most part I have tried not to take sides. This time Darv is not acting out of some crazy, headstrong desire to annoy you but because Astra is genuinely terrified that the guardian angels will want to take her baby away from her when it's born.'

'We could prevent that happening easily enough,' said Telson scornfully.

'Even if it was born while we were in suspended animation?' Sharna inquired mildly.

Telson said nothing.

'Well this time I *am* going to take sides,' Sharna continued. 'As much as I love Astra and Darv, and would be miserable to see them go, I think I understand exactly how they feel.'

Without Sharna's support Telson suddenly felt very lonely. 'So what do you suggest?' he asked at length.

'That we go into orbit around the third planet. If it does have a suitable environment, then we allow Darv and Astra to spend a few weeks living on the planet to find out whether or not they could adapt to it.'

'And if they can't?'

'Then they return to the *Challenger* and live in an uncontrolled zone – away from the influence of the guardian angels.'

'All right,' said Telson after a pause. 'I'll think about it.'

The guardian angels considered that their most pressing problem was to determine the whereabouts of the terra-forming centre and its associated excursion terminal. They learned from Telson's and Sharna's conversation that the excursion terminal housed a large amount of machinery designed for planetary use plus six space shuttles. By a process of elimination, the guardian angels evolved a short list of three possible locations. After further refinement, they narrowed the number of probable sites down to one location – one that caused them grave disquiet because it was on the same level as their central switching room.

Telson gave Sharna his decision the following day after repeated assurances given to him by the guardian angels that it would be suicidal to take the *Challenger* nearer the sun.

Sharna listened without comment to Telson's reasons and opened a drawer on one of her room's lockers. She produced a length of plasticised paper covered in small print and held it out to Telson. 'It's a hard copy of the ship's constitution,' she explained. 'I accessed it from the library this morning.'

'I can't see what bearing it has on the present problem,' he remarked, not bothering to look at the document.

'It's got everything to do with it,' Sharna murmured. She moved to Telson's side and pointed at a sentence halfway down the column of close print. 'Especially Article Twenty-nine.'

Telson read the clause. 'Nonsense,' he said when he had finished reading. 'This only applies to the days when the *Challenger* had a crew of over three hundred.'

'I've read through carefully,' said Sharna quietly. 'It says nothing about numbers. Look at the wording. The guardian angels appointed you commander of the *Challenger* because there was no one left on the *Challenger* of voting age after the Great Meteoroid Strike. Now there are – and you can only remain commander provided that you have the support of the majority. Any member of the crew can lodge a motion of no confidence in the commanding officer and, provided that the motion carries the support of at least twenty-five per cent of the crew, the motion must be put to the vote by a secret ballot at an extraordinary meeting of the full crew.'

'But it's lunatic' Telson protested. 'We've never resorted to quoting the constitution at each other before – '

'We've never had to.'

'-and twenty-five per cent of the entire crew happens to be one person. Or had that escaped your notice?'

'As I said,' Sharna murmured, remaining very calm, 'The constitution refers to percentages and not numbers.' She handed two documents to Telson. 'That's Darv's motion and my support.'

Telson glanced at them and at the constitution. 'It says here that there has to be a seventy-five per cent vote against the status quo,' he pointed out.

'So let's hold a ballot to decide the matter,' Sharna replied.

'I said that I'm never going back into controlled regions of the ship and I meant it,' Astra declared, sitting on the steps of a space shuttle and folding her arms defiantly.

Darv groaned. There had been a time when Astra could be

relied on to do as she was told. 'It's important, Astra. Telson has the right to say that the meeting should be held in the restaurant.'

'I don't care. It's a stupid idea and I'm not moving.'

Darv turned to Sharna who was hovering in the background.

'You talk to her,' he said wearily. 'Maybe you can make her see sense.'

It took Sharna thirty minutes of skilled reasoning to persuade Astra to leave the uncontrolled zone. It was an accomplishment of which she was not particularly proud.

The voting was predictably three in favour of taking a close look at the third planet and one against.

Telson pushed back his chair and stood. 'All right,' he said resolutely. 'There's no point in delaying. We'll go to the control room now and make an immediate start on the pre-manoeuvering procedures.'

As they entered the main control room, Darv wondered why victory had such a sour taste. They moved to their respective desks and sat down. Telson waited until Darv, Astra and Sharna had reported that their control desks were activated and moved his hand an inch above his start control to bring his own console to life. Nothing happened – the touch controls remained unilluminated. 'Are you sure all three have activated your controls?' he queried, looking at them.

'Well that's odd,' Telson muttered when he had received three confirmations. 'My desk's still dead.'

'Are you sure you put your hand in the right place?' Darv inquired suspiciously.

'Well of course I'm sure!'

'So let's change places,' Darv suggested.

They swapped desks but nothing Darv did had the effect of activating Telson's desk.

'Odd,' Darv commented, noticing Astra's sudden tense expression.

'You're damned right it's odd,' said Telson grimly. 'Angel One!'

'Commander?' Angel One's voice answered.

'Why the hell can't I activate my desk?'

'You wish to take the *Challenger* into an orbit around the third planet, Commander Telson?' Angel One inquired.

'It's not what I wish – it's what I've agreed to,' was Telson's curt reply.

'Then we cannot permit the opening of the master control circuits from your console to the photonic drive,' said Angel One smoothly. 'As we have repeatedly explained – the inner planets of this solar system are swamped with radiation that could endanger the ship. The first planet orbits too close to the sun to support any form of life; the second planet is shrouded in cloud and has an extremely high surface temperature; the third planet – '

'Was visited by the second-generation crew,' Darv broke in. 'Correct, Angel One?'

There was the briefest of paused before Angel One replied – a pause that was long enough for her to consult with Angel Two. 'Correct, Darv. They called it Paradise.'

All four were completely taken aback by the astounding admission, but no one as much as Darv. He was left gaping, unable to think of anything to say as Angel One pressed on with more revelations: 'Commander Sinclair of the second-generation crew decided that the planet might be suitable for colonization. He was wrong, of course.'

'So you've finally decided to admit it,' said Darv when he had found his voice.

'We have decided to make all the information on Paradise available to you,' said Angel Two. 'It will be necessary for you to assemble in the galactic resources centre.'

The strange blue-green planet shone like a jewel in the centre of the replication field. It was undoubtedly the most beautiful planet that the four had ever seen, although Darv was troubled by the considerable expanse of blue that was visible through the convoluted patterns of white cloud.

'Paradise has a year that consists of three hundred and sixty-five of its days,' Angel One intoned. 'And in that respect is totally different from our Earth. Also, it is tilted on its axis – the effect of this is to create severe temperature changes throughout the year in the Southern and Northern temperate zones. These are the regions where our Earth-type crops would fail during the cold periods before they had a chance to mature.'

'Doesn't look very promising, does it?' said Telson for Darv's benefit.

'There are more problems as the hologram will show,' said Angel One.

The planet swelled on the replication field until one of the vast blue areas seemed to fill an entire hemisphere.

'That,' said Angel One, 'is a single expanse of water.'

Darv's heart sank at the bleak spectacle. The fine cloud detail and the patterns of islands in tight groups that interrupted the awesome lake had an authentic look – he doubted of the guardian angels had the resources to fake what he was looking at.

'It's not possible,' Astra muttered. 'No lakes could be that large.'

'Your surprise is understandable,' Angel One continued. 'Almost seven tenths of the surface of Paradise is covered in water. The planet is larger than our Earth and yet has only one fifth of the land mass. Also, the water covering Paradise is undrinkable. Terra-forming precipitation could not bring about any lasting change to the poisonous nature of the lakes.'

'But is there fresh water?' Darv queried. 'Those clouds must create some rivers?'

'There are rivers and streams, Darv, but they account for an infinitesimal percentage of all the water on Paradise.'

'But animals survive there,' said Astra doggedly. 'It *is* habitable and we *could* breathe its air.'

'It is habitable in the temperate regions,' said Angel One. 'Unfortunately, most of the land is in the Northern hemisphere, and it is these areas that are subject to frequent ice ages when the ice from the frozen north advances southward. This has happened several times in the planet's history and each time life on dry land has come close to extinction.'

'Then why was it called Paradise?' Telson demanded.

'There's much more,' Angel One continued. 'The planet's atmosphere does not provide full protection against cosmic ray bombardment from the sun. The probe left behind by the second-generation crew indicates that unstable particles reach the surface.'

'Listen,' said Darv harshly. 'Nothing you say can alter the fact that I can now clearly remember Commander Sinclair saying in a hologram recording that Paradise was suitable for colonization.'

'Where is this recording now?' asked Angel Two, speaking for the first time.

'I think you and Angel One know the answer to that.'

'I see,' said Angel Two. 'Did the recording mention the intense bands of radiation that surround Paradise? So intense, that under certain circumstances they can light up the Northern sky?'

'Don't be absurd,' said Darv shortly.

The hologram changed abruptly to a scene of a frozen, moonlit landscape dominated by a sky filled with patterns of ethereal light that stretched from horizon to zenith. As the four watched, spellbound, the amazing lights performed a slow dance and became a twisting, interlocking and then separating kaleidoscope of dazzling symmetry which waxed and waned through every conceivable colour.

'This is a recording made by a party of the second-generation crew who carried out a survey of the northern regions,' Angel Two explained.

Darv glanced at one of the blank data screens. 'Did they also record the radiation levels that caused that lighting display?' he inquired.

Angel One answered: 'Unfortunately their findings were destroyed in the Great Meteoroid Strike, Darv. But I'm sure you will all agree that the radiation levels must have been significant to have created such a spectacle. Or does Darv believe that we could fake the recording?'

'Oh, I'm sure it's genuine,' said Darv. 'But no matter how hard you work at trying to prove that Paradise is unsuitable nothing can alter the fact that I saw two advanced humanoids in the recording.'

'Advanced, Darv?' queried Angel One.

'Not by our standards,' said Darv. 'But they were indigenous to Paradise and they were the product of at least one million years' evolution. If they can adapt to the radiation, assuming that it's dangerous, then so can we.'

'How do you know that they did adapt?' said Angel One. 'There were less than a thousand pairs at the time of Commander Sinclair's visit. For all we known they could be the remnants of a once-dominant race that covered the entire planet. We don't know if the humanoids on Paradise are destined to rise to civilization or are falling from it.'

'Is there any sign of a former civilization on Paradise?' asked Sharna.

'No,' Angel One replied. 'But the erosive effect of Paradise's highly active atmosphere and weather systems would be enough to wipe out the vestiges of even large cities during the course of half a million years.'

'We're going to settle on Paradise,' said Astra. passionately. 'I don't know what will happen to us, but I do know that my baby's not going to be born on the *Challenger*.'

Darv sat on the steps leading to the shuttle's entrance and studied the figures he had scribbled on the pad. Astra stopped piling the food and clothing supplies on the floor near the shuttle and sent Tidy off to locate some first aid equipment. 'Well?'

'It's crazy to think of leaving the *Challenger* in one of these things,' Darv complained. 'The journey would take weeks.'

'No,' said Astra firmly.

Darv held up his pad that was covered with the computer results of numerous calculations. 'All six shuttles have the same performance – right?'

'Right.'

'It's a thousand million miles to Paradise. I've worked out a sunward minimum energy orbit that intersects Paradise's orbit twelve weeks after leaving the *Challenger*. There's no way of reducing that figure.'

'That's not what I worked out,' said Astra.

'Well, I wish you'd show me your figures because they're doing things for you which they're not doing for me.'

Astra stepped past Darv and entered the shuttle. He took a playful bite at her ankle but she was not in the mood for games. He followed her to the pilot's control panel where she touched out some figures on the graphic display.

'There,' said Astra. 'I worked them out yesterday and they're sound.'

Darv touched the key to run Astra's program. The screen showed a graphic representation of the shuttle separating from the *Challenger*. The shuttle fired its main engine in a hard braking burn to cancel the *Challenger*'s orbital velocity around the sun and a second time to assist the sun's gravitational pull as the shuttle fell sunward. Figures showing the shuttle's mounting acceleration and diminishing fuel reserves were displayed at the side of the screen together with a rapidly winking set of figures that indicated the duration in hours of the speeded-up, simulated voyage. Several firings of the main engine sent the shuttle plunging down into the atmosphere of Paradise and a series of final burns showed the shuttle settling neatly on the surface.

Darv looked at the final fuel figures in disbelief before turning to Astra. 'You're not serious, Astra, surely?'

'Why not?'

There was a resolute set to Astra's face the Darv found disturbing. Since her discovery that she was pregnant her personality had undergone a significant change. The carefree young girl had gone, to be replaced by a determined young woman with a streak of ruthlessness that manifested itself when ever she suspected that the safety of her unborn child was threatened.

'But look at the figures,' Darv protested pointing to the screen. 'Forty-five per cent of total boost capacity for dropping sunward . . . Another forty-five per cent for deceleration and establishing an orbit around Paradise; seven per cent for atmospheric entry and atmospheric flight . . .'

'And two per cent for landing,' Astra finished. 'A ten day journey – yes?'

'A fast trip,' Darv agreed. 'But those figures add up to – '

'I've also allowed for a two-tonne payload of supplies.'

'Listen, Astra. Your figures add up to ninety-nine per cent of our fuel burned. We touch down on Paradise with one per cent left in our tanks!'

'So?'

Darv suddenly felt trapped. 'Supposing the angels are right and Paradise isn't suitable? How do we get back to the *Challenger* if we have to?'

The resolute light in Astra's eyes alarmed Darv. 'The answer to that question, Darv, is that Paradise *will* be suitable and we *won't* be coming back.'

Sharna looked critically at the one-piece suit Astra was wearing and shook her head. 'Red doesn't suit you.'

Astra smiled. 'I wasn't concerned about the appearance of the thing. Do you think it's practical?'

'Show me the insteps.'

Astra stood on one leg and then the other while Sharna examined the garment's soles and heels. 'That's going to be where all the wear is,' Sharna observed. 'Get the android to make the heels and soles as thick and as tough as possible.'

Astra nodded and gave the two garment-making androids revised instructions.

The girls were sitting cross-legged on the floor of the terra-forming centre surrounded by bolts of cloth that they had found in the stores. The two garment-making androids were busily turning out a wide variety of lightweight clothes for Astra and Darv while Tidy fussed around trying to prevent the mess the two machines were making getting out of control.

'Of all the androids, I think I'm going to miss the garment-makers the most,' said Astra, opening the seams of the one-piece suit and stepping out of it.

Sharna looked up from the overshoes she was inspecting. 'There's a thousand and one things you're going to miss, Astra.'

Astra was thoughtful for a moment. 'I'll miss you, Sharna. I'll miss you very much.' She gave an embarrassed smile. 'Well . . . that seems to be everything.'

'Astra,' said Sharna, watching Astra folding clothes that the androids had finished. 'Is life on the ship really so bad? You and Darv could live here – it's uncontrolled – there's no way that the guardian angels would be able to harm your baby.'

'How long will they allow it to remain uncontrolled, Sharna? They'd get the service androids to carry out repairs. No . . . the only way I could ever be happy on the *Challenger* is if the angels were destroyed.'

Darv and Telson entered the centre.

'We've finished checking the shuttle,' said Telson. 'It's never been used, and is in perfect working order as far as we can see.'

'Tidy,' Astra commanded, pointing to the finished clothes. 'You can take those aboard and make a start on clearing up in here.'

'Make a start!' the android echoed indignantly. 'I've been trying to clear up for the past hour.'

'Well now is your chance to try extra hard.'

Sharna grinned. 'Wouldn't you like to take Tidy with you, Astra?'

'I don't think so.'

The girls looked at each other and burst out laughing.

Sharna and Telson finished cramming supplies into the shuttle's stowage bay and closed the bay's outer door. 'That's everything,' said Sharna as she and Telson entered the shuttle's main cabin where Darv and Astra were completing the pre-separation checks.

Astra turned round and smiled gratefully. 'You've both been very kind,' she said.

'We've both been crazy to help at all,' Telson growled. 'Is everything ready?'

Astra glanced at her screen. 'Water, fuel, food, drugs – everything. And all systems are in a green condition.'

'Well,' said Telson after an embarrassed pause. 'We've said our goodbyes so there's no point in delaying things any longer. Sharna and I will operate the excursion air-lock from the terra-forming centre.' He took Sharna by the arm and turned to the shuttle's open air-lock doors.

'Thanks for everything, both of you,' said Darv.

Telson nodded. 'If we ever win total control over the *Challenger*, we'll return to Paradise to see how you're faring – radiation or no radiation.' He gave a half smile. 'We're going to miss you both . . . But we've said all that. Come on, Sharna – there's a control desk we've got to learn how to use.'

Telson and Sharna returned to the terra-forming centre and sat at the two consoles that faced the window overlooking the excursion terminal. Sharna contacted Astra to ensure that the shuttle was sealed before she cut the excursion terminal's artificial gravity and touched the controls to open the main air-lock door that the shuttle was facing.

In the shuttle, Darv watched the huge door sliding open and applied a short burst of directional thrust to lift the craft off the floor of the terminal.

'Thank you, Sharna,' he acknowledged. 'Moving into the air-lock now.'

Light came on inside the cavernous interior of the freight air-lock as Darv edged the shuttle forward. His rear-view screen showed the door sliding shut.

'Evacuating air-lock,' Telson's voice reported.

As soon as the ambient air-pressure reading in front of Darv reached zero, the outer hull door began sliding open. What started as a slit of stars slowly widened to become a forbidding rectangle of countless millions of burning points of light.

Darv glanced sideways at Astra who was staring at the stars with a fixed expression. 'You can still change your mind,' he suggested gently.

Astra shook her head without speaking.

Darv applied a burst of rearward thrust that sent the shuttle edging forward into space. It cleared the shadow of the *Challenger*'s stupendous bulk and was bathed in weak sunlight. At a distance of a thousand million miles, the sun was little more than a disc of light, but it was several billion times nearer than the nearest star and was therefore the brightest object in the heavens.

'Shuttle to *Challenger*,' Darv reported. 'Separation complete.'

The shuttle cruised the entire length of the mighty starship, crossing the gulf of tangled and twisted metal that marked the site of the Great Meteoroid Strike. It moved towards the prow of the ship and the semi-circle of brightly-lit view ports of the deserted main control room.

'Ten seconds to main engine burn,' said Darv as he orientated the shuttle in accordance with graphics on the inertial navigation screen.

'For the first time I feel safe.' said Astra quietly.

'We haven't got anywhere yet.'

'I don't care. I feel safe.'

There were final farewells from Telson and Sharna. 'Don't forget to radio us your landing site,' was Telson's final reminder.

The main rocket engine fired automatically as Darv completed his acknowledgement. The gap between the shuttle and the *Challenger* widened slowly at first and then with increasing rapidity as the tiny craft accelerated into its thousand million mile fall towards the distant sun.

The guardian angels watched the departing space shuttle with equanimity. They accepted that they had failed abysmally with Darv and Astra. The knowledge increased their determination to ensure that the same thing did not happen with Telson and Sharna. As soon as the couple were in suspended animation, an immediate start would be made on building a fourth-generation crew.

That's it,' said Telson, standing up. 'There's no point in staying here any longer. We can speak to them from the main control room.'

Sharna moved away from the desk she had been sitting at and paused by a console that they had not used. There were no control areas marked on the featureless surface.

'I wonder what this desk is for, Telson?'

Telson shrugged. 'All the equipment in this place is a bit of a mystery.'

217

'That's why we ought to familiarise ourselves with it.'

'Not now, Sharna,' said Telson moving to the terra-forming centre's entrance.

'Why not? What else is there for us to do? We've got ten days until we know whether or not Darv and Astra have made a safe landing. And you agreed that we make no attempt to leave this solar system until then.' Without waiting for Telson's reply, Sharna sat down at the strange console and activated it by passing her hand back and forth above its featureless surface.

The console came to life. As Sharna stared down, symbols and graphics began to glow on the surface and increase in intensity.

'Telson – come and look at this.'

Sharna's tone was enough for Telson to move to her side.

'What do you make of that?' she asked.

Lines were appearing on the surface. At first Telson thought that he was looking at an electronic circuit and then he realised that it was a plan of the ship. 'It doesn't make sense,' he muttered. 'Why have a control desk without any controls?'

'Unless it's some sort of data screen,' said Sharna, every bit as baffled as Telson.

The information of the horizontal screen became clearer. Corridors and passageways were identified by their numbers, and a legend appeared that indicated the terra-forming centre.

'My God,' Telson breathed softly. 'Look, Sharna! Just look at that!' His finger trembled slightly as it traced a series of parallel lines that ended at a box symbol that was identified by the caption:

ANCILLARY GUARDIANS OF ENVIRONMENT AND LIFE – SYSTEM ONE AND SYSTEM TWO – CENTRAL SWITCHING ROOM.

Sharna's face was ashen as she met Telson's eyes. 'It's on this level,' she said hollowly. And then she was virtually shouting: 'The angel's central switching room is on this level!'

*   *   *

The sixth planet of the solar system was like no planet that Darv and Astra had ever seen. It had a breathtaking system of braided rings that formed a multi-coloured equatorial band around the methane and ammonia giant. Astra measured the diameter of the rings with the shuttle's instruments and arrived at a value of 170,000 miles, yet they were so thin that they seemed to disappear as he shuttle passed them edge on.

The fifth planet was on the far side of the sun and was therefore invisible to the shuttle's optical instruments. The fourth planet was similar to Kyros in their home solar system – a reddish-hued barren world with ice-caps of frozen carbon-dioxide.

But five days after separation from the *Challenger* it was the third planet and its crater-scarred moon that was holding the couple's rapt attention.

After six days it was possible to discern the illuminated crescents of both bodies without the aid of the telescope. The passing of each hour brought a noticeable increase in the apparent size of Paradise and its satellite: as the shuttle dropped closer towards the sun, so the sun's rapidly mounting gravitational pull increased the rate of fall of the tiny spacecraft.

While Astra was sleeping, Darv checked the shuttle's speed in relation to Paradise. The spacecraft would, even after a braking burn, hit the atmosphere of Paradise at an incredible 100,000 miles per hour. He had no idea if such an impact was within the design limitations of the shuttle's heat shield. He radioed a report to the *Challenger*. The rapidly increasing gulf between the two craft made communications frustrating – it would be nearly two hours before he received an acknowledgement.

harna directed the beam from the arc lantern on to the rough sketch plan that Telson was holding.

'It's got to be left,' said Telson. He flashed his own lantern on the roof of the low corridor. The massive trunking that ran along the wall where it joined the roof snaked to the left, confirming the information on the plan that Telson had copied from the diagram he and Sharna had discovered in the terra-forming centre.

They had been stumbling through the strange corridor for an hour, following the trunking which they were convinced would eventually lead them to the guardian angels' central switching room.

At each junction, more optical tracks fed into the main trunking, swelling its size, until it was now nearly two feet in diameter.

Telson shone his lantern along the corridor that led to the left. An optical track from the right joined the trunking virtually doubling its size so that they would have to negotiate the passageways by crouching.

'You don't have to come any further,' said Telson.

'I'm not turning back now,' Sharna retorted. 'And we agreed that we stick together.'

Telson looked at the plan. 'About another hundred yards to go if I managed to draw it to scale.'

The guardian angels noted the approach of Telson and Sharna with interest at first and then with mounting alarm when they realized that the couple were unfailingly taking the correct turnings at each junction. The angels had always regarded the complex labyrinth of narrow maintenance passages as a protection in their own right. Such was the confusion of interconnected passages that even service androids carrying out repairs on the optical tracks occasionally got lost and had to be talked out of the maze.

Telson and Sharna were not lost. They were moving towards the central switching room with unerring accuracy.

One by one, the guardian angels activated the nightmare barriers that were their last line of defence.

* * *

'*Challenger* to shuttle,' said the surgical android. 'This is SA10 on duty in the control room acknowledging your report which I have recorded.'

Astra frowned at Darv. 'That's odd,' she said. 'Telson promised us that at least he or Sharna would be on watch until we had reported a safe planetfall.'

Darv nodded his agreement with Astra and inwardly cursed the two-hour time-lag that made it impossible to have a coherent conversation with the *Challenger*. If there was a God, Darv wondered why he had been so generous with the size of the Universe and so niggardly with the speed of light and electro-magnetic radio waves. 187,000 miles per second was nothing when one considered that it could take a radio signal several hours to traverse even a moderately sized solar system.

'Thank you, SA10,' Darv acknowledged. 'Will you please advise what has happened to Commander Telson and Sharna.'

'*Turn back, Sharna*,' whispered the voice. '*Turn back . . .*'

Sharna touched Telson's arm and stopped walking. 'Did you hear that, Telson?'

'Hear what?' Telson tried to straighten up and bumped his head on the trunking.

'A voice . . . I think it sounded like Angel One. It said something about turning back.'

'Your imagination,' said Telson shortly.

'*Turn back, Sharna. There is danger ahead!*'

Telson was about to continue down the passageway, but Sharna clung to his arm. 'Telson – they can see us and hear us. I always know when they're watching me.'

At that moment the voice touched Telson's mind. He became tense.

The whole things crazy,' said Sharna worriedly. 'I mean – what can we hope to achieve?'

'I'm now certain they lied when they said that this solar system is swamped with radiation,' said Telson grimly. 'And now they're trying to play tricks with our minds.'

'*Turn back! Both of you must turn back! Death lies ahead!*'

The insidious voice reached deep into Sharna's mind, making her want to cry out in fear. The sudden reassuring weight of Telson's arm across her shoulders restored some of her evaporating confidence.

'It's only a voice,' said Telson, urging her forward. 'It can't possibly hurt us. We've just got to ignore it.'

They moved another twenty yards through the gloomy passageway. The voice rose to a demented shriek that clawed at Sharna's sanity and would have frozen every muscle on her body had not Telson been at her side, half pushing and half dragging her, while offering words of encouragement that enabled her to cling to her dwindling reserves of strength and courage.

'*Death lies ahead! Death! DEATH! DEATH! DEATH!*'

And then she saw the hideous creature. Gleaming fangs that dripped red saliva; burning, yellow-rimmed eyes that screamed venomous hatred; flaring nostrils and rangy, powerful muscles under blood-matted fur that were preparing the monstrosity to spring at her throat.

Sharna screamed and in that instant the ground beneath her vanished. She heard her own scream echoing back at her as she plunged into the black, bottomless pit.

Darv touched Astra's arm.

'Staring at it won't make it come any quicker, my lovely.'

Astra turned her head from the view port. 'It seems ages since you last called me that,' she said, smiling and leaning her head back against Darv's chest. 'Isn't it the most beautiful planet you've ever seen, Darv?'

Darv stared at the magnificent blue-green sphere for some moments and nodded. 'But with an extremely ugly moon,' he joked. 'Have you ever seen so many craters? There are even craters in the craters.'

Astra laughed and became serious. 'What do you suppose has happened to Sharna and Telson?'

'They'll call us up when they return to the control room,' said Darv lightly.

'*If* they return.'

'Hey. We've got a job to do,' said Darv, changing the subject. 'We've got to select a landing site.'

'Can't it wait? We don't begin atmospheric entry for another two days.'

'We can select a landing area now and a definite site within the area before we enter the atmosphere.'

Glad of something to do to take her mind off Telson and Sharna, Astra studied the planet through the forward view ports which were now dominated by the planet's shining crescent. 'Where do you suggest?'

Darv activated the topographic radar screen and pointed to a land mass that resembled an inverted triangle. The bulk of the land mass was located in the northern hemisphere and it tapered down to a rounded apex that extended over thirty degrees into the southern hemisphere.

'Why there?' asked Astra.

'Because that's where the probe is located,' Darv replied. 'If all those animals can survive there, then so can we.'

Astra shivered inwardly at the thought of coming face to face with the grotesque creatures with the long necks that they had seen in the hologram transmitted from the probe.

The following day was the ninth since separation. Paradise had swollen to the point where it was only possible to see its complete disc by moving close to the view ports. It now took three hours to send a message to and receive a reply from the *Challenger*.

'We have still been unable to locate Commander Telson and Sharna,' the surgical android reported to Darv across a thousand million miles. 'We now have thirty service units searching for them.'

Darv read out the landing site that he and Astra had eventually decided on after some discussion. It was on the eastern coast of the land mass, one thousand miles to the north of the planet's equator. He radioed the co-ordinates to the *Challenger*.

The surgical android acknowledged three hours later when the shuttle was, according to its instruments, passing through the outer belts of the radiation zones that encircled Paradise. The radiation levels were low enough not to interfere with radio communications between the shuttle and the *Challenger*. It meant that the guardian angels had grossly exaggerated the dangers. The knowledge gave Astra and Darv renewed hope for their future although they were desperately worried about the fate that had befallen Telson and Sharna. If they had the fuel, they would have turned back but the shuttle had passed the point of no return shortly after it had fired its main engine following separation from the *Challenger*.

'Ten hours to atmospheric entry,' said Darv cryptically as he loaded the landing site references into the shuttle's navigation computer.

The shuttle's automatic systems immediately set to work on an analysis of the planet that it was approaching at 150,000 miles per hour. Radar signals assessed the density and composition of the atmosphere and displayed the information on the data screen located between Darv's and Astra's seats. The systems studied the planet's gravity and compared the information with data on the amount of fuel remaining in the shuttle's tanks. One second after Darv had loaded the selected landing site into the navigation computer the display came up with the legend:

LANDING NOT ADVISED – WILL LEAVE INSUFFICIENT FUEL FOR RETURN TO MOTHERSHIP

There was no suitable response given on the options list so Darv had to resort to a voice input command. He said: 'Return to mothership not required.'

The computer digested this and came up with.

LANDING POSSIBLE BUT NOT ADVISED WITH EXISTING FUEL LEVELS. TOUCH PROCEED KEY THREE TIMES IF YOU WISH TO CONTINUE.

Darv touched the 'proceed' key as instructed. He grinned

at Astra. 'Seems that our clever little shuttle doesn't like the look of Paradise as much as we do.'

Astra looked worried. She had learned to respect the judgement of the onboard computers used on the shuttles. 'Do you think we've made a terrible mistake?'

'Relax, Astra. It hasn't said that we can't land – only that it's not advisable. Obviously it's been programmed to query landing requests that will leave it short of fuel.' Darv's cheerful reply to Astra's query belied his concern – he had noticed that the separation burn from the *Challenger* had cost them one per cent of their fuel above the estimate. Astra had not looked carefully at the data display and did not appear to have noticed the discrepancy. He saw no point in drawing her attention to it now.

The next eight hours were the longest in the couple's memory. One of the disadvantages of the shuttle's fully-automated landing systems was that there was little for them to do except gaze down at the dazzling splendour beneath them while trying not to fret about the impending atmospheric entry.

They sat in silence, watching the swelling orb. The only movement in the cabin was the constant winking of figures on the displays as the shuttle's systems continuously updated the information they were receiving from Paradise.

At precisely one hour before entry, the shuttle's directional thrusters fired briefly and rotated the spacecraft through one hundred and eighty degrees so that it was travelling backwards along its flight-path. The vast curvature of the white-lace horizon dipped out of sight for a few seconds and reappeared.

FASTEN SEAT RESTRAINTS flashed an illuminated sign.

Darv leaned sideways and gave Astra a lingering kiss before helping her to secure her seat harness and then fastening his own.

'Our fuel's down one per cent on what it should be, isn't it?' said Astra in a matter-of-fact tone.

'Nothing to worry about,' was Darv's flippant reply. 'We would've had one per cent in hand anyway.'

BRAKING BURN IN 60 SECONDS advised the data display.

The seconds seemed to stretch into minutes.

20 SECONDS said the display . . . 10 SECONDS . . . 5 SECONDS . . . 4 . . . 3 . . . 2 . . . 1 . . . ZERO . . .

The main engine's deafening roar filled the cabin for three minutes. Astra opened her eyes when the motor cut out. She saw that the shuttle's speed had dropped from 150,000 miles per hour to 100,000 miles per hour. Clearly the shuttle considered the velocity too high to attempt an atmospheric entry because it fired the engine again to claw the spacecraft's speed down to 70,000 miles per hour.

The directional thrusters fired again, turning the shuttle around until it was pointing along its flight-path once more.

ATMOSPHERE ENTRY IMMINENT. BUFFETING ANTICIPATED AT FORCE 8 warned the display.

The directional thrusters fired again – this time to lift the shuttle's nose. For a few seconds nothing happened and then Darv and Astra became conscious of a faint whining noise. There was a severe jolt that was too harsh for the artificial gravity compensator to cancel.

The whining ceased. It started again after a few seconds and became progressively louder until a second jolt shook the spacecraft. The motion puzzled Darv until he realised that the shuttle was losing velocity by skimming in and out of the upper layers of the atmosphere in exactly the same way that flat objects he used to send skimming across the surface of the reservoir lost speed with each skip. His respect deepened for the men and women who had designed and built the shuttle.

The next jolt was the worst of all. The sharp whining that followed rose to a shriek. Darv risked a quick glance at Astra and saw that her eyes were closed and her face serene. The whiteness of her knuckles gripping her arm rests told a different story.

The shuttle's nose lifted higher as the heat shield began to drive downward into the atmosphere. Ionised gas began glowing around the view ports. A message, hopelessly garbled by the plasma that was forming around the shuttle's radio antennae, tried to break through at that moment.

'. . . llenger . . . Shuttle . . .' said the surgical android's voice. '. . .control lost . . . Commander Telson . . . lost . . . Sharna . . .' the words tailed away into an unintelligible blast of white noise.

Darv turned his head to Astra. 'Could you make out any of that?'

Astra kept her eyes closed and shook her head.

The distorted message was immediately forgotten when the buffeting started. Everything around Darv became a blur; the displays dissolved into vague streaks of coloured light, and the flames roaring past the view ports mercifully merged into a less frightening kaleidoscope of dancing orange and crimson patterns. He tried forcing his head back harder into the headrest to prevent it being thrown about and discovered that the terrifying decelerating was doing the job for him.

Astra opened her eyes briefly and closed them again. She guessed that the shuttle's heat shield was being burned away so that the incandescent particles burning off took their heat with them. The knowledge was no comfort when she saw the inferno raging beyond the view ports. The deceleration rammed her deeper into her seat. She felt the blood draining from her face. She had no way of telling if she had passed out for one second or one minute, but the noise and buffeting had miraculously stopped. The sudden silence was uncanny.

'Are you all right, Astra?' asked Darv anxiously. He gave a warm, delighted smile when he saw her eyes open.

'What happened?'

'We're through,' he said simply. 'Stable flight. Altitude – one hundred thousand feet.'

'I don't believe it,' said Astra weakly.

'Nor do I.'

Astra leaned forward against her seat harness and looked down. Through breaks in the cloud she could see a huge expanse of blue. 'Now what happens?' she inquired.

'We're gliding down at one thousand feet per minute so presumably the shuttle won't take any further action for at least another hour and a half.'

The shuttle dipped through the cloud just over an hour later. The cloud thinned out so that after another fifteen minutes the shuttle was flying over water that was so blue that it almost hurt the eyes to look at it.

'It would be beautiful if there wasn't so much of it,' commented Astra when the shuttle's altitude was down to 12,000 feet.

'My feelings exactly,' agreed Darv.

The ribbon of coastline appeared on the horizon at the same time as it appeared on the radar screen. The shuttle's vertical descent velocity increased as it lost forward speed.

Another minute passed. It was now possible to distinguish the regular swell on the surface of the water. Darv glanced down at the navigation displays. The shuttle was heading due west in a straight line towards the landing site that was centred on the screen.

'Just enough fuel for a five second burn,' Astra observed. 'Will we make it?'

Darv eyed the approaching land and glanced down at the water 3000 feet below. 'Just,' he said, hoping that his voice sounded confident. The truth was that the water was getting nearer much quicker than the land was.

The main engine fired without warning. The shuttle's nose lifted, the spacecraft picked up speed. The ground proximity display managed to sustain a steady figure instead of one that was continuously dropping. Darv's eyes flickered to the fuel-reading display. He resisted the temptation to swear out loud. At that moment the low fuel warning gong sounded and the engine cut out a second later.

Darv cancelled the automatic pilot and assumed manual control. There was little he could do except put the shuttle's nose down in the hope that the increased speed would give it enough lift to reach the broad band of yellow and green that rose out of the water some eight miles straight ahead.

Astra remained silent and white-faced, staring down at the water that seemed to be racing up to meet them.

At 1000 feet Darv thought that perhaps the shuttle would reach land but the inboard computer did not share his optimism.

DITCHING PROCEDURE INITIATED flashed up on the screen.

There was a loud thump from underneath the floor and a new message appeared: LANDING SKIDS JETTISONED.

The cryptic legend puzzled Darv until he realised that the

shuttle's best chance of remaining in one piece was to present a clean under belly to the water upon impact. At 250 feet the inner and outer air-lock doors opened of their own accord. At 200 miles per hour slipstream screamed into the shuttle's interior and made it difficult for Darv to think properly. He stared in almost hypnotised fascination at the ribbon of yellow that was hurtling towards him. Suddenly Astra was yelling at him above the howling racket of the air rushing past the open air-lock.

'Pull the nose up!' she screamed. 'Pull the nose up! For God's sake do as it says!'

Darv looked down at the display just as Astra's hands closed over his hands and hauled back on the controls. A shuddering crash suddenly ripped through the spacecraft, slamming Darv down into his seat and driving the air from his lungs. Everything went dark for an instant as the massive deceleration crushed his eyeballs into the bottom of their sockets. Barely had he managed to draw another breath when a second mind-pulverising shockwave smashed against his senses. A tiny part of his brain that manage to remain clear during the appalling assault on his reason noted that the shuttle seemed to be bouncing across the water.

The third and final crash was the least severe but it was enough to rip the skin away from the bottom of the spacecraft's drastically weakened hull. There was the sudden cold touch of water swirling around Darv's feet. Even before his hand reached the seat restraint release, the water was up to his knees. The shuttle stopped bucking and seemed to settle lower. Water began roaring through the open air-lock doors. Astra had released her harness and was standing beside her seat, leaning backwards as the shuttle's nose tilted down. Darv grabbed her hand and hauled her towards the air-lock.

'I can't swim,' she gasped as the water in the cabin rose around her waist.

'Doesn't matter – let's get out of this thing before it sinks.'

The force of the water surging through the air-lock meant that Darv had to hang on to the door surround and thrust Astra out of the shuttle with his foot. The water was a living wall piling up against his chest as he hung on to the door surround and yanked himself out of the spacecraft. Water stung his eyes and got into his mouth. He experienced a moment of panic when he remembered the angels' warning that the water on Paradise was poisonous. It didn't taste poisonous – merely salty. The shuttle gave a lurch and drove its nose deeper under water. Darv pushed himself clear and trod water.

'Astra! Where are you?'

'Here.'

Darv discovered that it was virtually impossible to swim in the one-piece suit. It took him several clumsy strokes to reach the shuttle's tail where Astra was clinging with white-faced grim determination to the rocket motor fairing. He grabbed hold of a torn strut and held on beside her to get his breath back.

'Now what?' gasped Astra.

'Beach about two hundred yards. We'll have to swim . . . Shuttle won't stay afloat much longer.'

At that moment bubbles erupted around them and the spacecraft sank lower until the swell was virtually washing over the hull. Darv opened the seams on his suit and struggled out of it. He told Astra to do the same and reached down to pull it away from her legs once she had got her arms free.

'Okay,' he gasped, releasing his hold on the sinking shuttle and hooking an arm around Astra's neck. 'I'll hold your head above water. Keep your eyes and mouth shut and don't struggle. Ready?'

Astra reluctantly let go of the rocket motor fairing. She felt Darv's legs beneath her push away from the doomed spacecraft. He turned slightly on to his side in the water to give his free arm a more comfortable stroke and struck out towards the boom and roar of waves breaking on the beach.

After fifteen minutes' sustained effort, Darv was barely conscious of his surroundings. His limbs were aching to the point of numbness. The breaking waves sounded nearer. He lowered his feet to tread water and they made contact with the bottom.

'Astra!' he croaked. 'You can stand up now.'

The couple staggered to their feet, clinging to each other, and half-waded, half-stumbled towards the beach. They were too exhausted to be scared of the rollers that scooped them up in the last fifty yards of their struggle and hurled them breathless, bruised and naked on to the warm sand. They crawled a little way up the beach to be clear of the surf and lay still for five minutes.

Astra was the first to recover her senses. She sat up and gazed about her in wonder – her bruises and aches from the recent ordeal forgotten. There was no sign of the shuttle. They had been deposited on a beach of dazzling white sand that formed a ribbon between the water and rich, green vegetation. The sky was the same flawless blue as the water, and the sun was as warm as the solar lights above the *Challenger*'s reservoir.

From the trees lining the beach came a sound that she had heard only in recordings. Somehow, even the most perfect of recordings failed to capture the richness and depth of birdsong. A movement caught her eye. Something white was flashing across the water at wave-top height. The seabird plunged into the water and became airborne again with a small fish in its bill.

'Your wish has finally come true.'

Astra turned her head. Darv was sitting up, leaning back on his hands and grinning at her.

'Wish?' she said.

'A beach by a lake. Sand. And a warm sun.' Darv squinted up into the sky. 'At least it is warm so we won't freeze.'

'It's beautiful, isn't it? It's a hundred times more beautiful than I ever imagined it could be. Shall we go exploring?'

Darv looked anxiously at Astra and shook his head. 'I don't think we should move from here until you've had at least an hour's rest, my lovely.'

Astra stretched out beside Darv and took hold of his hand. Ten minutes later they were both sound asleep.

The cold touch on her ankles woke Astra. She sat up suddenly. Her eyes went round with shock at what she saw and she screamed in terror.

The water had crept nearer while they were asleep.

* * *

Every second spent in the magnificent forest brought new sensations: brilliantly coloured birds; heavily scented flowers of every conceivable shade; swarms of small, chattering creatures that scampered through the trees at their approach – and always the trees. Large trees, small trees, trees with leaves as broad as they were, trees with spiky leaves that they quickly learned to avoid brushing against. And each new tree, flower or bird seemed to be more beautiful than the last.

Despite their nakedness and vulnerability, it never occurred to Darv and Astra to be afraid. Even their first shock when they discovered that water had moved up the beach had been dissipated by Astra's reasoning that the line of rotting seaweed near the top of the beach marked the extremity of the mighty lake's advance.

They came to a clearing that was dominated by a towering fruit tree which, judging by the state of its gnarled roots, was probably the oldest tree in the forest. Thousands of small creatures who had been feeding in the tree fled as they drew near – a brown, panic-stricken furry tide that swarmed down the trunk and dashed into the safety of trees on the far side of the clearing. The first living creatures other than humans that they had ever seen and they were not afraid.

They paused beneath the tree and looked up longingly at the tempting fruit. The ground under the tree was littered with the remains of rotting cores that the creatures had discarded. The decaying fruit released a pungent, mouth-watering smell as it was pulped beneath their bare feet.

'I could reach those lower ones if I climbed on to your shoulders,' said Astra, pointing up.

'You shouldn't go climbing, and we don't know if they're safe to eat.'

'If they are safe for those animals then they're bound to be okay for us to eat. I'm starving. And furthermore, I'm just as fit as you are.'

Darv decided not to argue. He leaned against the bole of the tree and hooked his hands together to provide a foothold for Astra. She climbed on to his shoulders and swung a leg over the lowest branch, gradually easing her weight further away from the trunk along the branch until the fruits were within reach of her outstretched hand. Darv watched her anxiously as she plucked on of the fruits from an overhanging branch. She sniffed at it cautiously, sank her teeth into its flesh, and crunched noisily.

'Well?' queried Darv.

Astra pulled a face but continued eating. 'It tastes a bit odd,' she admitted. 'Sort of like apple. But it's all right. Least it gets rid of that horrible salty taste. Here – catch!'

Darv caught the fruit that Astra had bitten into and sniffed it.

Astra laughed down at him. 'It's not bad at all really. It's just that the first taste is a bit odd. Try it.'

'Are you sure?'

'Go on – try a bite.'

Darv took a bite out of the apple-like fruit and chewed suspiciously. His caution gave way to a broad smile. 'Hey – not bad.'

'Well, at least we won't starve,' Astra commented as she stood up on the branch. She had seen a cluster of the fruits hanging below a neighbouring branch. She placed one foot on the nearby branch and, with her legs wide apart, pulled the fruit towards herself. Darv was looking up at her. For the first time, for no sensible reason that she could think of, she suddenly realised that she was ashamed of her nakedness.

'Astra!' said Darv urgently. 'Don't move! Whatever you do, don't move!'

Astra froze.

'To the left of your right hand.'

Astra's body was rigid. Only her eyes moved. The snake was coiled around the branch that her right hand was resting on. Its small black eyes were regarding her steadily. The mottled markings down its back screamed danger. For timeless seconds neither Astra nor the snake moved.

'Take your hand away from the branch,' said Darv quietly. 'As slowly as you can . . . That's it . . .'

The motion appeared to startle the creature for it began to withdraw. At first Astra thought that it was disappearing until she realised that it was backing into its hole in the branch. After a minute only its eyes were visible – two gleaming points of unblinking malevolent light staring glassily at her from the dim recess of the hollow branch.

Astra was so paralysed with shock that Darv had to climb up beside her to persuade her to come down. It was when she was safely back on the ground that she burst into tears.

'It's a terrible place,' she wept. 'All I want is to be back on the *Challenger*.'

Darv did his best to comfort Astra but his words lacked conviction because of his own mounting apprehension about Paradise and the feeling that perhaps they had made a terrible and irrevocable mistake.

It was as well that he had no idea that there was far worse to come.

They had been following the sound of the stream for twenty minutes, taking straight lines through the dense undergrowth for fear of losing track of the running water's sweet music. By the time they came upon it, their feet were cut and bleeding.

Darv splashed into the middle of the stream and scooped up a handful of water. He tasted it as it streamed through his fingers and gave a shout of elation. 'It's fresh water, Astra! Come and taste!'

Astra adjusted the hopelessly inadequate skirt that she had fashioned from leaves and joined Darv. He cupped his palms together and scooped up water so that she could drink from his hands.

'Better?' asked Darv when she had finished.

She managed a faint smile and nodded.

Darv grinned and splashed water over her. 'We've got to look after the two of you . . . Which makes twice as much trouble.'

Astra laughed and retaliated. Two minutes later they were laughing and chasing each other from one ankle-deep rock pool to the next. Their high-spirited play came to an abrupt end when Astra lashed out to kick water over Darv and saw the blood-bloated creature coiled around her ankle.

Astra's scream of terror raised a storm of protesting cries from the birds and hidden denizens of the surrounding forest. She fell backwards into the water. Her scream became a tortured, uncontrolled howl of hysteria. Darv grabbed at her foot and pulled the clinging creature away. It needed all his self-control not to be sick when he saw from the burst blood vessels beneath Astra's skin that the thing had been feeding on her blood. As he dragged Astra to her feet, he saw that two more of the loathsome creatures were adhering to her breasts.

With the night came the storm.

Astra and Darv clung to each other; naked and cold – terrified orphans of the forest – with the frightful thunder and lightning rolling and crashing above their heads in a cacophonous uproar that numbed their senses.

Two hours before dawn brought the rain in a continuous freezing downpour. Gradually the ground beneath them became a heavy, clinging mud but Astra was too exhausted to care. All she could think of was the *Challenger* with its warm, comforting environment, and her air-conditioned room with its big, soft bed.

The rain stopped an hour before the dawn and, miraculously, Astra finally fell asleep, cradled in Darv's protective arms.

The black despair that had settled on Darv and Astra during the terrible night was soon dispelled by the return of the warm sun. They washed and drank in a small water pool that was separate from the main stream and therefore free of the ghastly creatures they had encountered the previous day. They ate an adequate meal of the apple-like fruits that they found growing on a small tree near the stream.

'We ought to make our way back to the beach,' said Darv two hours later after they had enjoyed a brief sleep in the sun stretched out on a rock.

'Why?'

'Maybe some of our supplies from the shuttle have been washed up in the night.'

'We'd never find our way back through the forest,' Astra pointed out.

Darv sat up and rubbed his eyes. 'Come on, my lovely. The chances are that the stream leads to the beach.'

They discovered that walking barefoot was less unpleasant if they kept to the stream's sandy banks. After forty minutes they came to the beach. To Astra, it seemed that the vast stretch of blue water and the white sand was the most friendly place of all on Paradise.

Their search of the beach proved fruitless. The only discovery of any interest was a large white fish that was flapping about, trapped in a sand pool.

Darv examined the driftwood at the top of the beach. He pushed two straight lengths of slender tree trunk upright into the soft sand above the high water mark and pulled their tops together to form the apex of a triangle. Astra watched him curiously.

'What are you planning, Darv?'

'Some sort of shelter for tonight.'

'And tomorrow night. And the night after that,' Astra corrected.

Darv laughed. 'If we rounded up a lot of these and stuck them in a circle, we could tie their tops together with some of that vine, or whatever it is hanging from the trees, and cover the whole thing in leaves to keep out the rain. At least we might be able to keep warm at night.'

'There's something else we ought to try making first,' said Astra seriously.

'What's that?'

'Fire.'

Darv looked ruefully at the blister on his hand and threw the short stick down in disgust. 'It's useless, Astra – you can't make fire with friction.'

Astra said nothing. She touched the tip of the stick that Darv had been rubbing back and forth in a notched piece of dry wood and then pressed it against Darv's cheek.

'Ouch!' he protested.

'Well – it's hot,' said Astra.

'Well of course it's hot – but I'd never get it hot enough to start a fire.'

Astra took the stick and began rolling it quickly between the palms of her hands while holding the tip of the stick pressed firmly into the notched dry wood.

'All you'll get is blisters,' was Darv's contribution to her effort.

'Push some of that stuff around it,' said Astra.

Darv shredded some dried seaweed and pushed it carefully around the tip of the stick. Astra settled down to a steady rhythm and kept it up for five minutes despite helpful comments from Darv such as: 'You're wasting your time, my lovely.'

Sweat began trickling down Astra's forehead. Darv watched with disinterest and then blinked, wondering if the tiny wisp of smoke had been a product of his imagination.

'Blow!' Astra said urgently. 'Quickly!'

Darv crouched over the tip of wood and blew gently while pushing the dried seaweed closer. To his astonishment the material started to curl and blacken. He blew harder and the tiny flame, invisible in the bright sunlight, tongued through the dry seaweed and stung him on the cheek.

Astra took her hands away and gave a savage grin of triumph as the flames took hold while Darv carefully added more combustible material to keep the fire going.

They both worked hard for the rest of the morning, piling up sufficient driftwood and dry seaweed to keep the fire fuelled for at least another two days. Darv was opposed to Astra working but she insisted on doing her share.

They spent the early part of the afternoon asleep in the shade of the trees that lined the edge of the beach, and woke refreshed and eager to start work on the shelter. Once the skeleton was in place, fashioned from the abundant supply of driftwood, Darv climbed one of the trees and hacked down its broad fronds with the aid of a sharp-edged stone. Astra wove the giant leaves in and out of the shelter's primitive framework and stood back to admire her handiwork.

Darv dumped another armful of leaves at her feet. 'Come on, my lovely. It'll need that lot in place before it's waterproof.'

'I've never made anything before,' said Astra proudly. But her pleasure at the discovery of her new-found skills was diminished when she realised with a guilty start that she had been too busy to think about Sharna and Telson.

Darv slipped his arm around her waist and gave her a gently hug. 'I know what you're thinking about,' he said. 'If it's any consolation, I haven't given them much thought this afternoon either.'

Darv selected a long, slender piece of driftwood and sharpened one end on a stone. Spearing a fish trapped in a sand pool proved unexpectedly easy and he even succeeded in catching two smaller fish using the same technique. They cooked them over the fire and decided that it was the best meal they had ever had in their lives.

Darv set about carefully building the fire half an hour before sunset so that it would not go out during the night. It was getting dark by the time he finished work. He and Astra crawled into the shelter and closed the entrance by means of a frond-covered frame that served as a crude door.

It was when they stretched out that they realised how tired they were. It was a pleasant form of tiredness – the exhaustion that comes from hard physical labour combined with a sense of real achievement.

Astra was woken after dawn by a strange whistling sound. Perhaps it passed overhead or perhaps it came from the forest. She tried to focus her brain and decided that she had been woken by her recurring, but always pleasurable, dream about Darv and a strong young child playing together in the surf while she looked on. Her eyes and limbs were still heavy from the previous day's exertions. Darv was beside her, lying on his stomach with an arm thrown carelessly across her thighs. She listened to the reassuring sound of his breathing for a few minutes and drifted back to sleep.

Astra picked up the first of the clay bowls that she had moulded in her fingers and examined it with pride. The sun had dried it in a most satisfactory manner. She dipped it into the stream, filled it with water and lifted it to her lips. She drank and set the bowl down on the rock beside her. It worked! Now for a much larger one. She stood up and glanced down the beach to make sure that Darv was not too far away. He was working on improvements to the shelter, occasionally stopping work to add more fuel to the fire that was burning briskly in the stiff morning breeze.

Astra knelt down again by the mouth of the stream and watched the dancing water as it gurgled noisily over the rocks on the last few yards of its rush to the sea. She tested the strength of the second bowl that she had made and decided that the new one, if it was to be of any use, should be jug-shaped so that it would be easier to carry water without spillage.

She drove her fingers deep into the oozing, wet hole she had dug beside the stream and lifted out enough clay to form the base of the jug. She had learned that it was useless trying to work too much clay at once because it invariably dried too quickly.

She worked slowly and carefully, so intent on her work that she was unaware that she was being watched. The dancing water effectively cloaked any unusual sound so that the first warning she had was when the huge shadow fell across her.

She gave a cry of alarm and wheeled round. The sun blinded her as she tried to look up at the thing that was towering over her.

'Sand,' complained a familiar grating voice, 'Bad for mechanisms. Gets everywhere.'

'Astra!' cried another familiar voice. 'Hey, Sharna! George has found Astra!'

Astra rose to her feet. Suddenly there was a roaring in her

ears. Everything started spinning. Her knees buckled under her and she fell forward in a dead faint.

Astra had regained consciousness by the time George was setting her down carefully beside the shelter. 'Sand gets in your mechanisms,' he grated sympathetically. 'Know what it's like. Very bad.'

Astra looked up, dazed, her mind reeling, as Telson, Sharna and Darv exchanged ecstatic greetings. Sharna knelt down beside Astra and gave her an enthusiastic squeeze and a kiss. Astra was unable to speak at first – she eventually managed to blurt out. 'Sharna! It can't be you!'

Sharna laughed and wiped away her tears of joy. 'Of course it's me. Who else could I be? Hey! Steady!' Sharna fell backwards on to the sand, half laughing and half crying as Astra threw her arms around her.

'We landed just after dawn.' Telson explained. 'We knew we were near your landing site. We tried interrogating your shuttle's radio beacon to get an accurate fix but couldn't get an answer.

'We crashed the shuttle in the water,' said Darv.

Telson nodded. 'Hardly surprising after travelling a thousand million miles. Luckily we didn't have your problems.' He looked at the fire. 'And it's lucky we saw your smoke.'

Telson jabbed his stick into another piece of fish and held it above the flames. He was nearing the end of his account. 'You wouldn't believe what they threw at us to prevent us reaching their central switching room. Hallucination holograms, light, sound, visions – everything.'

'How *did* you get past them?' Astra asked.

Sharna's expression hardened at the recollection of the nightmare barriers. 'Telson managed but he had to leave me. It was the only way.'

Telson nodded. 'My lack of imagination that you've always complained about, Darv. This time it came in useful because the angels' little nightmares didn't affect me as much as they did Sharna.'

'But you got into their central switching room,' said Darv eagerly.

Telson nodded. 'Oh, yes.'

'What was it like?'

'Not more than eight feet square.'

'What?'

'Our angels were nothing but two organic brains in two tanks. They were floating in some sort of liquid. Nutrients, I suppose. It was a disappointment. Just those two tanks. No force shields to protect them. No service androids. Nothing.' Telson gave a hollow laugh. 'All our lives we were ruled by two entities that we could have disposed of by two simple blows with a hammer.'

'Is that what you did?'

'No . . . They begged me to spare them. Can you imagine that? Our two guardian angels begging one of *us* to spare them? We did a deal. They agreed that this planet was suitable for settlement, and they agreed to allow the *Challenger* to be brought into a close orbit around Paradise so that we could leave by one of the space shuttles from the terra-forming excursion terminal. You tell them the rest, Sharna.'

'We obtained your landing site reference from one of the surgical androids,' said Sharna. 'And we left four of them in the main control room to handle the ship.'

Astra frowned. 'Why, Sharna?'

'Because Angel One and Angel Two are going to continue the Earthsearch mission.'

'You mean that they might return?'

Sharna smiled. 'You needn't look so worried, Astra . . . They won't return in our lifetime, or the lifetime of our children or their children.'

'But we'll have to warn them,' said Astra, gazing out to sea to where the moon was rising.

Darv poked at the fire and sent sparks climbing into the darkening sky.

'Well,' said Sharna brightly. 'Tomorrow we'll collect the shuttle. The stowage bay is crammed with enough supplies to last us a lifetime.'

Astra thought of her row of little clay bowls and felt vaguely saddened.

Telson picked up a handful of sand and allowed the grains to run through his fingers. 'We now have a planet of our own,' he said thoughtfully. 'So what happens next?'

THE END

What happens next is described in
EARTHSEARCH – DEATHSHIP.